T0165368

The White Starched Apron

Saragene Stamm Adkins

iUniverse, Inc.
New York   Bloomington

The White Starched Apron

iUniverse books may be ordered through booksellers or by contacting:

iUniverse
1663 Liberty Drive
Bloomington, IN 47403
www.iuniverse.com
1-800-Authors (1-800-288-4677)

*Because of the dynamic nature of the Internet, any Web addresses or links contained in this
book may have changed since publication and may no longer be valid. The views expressed
in this work are solely those of the author and do not necessarily reflect the views of the
publisher, and the publisher hereby disclaims any responsibility for them.*

ISBN: 978-1-4401-8313-3 (sc)
ISBN: 978-1-4401-8311-9 (dj)
ISBN: 978-1-4401-8312-6 (ebk)

Printed in the United States of America

iUniverse rev. date: 12/31/2009

Dedication

The hand of God wrote this story, I prayed to God at the moment I had the idea of my book. I asked God to give me the time to finish my book and my prayer was answered.

I also dedicate my book to my little seven-year-old grandson, Lucas Anthony Lowe, who had the faith of the world and believed in his, MaMa Sara.

The Year was 1937; Maggie, Red and Glenda Faye had just graduated from St. John's Academy for young ladies.

The three girls were looking forward to their last summer of freedom. In the fall they would enter St. Ann's School of Nursing.

Maggie, Red and Glenda Faye had been friends since before they could remember. They were born and grew up in a small town called, SPEEDWAY CITY, INDIANA.

Come join the, "Fearsome Threesome," as they were called on their adventures into their futures.

There will be tears and laughter along the way, but you will be held fast and drawn in by the love and friendship, long ago lost.

FOREWARD

I stated in my dedication, the hand of God wrote this book, by this I meant He gave me the time to finish the book.

On January 22, 2008, after a serious operation due to lung cancer, I was told that there was nothing they could do for me except to send me to an oncologist. The cancer had spread outside of my lung, which did not show up before the surgery, I was angrier with this, than the expiration date they tried to give me! This was needless surgery for a condition that had no cure, just rounds of chemotherapy and radiation.

I would not let the doctors give me an expiration date, but when the oncologist was called in, I knelt up in bed and said in a very loud voice, "No treatment, get this chest tube out of me and let me go home!" I wanted to be the best that I could be for my family; I did not want them to see me waste away before their eyes like my two best friends. I truly believe their time was cut short because of the treatment, not the surgery or the cancer. That is one person's opinion we all have one.

My sister let it slip one day on the phone, "One year to live, how are you able to cope with this?" Now I knew, what do you do with one year? After I healed from my surgery, I had two choices, go to bed, cover my head and wait to die or live every day to the fullest.

I prayed to God for an answer, but in the mean time I went back to doing what I was doing before, I had started making what I called my, " Big Comfy Blankets." I had started making these blankets for my two friends going through chemotherapy themselves before I was diagnosed. My friends told me there was magic healing in my blankets, all the ladies they sat with everyday wanted one of my blankets, as did my family members.

I went back to making my blankets, I wrote and illustrated a children's Christmas book and wrote a short story called, "The Last Blanket." I was still praying to God for something really big to leave as my legacy to my family and friends.

One winter afternoon I was tying the yarn on one of my blankets while my daughter slept on the couch. She was recuperating from knee surgery, when Lil woke up I told her I had an idea. God gave me, not only the title of a book, but the last chapter. Lil smiled at me and said, "What about all of the in between?" I told her that was up to me, but I had it, as my grandson always says, "Grammie you have so much up there, you need to write it down."

All my life friends and family have told me I should write a book about my life, this due to the fact that I have been married 8 times, yes, that is correct, not a misprint. I did not want to write about those years in my life, they were not pleasant for me. One day, many years ago, I said to my self, "Enough is enough," my pivotal point, and totally changed my life for the good.

Almost immediately God started working in my life, first in small ways and as the years progressed things got better and better. If I were to go into all of this, it would be no big deal to most of you, but to me it was a miracle.

I wrote, "The White Starched Apron," for you the reader that loves a simple, but wonderful story. This book will have you reaching for a tissue one minute and then laughing so hard that you feel good for the rest of the day.

This book is a work of fiction, but based on my mother's nursing training days back in 1937, some of my characters are my real life friends. Some are still living, but two of my main characters, "Red (Sandra Kay) and Joseph Murphy," passed away from my dreaded disease in the past two years. Some names have been changed, but some remain the same that they carry to this day. I tried to weave my friends and family all through this book in the characters you will grow to love and care about as I have during my writing.

I myself became, "Maggie," in my heart, I would sit at my computer and cry about what had just happened in the lives of my three girls. I love, Maggie, Red and Glenda Faye, they are true, "Friends of my heart." These three girls were real people, Maggie was my own mother, Red (Sandra Kay) was my best friend in true life, but passed way in 2007, Glenda Faye was here yesterday for a visit, we are still real friends. (April 2009)

If you are a fault finder, fact checker or you like to naysay, this book is not for you, even my actual facts are a little shaky, remember I was working under pressure in a tight time frame. I just passed my expiration date two months ago, no I don't feel as well as I did 14 months ago, but I am still living through this book. These three girls kept me alive, and gave me a reason to get up in the morning and write this little piece of my heart for you. Keep in mind, I had written poetry all of my life, never thought of publishing, but this is my first, "Big Girl," book as I like to call it. There are three things I have done in my life that I am so very proud of, giving birth to my two beautiful daughters and now, this wonderful book that God gave me the time to write for you to enjoy and read. Yes, I am reaching for my tissue box once again, love and blessings to all of my readers.

Saragene Stamm Adkins
April 4, 2009

Chapter 1

Maggie Goes Back In Time

Once again, I am being pushed in my wheelchair, by my granddaughter, Lil, maybe I should start this with the full names of the people involved. Lil is really Lariann, but in a comedy of errors on a night out with her sister, Patti, someone asked her if her name was Lillian? Patti always gave everyone a nickname, from then on she was called, Lil; it stuck like gum on your shoe.

As she pushes me along and the wheels roll over tiny pebbles on the pavement, there is this rhythm of sorts that takes place that is soothing. She stops to adjust the scarf around my head and neck, she says, "Grammie, keep bundled up, you must not catch cold!" I just smile to myself as I look up at the name on the building we are about to enter, "St. Ann's Hospital," this building bears the same name as the institution where I took my nurses training so many years ago.

Today is my 90th birthday, Lil is soon to be fifty, and it seems like just yesterday I was fifty, where do all those wonderful years go? We approach the large glass doors, they swing open like magic, and there is no more sound under the wheels, now just the silence of the wheels rolling over charcoal gray carpet. Lil wheels me up to a beautiful wooden desk to check me in, we have been doing this quite a while now and she knows all the answers to every question on the clipboard. She finishes and hands the board to me, so I can sign and date the document.

Lil pushes me to the waiting area; she takes off my coat and scarf to make me more comfortable and pats my hand. This is a gesture of kindness she picked up from her mother many years ago. I watch all the people hurrying in and out of the big glass doors, if I were to take my glasses off, I could not tell if they were nurses or doctors, they all wear blue pajamas. Lil has corrected me on this several times, "Grammie, they are called, scrubs." Still they look like pajamas to me, what could all of these young people be scrubbing?

I hear my name called from the overhead intercom, Lil gets up and pushes me to the desk, the person there, tells her to follow the yellow line to the elevators and then to the basement. I will be having a procedure called a PET scan; we follow the directions given to us, and check in at yet another desk. Lil and Patti both work for St. Ann's in their research department, she knows the hospital inside and out, but we still have to follow their directions and do as we are told. A young man in blue pajamas comes to wheel me into the room where I will wait for my test. Lil helps the young man place me onto the table where I will be prepared for the actual scan, first I will have dye injected that looks like neon yellow soda pop. Lil knows about my fear of needles and holds my hand, soon the dye is in and the needle out. They bring in two warm blankets and cover me clear to the neck; I have to now lay here for an hour or so to let the dye travel through my system.

Lil says to me, "Grammie, are you sleepy," my answer is no, "If you are not sleepy, would you tell me one of your stories, you tell them so well." I agree to tell her a story, but I let her know in no uncertain terms, it is a story about me, but written down many years ago on white lined paper, that is now yellowed from

2

time. This story was written by your mother, and like most of her writing, never published. I will only be the narrator, strictly here for your pleasure.

We lost my daughter, Saragene, a few years ago to lung cancer, before her illness, we were four peas in a pod, spirits of the heart, as I like to call it. Patti, Lil and I sat at her bedside; we joined our hands, we four peas together. There was a crash in the room; it was the sound of four hearts breaking in unison. Then her hands went limp in ours. There was stillness then that had not been evident before, her breathing had stopped, Lil, Patti and I put our heads into the palm of her hands and we cried. Now there were only three peas in our pod, we knew this day was coming, but no matter how you prepare, you are never quite ready.

This is my story, as written by my daughter, Saragene Stamm. I kindly referred to her as, "My heart, and my spirit, my everything." I will try to do the story justice in my telling of it. After all I should be able to remember my own life!

Chapter 2

Maggie's Starts Her Life

Wow, wonderful, and every other great word you are able to come up with, myself, Clara Margaret Mann, but called, "Maggie," by family and friends, along with my two best friends graduated from, St. John's Academy for young girls, today.   Myself, Glenda Faye Kelly and Sandra Kay Murphy, were the fearsome, threesome, no one went anywhere, without the other! As I stated earlier, I was called Maggie, Sandra Kay was called, "Red," because she had the most wonderful red hair, not the kind that stuck out in cork screw curls, it was long and straight, no freckles and her eyes were a brilliant green. Then there was Glenda Faye Kelly, we called her, Glenda Faye, now that I think back on it, she should have had a great nickname too.   No, you know what, her name was perfect just the way it was.

I would like to give you a little background on the three of us girls, starting with myself: Clara Margaret "Maggie," Mann, born January 22,1919, in Indianapolis, Indiana, to Philip E. and Sadie Mann.   My father worked at the Speedway Lumber mill and mother was a homemaker to three children.   I had two older brothers, James and Joseph; I was their pet project most of the time.

Glenda Faye Kelly, born April 28, 1919, to Mary and Frank Kelly, Mr. Kelly worked at the General Motors Plant as a janitor, and having eight children, Mrs. Kelly was also a homemaker.

Sandra Kay, "Red," Murphy, born August 6, 1919, to Joseph and Irene Murphy, Mr. Murphy ran the local Green Grocery store on Main Street. Mrs. Murphy gave birth to Sandra late in life, which caused a continuing nervous condition causing her to be a little anti-social with strangers.

What a beautiful day in May, we were seniors, graduated; we got out of school early, because of this and now what to do with the rest of the summer of 1937? We did not want to waste even on second of this time, it was our last taste of freedom, before starting nurses training in September at St. Ann's School of Nursing.

We grew up in an obscure little town that sprung up overnight, like mushrooms in a forest; they called it the town that General Motors built, Speedway City, Indiana. No zip code at that time! Our town did not get named for General Motors, but for another attraction located on the outskirts of town, I cannot recall the actual name at this time, we all called it, "The Speedway." This attraction was a large oval racing track, the only one of its kind in the whole world. The Indianapolis Motor Speedway was built in 1911, a year later; Mr. Lem Trotter drafted plans for Speedway City. This would be an industrial community adjacent to the new Motor Speedway that was also a testing ground for automotive technology.

Its creators envisioned a utopia, Mr. Carl Fisher, one of the town's four founders, said in a 1909 interview that in Speedway City "the homes would be homes and not the kind of shacks that usually infest an industrial center." They advertised this city as, "Beautiful Speedway City," this encouraged people like my own parents to purchase land and build new homes and businesses there. The city advertised a horseless community with sidewalks, water, gas, electric lights, interurban train service and "wonderful gravel roadways."

Soon new industrial plants sprang to life in Speedway City, The Prest-O-Lite Company, Electric Steel Castings Company, Allison Engineering Company, American Art & Clay Company and Esterline Angus Company. In four short years the population increased from 507 residents to 1,400, due to the rapid industrial expansion.

The, "Speedway," racing track went through many changes over the years, today, it is referred to as, "The Greatest Spectacle in Racing," The Indianapolis 500 mile race, this year, 2009, will be the 100th running of this race. As for me, I had absolutely no interest in this attraction, I was never to pass through the main gate in my lifetime.

The local high school, Speedway High, has a sparkplug for their mascot, called, "Sparky." He has huge eyes and stick legs and arms. Everything centered on the racing track or the General Motors plant. My great-granddaughter, Bailey is getting ready to graduate from Speedway High this very year.

Chapter 3

Summer Fun

Just a little bit of history, I am so proud of my, "Speedway City," every child should have the opportunity to grow up in a wonderful, safe town where everyone knows you by your first name. My self, Glenda Faye and Sandra Kay "Red," had that opportunity, but to us it was just normal, we knew nothing else but the happiness of being friends in 1937.

The summer seemed to pass too fast for the fearsome threesome, we went to Westlake to swim and dance under the stars and my brother was a lifeguard there, so I had to be on guard too. Every night we would get cleaned up, meaning, washing our faces and brushing our hair, then arm in arm, we would head for the local soda fountain. There were two drugstores in our town, believe it or not, so we had other alternatives if there were no boys at one drugstore, we would just skip on down Main Street to the other drugstore. Hanging out at a soda fountain might sound boring to the teenagers of this day and age, but to the three of us, it was exciting and we were happy.

Our favorite soda fountain was located at the corner of Main and 15th Street; inside there were small round tables and pretty chairs with heart shaped wire backs. The, soda jerk, as he was called, would take our order and then go behind the counter and whip up whatever concoction we had dreamed up that day. We hardly ever changed our order, it depended on the funds we had in our little silk change purses we kept in our pockets. Some days it was only a cherry phosphate, this was made with soda water, lime syrup and cherry flavoring. When we were flush with coins, we would have our special banana split. The soda jerk would slice a banana in half, then place it in a clear glass boat shaped dish. He would then scoop three balls of ice cream, chocolate, strawberry and vanilla, and place these balls in the glass dish. Chocolate, strawberry and pineapple flavorings would be poured over the ice cream, but the best part was, watching him squirt whipped cream in high peaks, on each ball of ice cream and top it with candied cherries and crushed nuts. When this order was placed in front of us, there were not three banana splits, only one with three spoons. Red, Glenda Faye and I would gossip and sometimes laugh so hard our ice cream would shoot out of our noses!

The only part of the racing track being in our town that gave me interest was, each Memorial Day when the race was held, a carnival came to town. Again, here was an opportunity to get dressed up in our best sundress, a bow or barrette in our freshly washed hair and head to the Mid-Way, as it was called. The big attraction was boys, we were all boy crazy at this age, as were most young girls. We had some of the best summers at the carnival, eating cotton candy and drinking Coca Cola till we were sick to our stomachs. We loved stopping with a rocking motion, at the top of the Ferris wheel. We could see from one side of town to the other, if you looked hard enough, you could see the faint outline of downtown, Indianapolis. Here we would sit, three peas in a pod, sound familiar, that is the way my life has always been. Surrounded by the people I loved and the ones who returned that love. The way we lived our lives as friends during these summers, would seem really boring to the teenagers of 2009.

Chapter 4

Reality Sets In

As September came rushing in on the three of us, we started to feel the pressure of what lay ahead in the next four years. My mother gave me a beautiful brown alligator suitcase outfitted with a hairbrush, hand mirror and empty bottles to be filled with whatever lotions or creams needed to make a young girl beautiful. There was a divider in the middle, and as I flipped it over and looked at the empty space I knew exactly what to put in there. My mother was an excellent seamstress and she made me two beautiful taffeta full length under slips. She made the straps of white satin and stitched little bows, each with a seed pearl in the middle around the neckline. Of course, I had my satin chemise undergarments with tap pants to match, the runway fair of 1937. Under my clothes, I placed a photo of my mother and daddy, I could not leave home without them and this was the only way I could think of to take them along.

Being a student nurse, for the first year we did not wear a formal nursing uniform, that would come starting our second year. The second year students wore, blue and white striped dresses with the usual issued matching items. The graduate Registered nurses were the only nurses allowed to wear all white. We could not wait to wear our white shoes and hose with honor when we graduated. For the present we would have to be satisfied with the fare allotted to us as students.

A cool day in September, I stood on the front porch of my family home, this will be my first time leaving home for longer than an overnight stay. My daddy is driving me to my new school; mother will stay home and cry. I will be spending the next four years of my life at this institution of learning. I will spend every day and night, except for one Sunday a month and summer vacations. I was filled with fear and anticipation, I knew I would not be alone in this endeavor; the fearsome threesome would be together in it. My two friends and myself would be roommates, comrades in arms.

When daddy pulled up in front of the multi-storied brick building, my heart started skipping beats until I saw Red and Glenda Faye. They both had the same look of terror on their faces, which must have reflected on my own. Daddy got out and went around to the trunk of the sedan and retrieved my new suitcase and a few other boxes of needful things for my dorm room. Mother had packed each and every item on the list given to us by the school, I thought to myself, what if my friend's mothers had done the same? If this were the case our possessions would be spilling out into the hall? Daddy helped me carry my things to the second floor hall, we found my room number and he sat my things down. This was where his official job as my watchful parent came to an end; there were tears in his big brown eyes that I had never seen before. I threw my arms around his neck and hugged him so tight and placed a big kiss on his cheek hoping it would last till I could replace it again! As I watched my daddy walk down the hallway, his shoulders were slumped and there was slowness in his step. I thought at any moment he would turn, come back and rescue me from what was to come.

Just as I was reaching to turn the doorknob, Red and Glenda Faye came busting down the hall, with parents in tow. They could not wait for their parents to drop everything and get out of their way to the future! I was still a daddy's girl, unlike them; I would never be anything else for the rest of my life. Like most young women of the day, we had to stop everything and jump up and down, let out a few giggles and a little low-pitched scream. We were finally here, beginning the rest of our lives, turning from children to young adults, ready or not.

Finally we opened the door slowly, not knowing what to expect, after the door swung open on squeaking hinges, it was not much to behold. There was one small dripping sink on the wall with hot and cold-water faucets. The hot water faucet was deceiving; we found out later, the hot water faucet hardly ever produced hot water. We continued the discovery of our abode; there were three iron cots, which looked to be World War I, army issue. The mattresses were rolled up to one end of the cots, we all looked at each other and made an awful noise that cannot be described with words. Red, being the jokester of our group, said, "Looks like it will be the floor for me tonight," of course this never happened. We explored every nook and cranny of the large room, which got much smaller with three girls living there.

The three of us had decided to take advantage of the early week check in. This gave us the time to fix our room just the way we had planned it out together. We had a diagram on how to take clothesline and partition three separate spaces for each of us by hanging sheets. Big mistake, little did we know, Glenda Faye was a sleepwalker and almost choked to death the first night getting tangled in the clothesline. I know it was not funny, but we could not help laughing later when we saw the rope burns on Glenda Faye's neck. We needed help, we needed space, what to do? I went downstairs and stood on the little stool that was placed under the only wall telephone in the entire school and called my daddy. I relayed our problem to him and asked for his help; daddy said he would come by to see what he could figure out.

Daddy showed up, his folding wooden tape measurer in his back pocket, carpenters pencil and a pad of paper. He was never one for a lot of words, just a nod now and then as he scratched the side of his head while thinking. He did his work, kissed me good-bye and told me he would see what he could find at the lumberyard, where he worked, to fabricate something for us.

Believe it or not, my daddy invented the first cubbies, as we call them now! He took orange creates and scrap lumber that he attached little wheels to and made the first under the bed storage boxes. He made three small writing desks that could be folded down and stored in a little area where the chimney came through our room on the way to the next floor. The school provided a small table with three chairs. Daddy brought a folding wooden chair that he pulled from the trash along his route to somewhere. We could put our desks together with the small table and entertain our classmates in style, thanks be to my wonderful daddy, what a guy.

We would spend many a rainy weekend playing cards and board games on those little desks pushed together. Our friends envied us having such wonderful storage facilities, which meant, my daddy made many orange create boxes with little wheels that year. We had a little electric hot plate for cooking in, one pot at a time; we got real inventive over the next four years. We would use this little devise for boiling water to wash our hair, clothing and many more things too numerous to mention.

Chapter 5

Our First Year Woes

None of us was what you would call well off, I know my mother took in sewing and daddy did side jobs to pay for my tuition. Red's father was the green grocer and ran the local bootlegging business out of the back of his store. Glenda Faye, if the truth were told, was poor and didn't even know it. She came from a large catholic family with eight children to feed and clothe. She had won a scholarship to St. John's Academy funded by the local Catholic Charity. Once again she won the essay contest in her senior year on what it would mean to her to be a nurse. This scholarship paid her tuition, room and board, we were all so happy to know that the fearsome threesome would not be separated.

Still knowing all of this none of us considered Glenda Faye or myself poor, Red was the only one who had store bought white blouses. My mother made the white blouses for Glenda Faye and myself out of the sleeves and useable parts of men's old white shirts. I don't know where mother went begging for the shirts and we were just grateful to her for working so hard to make us fit in. The first year of school we wore, white blouses, navy blue skirts, ankle socks and a cardigan sweater in the same shade of navy blue. The sweaters for Glenda Faye and myself were presents from my great aunts, Leana, Beana and Rose. Yes, those are true names; these three ladies were wig makers and milliners. Did I mention my great aunts were, "Old Maids," or to use the proper term, spinsters?

Each week mother and daddy would come by and collect the laundry that we could not wash out by hand in the small sink on the wall. Mother said we needed to learn to make our way in life to some extent and that turned out to be hand washing underwear and socks! There were times when we had clothesline strung crisscrossed all over our room, which meant ducking when you entered the door. Be prepared was our motto and we informed the other girls of washday by hanging a laundry ticket on the doorknob. This prevented a lot of accidents in the years to come and who wants to be slapped in the face with a pair of wet undies?

The first Sunday we got released to go home, the three of us were waiting on the curb for my daddy to come rescue us. Each girl went her separate way to go to Sunday Mass with her family and then home to a magnificent hot meal prepared by their mothers. Most of us had ham or fried chicken, the chicken was most likely alive earlier that morning in the backyard of someone's home. The side dishes were many in number, boiled potatoes, gravy, green beans, corn, hot biscuits and a homemade pie or cake using their mothers secret recipe. I know when we returned to school that night, not one of us could button the waistbands on our skirts. What a wonderful day we all had, I feel sorry for the generation growing up now; they will never experience what we shared that day in 1937.

There were never three girls that worked any more diligently on their schoolwork than we did, we had pride in ourselves and wanted to make our parents proud. There were many nights, after lights out, that the three of us were under the blankets with flashlights in hand giving the test manual one more going over.

Chapter 6

The Troll Under The Stairs

I have not mentioned the other people, adults that lived in our building. There was Sister Mary Johns and Mr. Higgins, also known as, "The Troll." Sister Mary Johns had her own room on the first floor right inside the front entrance hall, this way with her eagle eyes and ears, no one made it in or out, without her knowing. Mr. Higgins, who I will refer to from now on as, "The Troll," lived in a space in the basement, under the stairs.

No one who valued her life ever explored the space where the troll lived. We would rush down the stairs to the tunnel that led to the hospital as fast as possible, but it seemed that the troll was always there to try to have a peek up our skirts. When the weather was fair, we would walk across the campus to the hospital, this is where we took our meals in the main cafeteria. We ate the same fare that the paying patients were given on their trays. It did not take us long to realize our best friend, Glenda Faye, who had to eat in the Charity Ward cafeteria, was becoming thinner.

No one ever thought of Glenda Faye as being a charity case, but the foundation that awarded her the tuition, room and board, did! We approached Glenda Faye and asked what they served her in the basement cafeteria; she gave out a small sob and broke into tears. She explained that there was no cafeteria, only a small table in the kitchen, where she and five other charity students ate together. Just a small sample of her menu: thin watery gruel, if this had been prepared correctly, you would have called it oatmeal, dry toast and half a glass of milk. Lunch consisted of the same items every day, a sandwich of butter bread, which she said tasted like lard and again, half a glass of milk. Supper was a mixture of unidentifiable contents, slopped in a bowl beside, the famous, "Lard Sandwich!"

If you have figured out my personality by now, you know I was once again standing on the small stool that set under the wall telephone calling for help! Mother answered the telephone, I guess I was half screaming and talking so fast, she could not make head or tails of what was going on. Mother turned and held the receiver out in the air and yelled, "Daddy, come here, Maggie is on the line." My daddy calmed me down until he could understand what was happening in my life at that moment, he told me he would talk to mother and get back to me as quickly as possible.

Now, you would had to have known my mother, she was the first president of the Catholic Alter Society, involved in absolutely everything that went on at our church. When mother spoke, everyone listened, I am not saying my mother was an angry or mean person. Mother just knew how to command respect and got it with a smile from her audience. I do not know and never asked what went on at the Alter Society meeting, but Glenda Faye never ate in the kitchen again, nor did her family know of her circumstances. There are no people in the whole wide world with more pride than, Irish Catholics. My mother was an Irish Catholic, her maiden name was, Kelly, but Glenda Faye Kelly and I were not related.

Chapter 7

Learning The Rules

Our nursing program was called the, "Diploma Program," a three-year course, but there was an advanced course of one year that prepared you for the actual Diploma Program. This would elevate having so many written subjects during your floor-nursing program with many sleepless nights, we all chose to do this course together and have more free time in the next three years.

The next few months passed so fast, we were schooled on the top floor of the nursing student building for the first year. Only in the second year were we allowed into the hospital to start the Diploma Program, unless you had family or friends as patients staying there. I only wish I had a photo of the fearsome threesome during bandage wrapping class; there was a moment when we all looked like mummies from Egypt. We had to contain our laughter, muffled in our bandages, Sister Francis Carl, would not hesitate to take the ruler to the palm of our hands if we were caught making fun of anything. Why is it that nuns take the name of a male saint when they are given their final vows? Sister

Francis Carl was a mean and angry woman, unlike my mother; this nun received no respect from any of her students.

We spent a lot of time with oranges and pigs feet, are you laughing? The oranges were to practice the art of giving a patient an injection; the pig feet were used to perfect our suturing expertise. One afternoon, I came bursting through the door as usual; there on the table was an orange with pig feet sewn onto the bottom of it and buttons for eyes. There was only one person who could be responsible for this hilarious stunt, it had to be Red, and she jumped out of the closet laughing so hard she peed her pants. When Glenda Faye came in, the whole scenario was repeated, without the peeing of her pants. If it were not for Red's comic relief, the three of us would never have made it through those four years.

The mid-term exams were given right before Christmas; this meant we would have to wait until after the New Year to receive our grades. I decided that we would try to put this out of our minds and enjoy our two weeks of freedom doing what we did best, hunt for boys. Once again, our hunt was fruitless, the town girls had snapped up all the available young men that had not joined the armed forces, while we were away at school. This was really not troublesome to us, we had so many wonderful times just being together out of the watchful eye of Sister Mary John.

Chapter 8

The Holidays

Mother made me an amazing yellow dress for my Christmas gift, it was as light as a butterfly wing and would move with the slightest breeze. There was a yellow satin slip to match the see through dress, so popular in this time period. I could hardly wait for spring to arrive; I would wear this yellow dress for Easter Mass. Red received a real gold locket from her parents; she would later place a photo of the fearsome threesome in the oval frame of gold. Glenda Faye came to my house sporting a new pair of warm wool mittens and scarf to match, made by her mother. Glenda was as happy with her meager gifts from her parents as Red was with a solid gold locket. This was a time when people cherished what was given to them; some knowing there was a great sacrifice behind the buying and making of the gift. Mother told me many years later that Mrs. Kelly would go to the basement of our church where they kept clothing and other items to dole out to the poor families. She would pick out a bag of unmatched wool socks, bring them home and unravel them and wind the yarn into balls. When she had enough yarn she would then knit the mittens and scarves for her children's Christmas presents. I hugged my mother, as the tears ran down my face, I had no idea just how hard the time we were living in was!

New Year's Eve, all three of our families got together to celebrate baby New Year arriving in, 1938. We all wore paper hats that made us look stupid, but here again, we did not know it, there were horns that rolled out when you blew into them like a snake, then they would snap back in place. Mother, Mrs. Murphy and Mrs. Kelly had set a table full of superb food, my older brothers and their friends stood like sentinels guarding their favorite treats. Each of the young adults were given a small glass of my mother's homemade grape wine, after consuming this small bit of beverage, our heads felt a little light and dizzy.

I stood in the hall waiting to use the bathroom, my daddy and his cronies, as I refer to them were smoking their cigars and drinking brandy in the parlor. I heard Mr. Kelly speaking of Germany and rumors of war going on over seas in Europe, this was the first I knew of any war anywhere! Remember this was a time of no television or internet, you had to listen to the radio or read the newspaper to know what was going on in the world outside of, Speedway, Indiana. I finished my business in the hall and stood in the doorway of the parlor and asked my daddy about the war. He just looked up and said, with his cigar still in the corner of his mouth, "Maggie, don't worry your pretty little head over the war in Europe, it will not have any effect on the United States." Little did he know what lay in store for the United States in the very near future, our world would be turned upside down.

Our holiday vacation ended way too soon for the three of us, before we knew it we were back in school. The three of us were huddled around the big cork bulletin board where our grades were posted for the whole school to see. Myself, I was not a good student, just passing was my goal, Red was above average, but Glenda Faye was the wiz kid of our group! We all made it through, me by the skin of my teeth as some people quoted, Red did much better and Glenda Faye was once again a straight A student.

We were sitting around our make shift table making our New Years resolutions one by one. I vowed to be a better student and put my nose to the grindstone, Red had a better resolution, she was going to meet the man of her dreams this summer, Glenda only ask that she could help in some way to have world peace. This statement would one day be used at almost every Miss America pageant held in the United States. Glenda had a good reason for wanting to help this come true; she had three brothers who would have to go to war, if in fact there was a war involving our country.

Chapter 9

Second Semester

Our second semester classes started with a bang, we were in the chemistry lab, and Red was mixing chemicals to make a certain compound listed in our manual. As Red held the glass beaker over the Bunsen burner and twirled the liquid around until it had dissolved, she then set it on the metal rack to cook. We all had our chemicals mixed, and then Sister Margarett Clair drew our attention to the chalkboard for further instructions. The next thing we heard and smelled was Red's glass beaker shattering and the smell of rotten eggs! Red had used sulfur, instead of the called for ingredient, the two bottles set side by side on the shelf above her head. From that day, until the day we graduated the smell of Red's mixture never completely left the chemistry lab.

Our days passed quickly and before we knew it, spring arrived early in 1938, the snow melted, the pussy willows started to break loose from their buds and the robins had returned. We were finally able to open our window and air out our dorm room, believe me, with three girls washing and cooking all winter long, the room really needed it. We were looking forward to our spring break and the Easter holiday, I would be able to wear my new yellow dress that I had received for Christmas.

We all loved the Easter holiday; our family and friends got together and attended the required church functions. My mother and Mrs. Kelly were the best of friends, just as Glenda Faye and I were; they too had grown up together as girls. The two of them worked together embroidering the new alter cloths; the first one was made of purple silk with white lilies surrounded by beautiful green stems and leaves. In the middle of the cloth there was a huge golden cross entwined with complicated stitched vines. This alter cloth would be used from Good Friday until Easter Sunday morning. Then they would replace it with a stark white cloth with yet, another gold cross, signifying Christ's resurrection from the tomb on the third day after his crucifixion.

Easter Sunday mass, was what Catholics called a high mass, it took forever to sit through and was all spoken in Latin. Even the choir sang in Latin, no one understood what was being said or sung. Glenda Faye and I had a brother or two that were alter boys, these boys helped the priest with his duties while saying mass. We were so glad when all this was over and we could go home and have the biggest feast of the year!

As I stated spring came early and it was warm enough to set up long tables borrowed from the church, in our side yard. The three families were once again united in the festivities, as were friends and the Great Aunts, each with an amazing new Easter bonnet of their own design. There were more than a few giggles concerning the Great Aunts Easter bonnets. The younger Kelly children and a few more from the street that I lived on came for an Easter egg hunt; my brothers were in charge of hiding the eggs before we went to church. Each child was given a paper basket that Glenda, Red and myself had constructed by weaving strips of colored paper together and using staples to hold the whole thing together, the little children were thrilled with the big event.

After the egg hunt was over and everyone settled down we all joined hands and thanked God for this beautiful day and the friends to share it with. All the ladies had prepared their famous side dishes, but my daddy always provided the huge ham. He made arrangements each year in advance with Austin Bates, Austin worked with my daddy at the lumber mill, but was also a farmer of sorts. Austin would put daddy's name on one of his hams when he butchered his hogs and hung them in the smoke house. I can still remember to this day what a wonderful flavor Austin's hams had; I believe it was called, "love."

We had iced tea, lemonade and homemade ice cream churned by the young boys. These treats were very delicious and only served on very special occasions. You had to advance order the ice from the local ice company in Indianapolis. No one that I knew had an electric refrigerator, we all had ice boxes. You would put your orange card in the window twice a week and the company truck would stop and the iceman, as he was called, would fill your wooden icebox with a huge block of ice. This was so much fun in the Summer, while the ice man was in the house, the children would run up and steal a small chunk of crystal clear ice off of the back of the truck. Do you think the iceman knew of this small indiscretion, I believe so, you could see his side-ways smile as he came towards his truck and we would all scatter in different directions.

After all the Easter meal was consumed, we would play croquet, ring toss and bat mitten. The grown men would light their cigars and pull an ice-cold beer from a large metal tub. This beer had been procured from the back door of Mr. Murphy's grocery store earlier. Then the men would start a game of horseshoes. All the women would do the cleaning up and then sit and gossip about everything under the sun. For some of ladies this was the only time of the year they got to see each other until the next Easter gathering.

No one ever explained to me why Easter was the most important holiday; I just figured everyone was sick to death of the winter months. There was really nothing funny in using the phrase, "sick to death," we had many deaths the past winter due to the flu. My daddy was very ill for almost a month and my mother never left his side, spooning in hot clear broth and changing those foul smelling wool flannel compresses on his chest. I can only imagine how heartbreaking this was for my mother; she had lost her first-born son, "Little Harold," as he was called to an epidemic when he was only six years old.

As the sun was hanging low in the spring sky, the colors were beautiful, you could still see through the trees that were just starting to leaf out. All of the women started packing their baskets and folding the linen they brought with them, the men took down the tables and loaded them onto Mr. Murphy's delivery truck. There was a nip in the air, we all put on sweaters while the men and young boys built a fire for roasting marshmallows, this was my mother's new recipe from a magazine she subscribed to. The soft sweet marshmallows were roasted on twigs pulled from trees in our back yard. We had a tradition of telling stories, each person would start the story and the next person would continue until we finally reached what would be the final chapter. We all said our good-byes with hugs, kisses and blessings until we met again next Easter.

Chapter 10

We Can Smell Summer

Daddy delivered the fearsome threesome back to school at least five pounds heavier than when we left for spring break. We spent the next two months in serious study; there was no time for pranks and goofing off, as you would say. We got up early and went to bed late, this was do or die time when it came to exams given in the middle of May. If we did not pass our classes, we could not go on, there was no summer school to make up a grade missed and Glenda could not afford to lose her scholarship. For the first time I really applied all of my skills, I was a hands on type of learner, studying from a textbook was really hard for me. I later learned I had an eye-tracking problem, which did me no good those many years ago.

Here we were again, huddled around the big cork bulletin board, Glenda Faye was head of the class with straight A's, Red kept a constant B average and I trailed behind with a passing B and C average. I was tickled pink; you would have thought I had won the gold medal in nursing that day.

We only had two weeks to suffer through until we could leave for our summer vacation. The week before we left, Sister Mary Johns informed us we were to report to the hospital to be measured for our student nurses uniforms. We were so excited, Glenda looked as if she had swallowed a peach pit whole and started choking. Red and I went over to see what the trouble was, again here were those famous tears in her big blue eyes. She whispered very low, "I have no money for the uniform," my mother and father worked so hard to raise enough, but we are still short by $5.00. I told her that we only had to put down a deposit and pay the balance in September, Red and I promised we would work along with her this summer to earn the $5.00, how hard could that be?

Red, Glenda Faye and myself had made an outline on paper for what we would be doing for the summer that lay ahead of us. When daddy picked us up from school, he had to bring an old trailer, borrowed from Mr. Bates, to haul our entire belongings home. Daddy dropped Red and Glenda Faye off at their homes where their parents were anxiously awaiting their arrival.

Daddy pulled the old sedan up to the tiny garage where my older brothers unloaded all of my belongings. The boys unhooked the trailer and daddy pulled the sedan into the small garage, there was barely enough room to open the car doors. This was a big point with my daddy, never, but never put a scratch on his old sedan, he kept it polished and clean every week. This old car was his pride and joy; there were very few people who even had transportation in those days.

As I walked past the grape arbor where the old fashion water pump was still standing, I thought back to the wonderful steaming hot summer days when all of the children would pump and play for hours in the ice cold water. I looked up to see my mother standing in front of the kitchen window, it seemed to me she spent most of her life, either in front of that window or sitting at her sewing machine. My mother had a sort of magic when it came to sewing, she could take an old garment and make

27

something beautiful from it. Just a new piece of lace here, a row of buttons there and the hem shortened just a bit. I loved her sewing machine, I used to sit and pretend it was everything from an automobile to a race car. I would pump the old treadle plate so hard with my little feet, daddy would say, "Maggie, you better slow down or you are going to take off and we will never find you again!"

My mother was so glad to see me, when I walked into the kitchen, she was winding a piece of string onto a ball of twine, and she saved absolutely everything. This was due to the fact we were just coming out of the, "The Great Depression," these years had been so hard on everyone. No one had been excluded from this dreadful period in time; my mother would never get over it. Mother had canning jars buried between her rose bushes, filled with coins collected in secret. I in turn learned from a young age how to save and look to the future, as being unstable at any moment and this was to be a great tool of learning for me in the years to come.

Daddy came in behind the boys carrying all of my suitcases, books and other needful things that I had collected over the past year at school. All of this mess was deposited in my room to be sorted through later. One thing I did not understand was why my parents bought a two-bedroom home, when they had two boys and one girl? Of course, it was do to finances and my mother's ability to make do. My daddy had added a room onto the kitchen for the boys to sleep in; they had half of the room, just one bed. Daddy made a folding screen to hide the bed; mother painted it her favorite shade of cream and green. In the center panels she put left over wallpaper from the dining room makeover. This rolled up paper was just one of many things mother kept in the closet that went over the basement stairs comprised of many stair steps to make more storage room. I used to call this closet her treasurer chest; you just never knew what might be hidden there! I didn't realize it at the time, but I was a very fortunate young woman to have her own room. This was a time of large families, like the Kelly's; you were lucky to have a bed, much less a whole room.

After much hugging and kissing by my mother, she always smelled of a mixture of talcum powder, Life Boy soap and oil of winter green. The oil of wintergreen was her topical medication that she rubbed on her knees to help relieve the pain. Did it work, it doesn't matter, and she thought it did and that was all I cared about. I loved my mother's knees, this is where I sat when I learned to listen, sew, read and just rest my head when the world was closing in on me.

Mother sat me down at our kitchen table, another construction project of my daddy's, I loved that table, I used it when I first married, as did my own daughter many years later. Mother poured hot water over tea leaves, into her treasured teapot, put a tea cozy over it and then set out our cups. When the tea was ready, she held a small strainer over each of our cups to catch any stray leaves. We had two very special cups; they were all that was left of a complete set, hand painted by the Great Aunts many years ago. We would, over the years, discuss many important as well as mundane subjects over our little hand painted teacups with the beautiful violets and green leafed stems. These little cups are wrapped and sealed away, by the time my own children were old enough, tea was not in fashion, nor was talking to your mother.

Today the subject was my summer vacation, I told her all about the plans that Red and Glenda Faye and I had made. That was a huge mistake, really huge!! Unbeknownst to the three of us, our mothers had their own plans concerning how we would spend the next three months and it had nothing to do with boy hunting or goofing off!

By the time Red, Glenda Faye and I got the time to get together over a banana split, we were all three in tears. Red's father had a working schedule for her in his green grocery store, Glenda Faye was to help her mother with the little side business she had doing laundry for other people. My mother had volunteered me for everything you could think of, she was too proud to have me work for money. Mother also told me this was the summer I would learn to read a pattern, cut cloth and sew a garment that I could actually wear out in public. There went our earning capacity for the $5.00 we needed for Glenda Faye's uniform, we would have to come up with something else. We ate the rest of the banana split in silence, dried our tears and took a walk down Main Street to find out all the gossip that had taken place over the school year.

Chapter 11

Summer of 1938

I am not saying that absolutely every minute of that summer was planned out for us by our mothers, we had a lot of free time and made even more by helping out each other in our duties. We were looking forward to the Indianapolis 500 mile race week and the carnival coming to town, some of my favorite memories were of these nights, arm and arm with my friends.

If I were able to sneak away from the watchful eye of my mother while she sat and talked on the telephone, her favorite pastime and one luxury, I would head straight for the green grocers. Red would be there, dancing around the store, feather duster in hand looking busy, but doing nothing but moving dust from one place to another. Mr. Murphy would come over with a metal pail filled with soapy water and hand us two rags, which meant real work. We would wipe all the shelves to be stocked and be constantly reminded not to forget the corners. Mr. Murphy would say remember, cans are not square and the corners are important. Then we would put the price stickers on the cans, these too were scrutinized he would not stand for crooked stickers on his cans. Today he would be a type A personality, but I could always call on these memories to help me later in my life. Each day before we left, Mr. Murphy would hand us a basket of apples, he knew we were on our way to the Kelly's.

Red did not like working at the Kelly's, this was real work, which meant getting your hands dirty and wet. When we arrived, Glenda Fay and her mother were already hard at work doing laundry. This was a great summer, it was the first time that the Kelly's had indoor plumbing, there was a small room built by Mr. Kelly and my daddy to house a sink, toilet and the smallest bathtub I had ever seen. I know this will not impress you, but up until this time in the Kelly's life, they had to walk to an outside toilet and bathe in a number 3 washtub. When you have eight children, you do not want to be the last one to step into the tub. Mrs. Kelly usually started with the girls and went from there; boys could care less about the water being clean or murky. Remember, each bucket of water had to be heated on a wood burning stove and carried to the tub for this weekly ritual of bathing for church on Sunday morning. Now, there was city plumbing and a gas water heater installed, this is where having true friends comes into play, Mr. Kelly knew everyone by name that worked at the Allison General Motors plant and Mr. Kelly was well liked and respected. You would not believe what could be carried out in a large lunch pail to help construct Mr. Kelly's indoor plumbing project. One day Mrs. Kelly came out and there on the lawn was an old gas stove with an oven door that was rusted and made an awful noise when it was opened, but to this precious woman it was a wonderful gift from God.

As Red and I walked up to the house, we started passing out the apples her father had sent for all the other children running all over the yard and hanging from tree limbs. I loved Mrs. Kelly as if she were my own mother, in fact out of respect; I called her, "Mother Kelly." I knew that if I had a problem, I could go to her and my confidence would never be broken, even to my mother. I think back to that actual time and picture this wonderful woman in my mind and I see her worn face with so many lines and her gray hair pulled back in a bun, always with stray strands of hair escaping. Not once did I ever hear her complain or show a frown, just smile lines, as she liked to call them. She would stand up and put her hands on the middle of her back and give me a huge hug with wet soapy hands. What I would give to once more feel those wet handprints on the back of my blouse.

Glenda Faye, Red and I would push up our sleeves and start separating laundry by colors and families they were to be returned to when washed and dried. Again, Mother Kelly was like Mr. Murphy, she wanted her work to be respected by the people she worked for. The old electric washing machine on the back porch was filled many times over and over, water drained and filled again. This was not an easy chore, after the allotted time in the washing machine; the laundry was then put through two wooden rollers, called ringers. The clothes then went into a tub of clear water and back through the ringer and on to the clothesline. The white clothes washed with Ivory soap flakes and bleach, the colors with Oxodol. I loved the smell of soap powder and bleach, I still do, and Mrs. Kelly taught me everything I know about getting out stains and being proud of having the whitest line of washing in the neighborhood!

By the time we finished our work we were too tired for anything but the walk home in time for supper and maybe to listen to a radio program. There was more and more news of the war in Europe, my oldest brother was getting married and moving out with his bride. He worked at the International Harvester plant, he said they were gearing up for a big government contract that was really hush, hush in whispers around the plant. My other brother was working at the Eli Lily Drug Company and he too was going to join the army like so many other young men. He had a sweetheart too, she was beautiful and blonde, her family was like the Kelly's, you could not keep track of them all.

Today is the first day of the carnival, the fearsome threesome, have changed and exchanged clothes so many times we have forgotten whose clothes belong to who. I snuck into my mother's bedroom, found a tiny tube of lip rouge as it was called, we now call it lipstick and put it in my pocket for later. I guess that sounds like nothing to you, but we were not allowed to wear lip rouge yet, this was a big deal to us at the time. We finally got dressed, said good-bye to our parents and ran out of the house free spirits once more. As soon as we were far enough from home I pulled out the tube of lip rouge, it looked strange, it was light orange, but once applied it turned a different color of pink on each one of us. Boy, did we think we were hot stuff that night, did I forget to tell you, we had also pinned our hair up on top of our heads in big loose curls tied in a pretty ribbon. We fixed our hair by looking in the back garage window, so no one could see us do this. Only older ladies wore their hair up.

We were now off on our first adventure of the summer vacation, boys, boys, boys, where are you? Remember this was a time when you could still hold hands with your best friend or lock arms and people would not give it a second thought. Every where we looked that was all we saw, our other friends, all girls, arm in arm, it seemed the only boys around were working at the carnival or using a cane to get around. We stopped to buy a coke and a cotton candy; we talked to Alice Marie Sullivan, Mary Rose Farley and Dianne Marie Miller. These were our friends who were attending other colleges or engaged to boys in the army. Being away for 9 months really put us out of touch with what was going on in the real world. The girls filled us in on just how bad things were here on the home front. There were a few boys around, or maybe I should start calling them men from now on, but not the kind you would take home to your mother and father.

We did not let this stop the six of us from having a wonderful time, we rode all the rides, some of them twice, all it took was a wink from Mary Rose and the men would just melt. She was a beauty and she knew it and used it to her advantage any time she could. I don't remember anyone who had blonde hair like hers that didn't come from a bottle, and those big blue eyes with lashes that curled clear up to her eyebrows. Needless to say, that night we ate, rode rides and did just about anything we wanted with just a wink of Mary Rose's beautiful blue eyes.

Chapter 12

Mother Makes A Plan

The rest of the summer seemed to drag on until August, all at once we realized we had not earned one penny to pay on Glenda Faye's uniform. This was a time when men were making $5.00 a week, so it was no small amount of money! I finally went to my mother with the problem, she wanted to go to the rose garden, shovel in hand and bail us out. I said, "No," we are in this together and we need help to find a project to make some money. Mother said, "Give me some time to think, and I will get back to you."

A few days later, mother called the three of us into the kitchen, there lay red, white and blue rolls of crape paper left over from some project mother had volunteered for. This too probably came from the closet with the stairs, her treasurer chest of goodies. There was a large box containing thin strips of wood that my daddy had made for our project, of course we had no idea what that was yet. Mother said there is a large fund drive for the people in Europe who need our help, it is downtown and it will be huge. I want you girls to make small flags for the people to wave and cheer after the mayor speaks. You may charge a nickel for your flags, but remember half of that goes to the cause in Europe. Wow, what a great idea, do you realize how many flags you have to make to earn $5.00, clear money? By the end of the day our arms were covered to the elbows with rubber cement and home made glue (flour and water mixed). This was not a pretty sight by any means, but we really worked hard on our project and when daddy came home he was so proud of us. He said he would take us downtown in the old sedan so we did not have to ride the bus with all of our flags.

Daddy made us another little folding table; boy did he come in handy, when we really needed him. He dropped us off and pulled away and would come back at 6:00PM. When we took a good look around, we realized other people had a similar idea to ours, but they all had made lapel buttons. Our flags were a hit, some people who only wanted one flag, but only had a dime, told us to keep the change. When this happened, you know where that extra nickel went, not half to the cause, it went in our secrete pocket. We needed every nickel we could beg, borrow or short of stealing. After all was said and done, we were still short $1.50.

We were just folding up our little table and it was 5:45PM, we were looking for daddy to come around the corner in the old sedan. A man came up to us and said he had been watching us from his office window and was proud of us for our effort. We kind of looked down, but told him half was for the cause and half was for our friend to buy her nursing uniform. He asked how much we needed, we told him the amount, he handed us a $10.00 bill and said, "She will need shoes to go with that uniform, and if you need anything else, come see me. My name is Mr. Fredrick M. Ayres, you are standing in front of my department store." Mr. Ayres just tipped his hat and strolled on down Meridian Street, as big as you please! We did not know at the time, but Fredrick M. Ayres would die in 1940 and be replaced by his son-in-law, Theodore B. Griffin. We could not believe our luck, we took the extra nickels out of our secrete pocket and donated them to the cause immediately. We all looked up, and sure enough we had set our table up right under the Ayres clock that was erected in 1936. Many years later there would be a 1,200 pound bronze cherub that would appear at Thanksgiving and remain on the clock until Christmas Eve. Each year this was like magic to most people, they never saw who placed the beautiful cherub on the corner of the clock. We all looked at each other and said at the same time, "We never thought of shoes!"

When daddy stopped the old sedan, we were all talking at once about what fantastic luck we had with our little project that turned into a miracle for Glenda Faye. My daddy just looked into the rear view mirror and gave me a big smile that made his brown eyes twinkle. He said, "When you are doing God's work, you cannot fail." We all felt a little guilty because of the secrete pocket money we would have used, but maybe God will forgive us that one indiscretion, after all it was going for a worthy cause of our own. Daddy left us off out in front of the house and we all went running in to retell our story to mother, who would have to keep it a secrete because of the pride of Mr. and Mrs. Kelly. Mother said, "I am glad I shop at Mr. Ayres' department store, even if it is in the bargain basement, but still I am more proud to know that he is an upstanding person with a generous heart, as his father before him, Mr. Lyman S. Ayres.

This was a big load off of our minds, now we had to start preparing for our future school year to begin.

Chapter 13

We Begin Our Hospital Training

When September of 1938, arrived we were once again nervous as we arrived at the big brick building that would be our home for the next nine months. The fearsome threesome were roommates, better prepared this time, we had plenty of clothesline and a few more cooking utensils to get us by. Everything we had to leave behind in our room was still there, Sister Mary Johns let us know that it was no easy feat to protect our precious objects from the troll, as we had come to call the janitor, Mr. Higgins.

We were called to the hospital auditorium for a short lecture and to receive our uniforms. We were given two blue striped dresses, two sets of white collar and cuffs, one white cap and two white starched aprons. We provided our own black cotton stockings and shoes, and then there were the unmentionables everyone owned. We listened to the lecture and then carried our boxes back to our dorm room we were so excited. For the first time we would dress as nurses while we worked in the hospital, for class we still wore our old school uniforms.

The first year of school we would be working in the Charity Wards located in the basement, yes, the same place Glenda Faye had invented the famous, "Lard Sandwich." We had no idea what we were in for, which was probably for the best or we would have taken off like a rocket to the moon.

We set our alarm early to put on our new uniforms and make sure everything was just right and we looked professional. As we put on our dresses, buttoned our collars and cuffs in place, we then reached for our white starched aprons. I don't know why, but this apron was my favorite piece of my uniform, I loved the way it felt, all smooth and crisp tied in a large bow in the back of my dress. Finally each one of us placed a cap on the other, we all turned and looked in the old mirror above the sink, we were nurses.

Our pride was to be short lived, the bell was ringing for morning prayers before breakfast, and we hurried down the stairs to the first floor and ran across the grounds to the hospital. There were rows and rows of tables all set for breakfast, we stood at attention, said the blessing and then were allowed ten minutes to gulp down our meager meal. The bell rang again; the Mother Superior stood and gave directions to each table of nurses according to their rank. She came to our table and led us to the basement and introduced us to the head nurse of the Charity Ward, Sister Ann Marie. Mother Superior turned on her heel and marched away with the clicking of her rosary beads tied at her waist and the heels of her shoes on the concrete floor.

We had no idea what to do with ourselves, there were twelve of us in the first year Diploma Program that year. Our first duty was to start at one end of the ward and work our way down to the end. Each patient had to be bathed and his or her sheets changed from the night before, I know this sounds like an easy job, not so in those days. Bathing a patient, meant just that, you had a basin of warm water and a foul smelling liquid soap, I found out later this was to help kill any lice that might be on the patient. They were washed, dried and smoothed with a fine talcum powder to keep down the odor. If they could stand or sit, you would then strip the bedding and remake the bed, there was a rule for this to, and you learned to make perfect hospital corners on the top and bottom sheets. If your patient could not get out of bed, you rolled them to the side with the help of another nurse who would make one side of the bed, then roll them back and make up the other side of the bed.

While all of this was going on, the nurses' aids, as they were called, served the patients their breakfast, by the time the aids got to the end of the ward the food was hardly palatable and cold. I could not get this out of my mind, I don't care how poor you are, and you should be given decent food and be treated with respect. I stored this in the back of my mind to talk to my mother about when we next went home for a break. After all the order of nuns was called, "The Sisters of Charity," and I did not feel this was being charitable serving food that even a dog would not eat!

After everyone was clean, dry and fed, "The Gods," of the hospital would make an appearance, otherwise known as doctors. These men demanded so much respect that we actually stood at attention with our eyes downcast, unless we were spoken to directly. Sister would go over each metal chart that hung on the end of the patient's bed with the doctor, and then he would write out the order of care for the day.

We were assigned by fours to an individual senior nurse, she would explain each problem and how it was to be handled. There was every kind of disease known to man in this ward, from broken bones to bedsores. When you are a brand new nurse, you want to spend time with your patient, but you learn quickly that this is a big no, the less spoken the better. That did not set well with me, I loved people and genuinely cared about their pain and suffering. I did as I was told, I did not want a reprimand from the Mother Superior the first week of my training. Red and Glenda Faye were fairing much better than I was, they took orders and never questioned anything they were told to do. Glenda Faye was a natural, having seven brothers and sisters she had seen it all and fixed it with the help of her mother at home. All of the Kelly children were born at home, her mother did not trust hospitals, and she had heard horror stories about something called, "Child Bed Fever," that was contracted at the hospital. Later it was found to be due to the doctors not washing their hands when going from patient to patient. This was discovered and corrected by a great doctor, called Joseph Lister. Doctor Lister was the genius who found and named, bacteria, there is even a bacteria named after him, it is called, Listeria and very deadly if left untreated.

We finished our first day of training and instead of running across the campus, we were barely able to walk. Our feet hurt so badly, all we could think of was filling a basin with Epsom salts and soaking our feet for hours. As we entered our room we looked at each other and took off running for the only basin we owned. Glenda Faye was the sprinter, she had to chase down so many of her little brothers and sisters, and she got to the basin first. Being the saint that she was, she filled the basin with hot water and Epsom salts and sat three chairs around it; we all squeezed our feet in together. Here again, friends make room for friends, even if it is their feet.

Chapter 14

Solving Problems Over Tea With Mother

The first month of training was a real challenge and we were all so glad when our Sunday day off came around. Daddy picked us up in the old sedan and we were very quiet, he looked in the rear view mirror, our eyes met and he knew something was very wrong. We dropped the girls off and went home for Sunday dinner, mother had all of my favorite dishes prepared just the way I liked them, even the lumps in the mashed potatoes. I sat there kind of moving the food around on my plate with my fork, all of a sudden a tear rolled down my cheek. Mother jumped up and came around the table, knelt down beside me, which must have been hard for her poor sore knees. I just threw my arms around her neck and cried for what seemed to be hours, but only a minute or two. The rest of the family sat like statues, they had no idea what was up with me, there was always something going on in my life that was a live or die situation to me.

I composed myself, whispered to mother that we would discuss my problem while we sat at the kitchen table and drank our tea. We cleared the dining room table, washed the dishes and mother put the kettle on for tea. I got out the beautiful cups and we sat down together to take care of my problem. I explained about the food at the Charity Ward and how the patients almost gagged when they had to eat their meals. Mother remembered the problem with Glenda Faye and having to eat this food the first year of school. Did we not think about the others who had no menu choice? Mother said, "I know where to begin, it all starts with money and those who have it!"

Mother remembered Mr. Ayres saying to call him if we needed any help in the future and believe me she would stop at nothing to get things taken care of. This was a time when you could pick up the telephone, her instrument of choice, and call the L. S. Ayres department store and talk to an actual person. When the switchboard operator answered mother's call, she told her she wished to speak to Mr. Ayres; he was a personal friend of her daughter's. Mother was immediately connected to his office and I don't know what transpired between them, but Mr. Ayres would be getting back to mother as soon as possible.

Chapter 15

Pink Ribbon For Nora

We returned to training after our Sunday off, it did not take long to get into a rhythm from day to day care of our patients. There were no walls in the charity wards, only folding screens with linen cloth to hide what ever was going on in the next bed. There was a kind of structured chaos to how patients were placed when being admitted, short stays, surgeries, terminal cases and a small private maternity ward. This was my favorite place to work; I loved the mothers and the babies. The first birth that I assisted with was like a miracle to me, I knew absolutely nothing about how a baby came into this world.

My first maternity patient was a middle aged woman named, Nora Baker, she could see the fright in my eyes, she said, "Take a deep breath, I will talk you through this." I did not know this was her 8th child, the little one slipped into this world without a whimper from her mother, the little girl was laid on her mother's stomach, cord clipped and then she was wrapped up and taken to be cleaned, weighed, measured and foot printed. The doctor finished up with Nora and I cleaned her very carefully, dressed her in a fresh gown and laid her head on a starched pillowcase that felt cool to the touch. She was so grateful for my gentle care that I only wished I had more to offer this wonderful woman.

We heard the head nurse returning with Nora's brand new little gift from God's hands to hers. I asked Nora what her name would be, she looked at me and said, "I will name her Maggie, a good Irish name, after a good Irish nurse!" I leaned over Nora and broke all the rules, by placing a light kiss on her forehead and then on little, Maggie's, too.

The next day when I returned to the maternity ward, I carried blue ribbons in one pocket and pink ribbons in the other, then mixed in were little tubes of lip rouge given to me by my mother on my last visit home. I stopped by to see how little Maggie and Nora were doing; there was a smile on both of their faces. As I bathed Nora she and I softly hummed an old Irish folk song together behind her screen. When I finished brushing her beautiful dark hair I pulled a long pink ribbon out of the pocket of my white starched apron. Nora's eyes lit up, you would have thought it was Christmas or some great event. I tied the ribbon around her head with a pretty bow at the side of her cheek, then, after looking both directions, I pulled out the little tube of lip rouge. I put a very thin layer of the orange rouge on her lips, told her to press them together and then held up the mirror in front of her face. I was glad there was no mascara involved or there would have been black streaks down her cheeks. Nora told me this was the first time she had ever had lip rouge or time to tie a pretty ribbon in her hair, these were luxuries she could not afford. As I turned around to leave Nora, I bumped right into her husband, Frank. The look on his face was amazing, if only I had my Kodak, what a moment this would have been. Frank looked at me and said, "See that beautiful woman, she is my bride and as pretty as the day we wed!" I silently walked away and left Frank alone with his beautiful bride, but I felt so much pride that one moment of kindness had brought to me.

Many years later in my nursing career, I ran into a young nurse who looked scared to death, I stopped her and asked what the matter was. She lifted her head and said, "My name is Maggie Baker, I am a first year student and I am lost!" I put my arm around her shoulders proudly and told her, "I brought you into this world, and my name is also, Maggie." Maggie told me that her mother still carried the pink ribbon that I had tied in her hair those many years ago. Maggie said she pressed it in her Sunday prayer book that she took to mass. I showed her on her way and as I walked down the corridor I felt my back straighten and I walked with the same pride I felt that day I made her mother look like a bride again.

Chapter 16

Home For The Holidays

The time seemed to fly by for the three of us; we were so busy that we hardly had time to think. The holidays were soon approaching, being first year student nurses; you had to work one of the two holidays. This meant picking a piece of paper out of a hat, you either got Thanksgiving or Christmas off, it was the luck of the draw as they say. Glenda Faye, Red and I all were to work on Thanksgiving, we were so glad; we all loved the Christmas holiday with our families coming together as one.

It seemed that no one got sick over the holiday, but the next week or so everyone was ill with many gastric problems of one kind or the other probably due to poor refrigeration. By the time Christmas holiday rolled around we were all so tired that we didn't care if Santa came or went. Daddy picked us up as he always did, it was now a routine that we all knew so well, first Glenda Faye so that I could give, Mother Kelly a huge hug and then to Red's house where her mother was waving from the window. She must be having another problem with going outside, now it is called, either a panic problem or agoraphobia.

It had been a very mild Fall, just a few light snows so far, as we turned the corner of Ford Street and Auburn, I could see our Christmas tree in the window. Immediately my spirits picked up, I felt renewed, I am so glad mother didn't wait for me to decorate the tree. I bet she knew in her heart that I would need a surprise to cheer me up and get me kick started for the season ahead. Daddy had so many lights strung all over the front of the house you could probably see it from outer space, as if that would ever be possible! Daddy let me out in front of the house while he drove the old sedan around to the garage; he knew I could not wait one more minute to be held in my mother's arms.

I rushed up the front steps skipping every other one on my way, mother was waiting with the front door open, and she grabbed me and pulled me in and hugged me so tight. This year was different; we did not get two weeks at Christmas like when we were just going to the academic program last year.

I was home, the smell of the pine, mother's homemade cookies, and hot buttered rum simmering on the stove. Lovely, that is the only adult word I could come up with, something had happened to me during these past four months, I had grown up.

After much hugging my brother and his wife, my younger brother and his intended, their wedding was planned for June of next year, 1939. We all sat around and ate like pigs, on this visit it was mostly about my family, I saw enough of my friends living with them. Tomorrow everyone would be calling, it was a tradition, each family would host and this year it was the Mann family. All day and evening our friends and family would come with food and presents. The Great Aunts would be picked up in daddy's old sedan and they would spend the whole day and evening. My burst of energy did not last long, I had to excuse myself and go to my room and drop from exhaustion onto the bed, clothes and all. I knew my daddy came in and covered me up with my quilt, I could smell his wonderful pipe tobacco, I smiled in a half sleeping state of mind.

I woke up to a chill, the temperature had dropped over night and the old coal furnace was running full blast. I got out of bed and slipped into my house shoes and chenille robe and shuffled to the bathroom. I came into the kitchen where mother already had a pot of tea ready, we did not use our special cups today, it was big stone mugs to keep the tea hot. Mother was baking a small ham, stewing a chicken for noodles and our favorite corned beef that would have cabbage added later. What was an Irish Christmas without the famous dish of Ireland on the table?

Mother took a moment to sit down with me at the table before I got dressed and started helping her with the rest of the preparations. She said, "You would not believe the Christmas present you are going to receive, it is so special that it must have been sent from an angel." Of course, my mind went to all the handsome young men I had taken care of at the hospital and they promised to write to me or call at least. Now I had to wait until after Midnight mass to open my presents, that was also a tradition in our family, Santa came while we were at mass. The little ones, if there were any at the time would fall asleep in their mothers laps and be ready when we got home. I tried to put this out of my mind all day, but it kept popping up every hour or so. I told Red and Glenda Faye about it when they arrived with their families. Mother wanted or should I say insisted they be here too, when I opened the gift. The rest of the day was wonderful, our house was like magic, and no matter how many people came there was always room for more. We ate, sang songs while Great Aunt Beana played on the old upright piano; she wore a beautiful hat of course. This hat had red and deep green velvet bows and little springs of artificial holly tucked here and there, she had sprinkled a tiny bit of glitter powder to make the leaves sparkle. Another Kodak moment lost in time, if it were not for my mother and her obsession with taking photographs, I only wish we had color film back in those days.

Before we knew it, the time to get bundled up and go to church for mid-night mass was upon us. As we walked outside to get in the old sedan, snow started falling, not normal snow, but the kind of snowflakes that were the size of nickels. The moon was full and bright making it look like diamonds falling from heaven to the earth. I was wearing a new Christmas coat, an early present from the Great Aunts; it was red with real ermine fur trim at the neckline. My Great Aunts spoiled me rotten having no children of their own and being partial to girls, there was a round hat called a, tam to match, I think it was a French thing. With my brothers having automobiles of their own now, we did not have to squeeze in until we turned a bright shade of blue any longer. Just joking, but it used to be quite uncomfortable in the past with all of The Aunts and us.

By the time our whole group arrived at St. Christopher church it was pretty much filled by one-third capacity. For the first time in my life, I actually listened to Father Linderman as he gave his sermon and knew I could use so much of his advice in my future as a responsible person. We all put on our coats and filed out after the Christmas blessing by Father Linderman.

Chapter 17

The Beautiful Woman

Daddy pulled the old sedan up in front of 4986 Ford Street, there in daddy's parking place sat a very large black sedan, mother said for me to get out and ask if they needed help or to use our phone. As I knocked on the window, it was slowly rolled down, there in the huge back seat sat a middle-aged couple, she in a beautiful mink coat and hat to match. Her husband was dressed in a black cashmere overcoat. He tipped his hat to me and asked how I was getting along and was I having a good holiday so far? I could hardly speak, I asked if they would like to come in out of the cold and have some hot buttered rum or other libation with my family? The lady was so gentle and soft-spoken, as she reached beside her on the seat, I could see the biggest diamond ring in the world on her finger. She handed me a large rolled up document and three small packages. I took the gifts and did not know how to respond; I was dumb struck, they finally said, "Merry Christmas to my three favorite girls and to pass the wish on to all of your families, especially my mother." I leaned in the window and gave her a big hug and kiss and thanked them for the gifts they brought to us on this cold Christmas Morning. Remember by now it was almost 1:30AM, in the morning, they said a final good-bye and rolled up the window as their chauffeur pulled away from the curb.

I ran into the house, scroll and the three gifts in hand, everyone was so excited to find out what was going on! I explained everything up to this point; I shrugged out of my hat and coat and called Glenda Faye and Red over to sit beside me on the couch. Together we broke the seal on the scroll, inside was a declaration stating there was a brand new Nutritional facility to be built on the campus. This facility would provide all the meals for every patient admitted to the hospital; no one would be excluded because they could not pay. The meals would be hearty, hot and palatable by everyone at the hospital, there would also be a lounge and cafeteria for the visitors to rest and relax while waiting for their family or friends to be taken care of. The person responsible for the donation of this great building was anonymous; it only stated that a doctor saved one of their children at St. Ann's many years ago.

I now know that Mr. Ayres knew many wealthy people who sat on many boards in our city of Indianapolis, I am sure it was one of his best friends that heard the story and wanted to help give back to the community. We then remembered the three packages all wrapped in beautiful paper with big bows and jingle bells tied on to the ribbon. As we opened the packages, we did it slowly wanting it to last forever. There was a small envelope and a jewelry box that contained a real 14K gold chain with a small nurses cap pendant hanging from it. Inside the envelope was a receipt for tuition paid in full for each of us to include room and board. There was also a gift certificate to the L. S. Ayres department store for each of our mothers to purchase any of our basic needs for the rest of our semesters at school. Needless to say, there was not a dry eye in the house. Just think, all these gifts from one young woman's need of $5.00 to buy a school uniform.

My mother helping three young women learn the lesson of taking the responsibility and working for what you need.

We were wrapping up our own gift giving and saying how we just loved everything we received, which was really true this year, when daddy gave mother a small box. This box was wrapped in the same beautiful paper as our necklaces had been wrapped in; when mother opened the box there was a white gold wristwatch with tiny diamonds all around the dial. I thought my mother was going to faint dead away, before daddy grabbed hold of her. Inside was a hand written card stating, "You are a diamond of a person and may you always watch over your family with love." A little play on words by Mr. Ayres, that Christmas this meek mannered man made me believe there are really angels on earth. Thank you God!

It was so early in the morning when everyone was packed up and on their way home, the Great Aunts came prepared to spend the night. My brothers brought the old rollaway bed up from the basement and set it up in the living room for the three of us to bed down. The Aunts slept in my room and one of them on my brother's bed behind the folding screen off the kitchen. We all stood at the picture window waving good-bye to everyone leaving we could not help laughing at the Kelly's and the Bate's. Mr. Bates had picked up all ten of the Kelly's on his way over, he had spread a thick layer of fresh hay all over the bed of his panel truck and covered it with some of Minerva's wonderful yarn tied blankets. Mr. Bates and his wife Minerva, along with their son David, road in the cab of the truck, the Kelly family all laughing and crawling in the back of the truck was a sight to behold. Another Kodak moment that was lost, but the next day Glenda Faye said they had the best time on the ride home. The little tykes fell asleep immediately and they all sang Christmas songs, warm and toasty under Minerva's blankets.

Chapter 18

Learning From The Best

This brings back a memory I need to share, I spent a few days on the Bates' farm with Minerva, she showed me how to make yarn tied blankets along with other things like canning peaches, etc. I taught my own daughter how to make these blankets, but she preferred hand quilting, later when time grew short, she started making these wonderful blankets for all the people who were going through chemotherapy. Her friends, family and patients told her there was magic in her blankets. I know it was the love she put into the making of them, she said a prayer every time she tied the yarn. She made so many the last years of her life that we lost count; Saragene was able to write a short story called, "The Last Blanket." Each time she would sew a blanket and turn it for tying with yarn, she would ask herself, "Is this the last blanket?"

The aroma of fresh brewed coffee woke me up along with bacon frying in mother's big iron skillet. The Aunts had been up as long as mother, it took the three of them over a half hour to just fix their hair. The Aunts had never really cut their, only a trim now and then, the length was to the bend in their knees. Each one would fix the other, while today my mother stood behind Great Aunt Lena and did hers to save time. Their hair was always braided and piled high upon their heads, it was a treat to see all three of them with their beautiful hair hanging loose and free, they looked like young women again. My heart ached for the love of these special women that God had given me in my life.

It was nine o'clock on Christmas morning, mother even let daddy sleep in on this special day, so unusual for him. Daddy came out of the living room stretching his large hands over his head and saying, "Something sure smells great in the kitchen this Christmas morning!" He knew exactly what it was, always the same menu, sliced ham, cream gravy, Minerva's secrete hand rubbed smoked bacon, a platter of fried eggs and mother's yeast sticky buns.

I have to stop and tell you about these buns, she made everything from scratch, she would put a pat of butter in the muffin pan followed by chopped pecans, brown sugar, all mixed with a tiny bit of sifted flour and then three round balls of yeast dough that made the bun pull apart with ease. These would rise setting on top of the oven covered with a red and white checked dishcloth, then popped in the oven about a half hour before we sat down. Mother had a special platter she used to turn the buns out on, I could never figure out why the sticky part did not slide off onto the platter and then drop on the tablecloth, and mine always did?

My daddy was a great man; he had such a routine, that if he would take one step out of line he would get caught. Yet, no one did surprises better than he did, like getting the new electric coffee pot into the house for mother this Christmas. Mother did not trust the new coffee pot and also put her old one on the stovetop, just in case. One thing daddy did that I still do today; he would eat his Christmas gravy on a fresh piece of bread, but leave on piece on the plate. I asked him when I was very young why he did this at every meal? All he said was, "It is a bite to be done on." I still have no idea what that meant and never brought it up again.

Christmas Day at the Mann's was a relaxed affair; we mostly sat around playing card games, checkers for my daddy and my older brother, with the radio playing in the background. People would stop by to wish us a happy holiday and be on their way, and then mother and daddy would do the same. That left me to my own devices, I would call Red and Glenda Faye to see what they got for Christmas and I would tell them what I had received and we would make a plan. This year it was to take the bus downtown to see, "Jezebel," starring, Bette Davis, for the fifth time, playing the Indiana Theatre. We sat in the balcony and threw popcorn at the lovers smooching in the row below us. The snow was deep, but we had on our boots and fun stomping through the drifts at the curbs. When we past the Ayres department store where we would catch our bus home, we could not help but think of our Christmas miracle!

When we arrived home the snow was still falling, we only had to walk a block to get to my home, but daddy had to get out the old sedan to take the girls to their homes. Poor daddy, not once in my life did I ever hear him complain or raise his voice, no, I recall there was a time when I tried to take my daughter's blanket away from her. He let me know in no uncertain terms I was to give it back to her and that was that! He loved Saragene more than he loved his own life; he called her, "Genie," his little sweetie.

It was getting late and we had a light supper and I started packing to return to school the next day. We would start working with more difficult cases this week, we would not have the New Year's holiday off, it was not considered a Christian holiday at St. Ann's.

Chapter 19

The Blizzard of 1939

The snow was still falling when daddy dropped us off at the entrance of St. Ann's school of nursing. The snow was up to the hubcaps of daddy's old sedan, he had been driving in deep ruts down Meridian Street; thank God there was no traffic this early in the morning. We came through the door shaking the snow off of our hats and coats; Sister Mary Johns was there to greet us. For some reason she actually had a smile on her face, maybe she was getting used to our shenanigans and us. It did not matter, we were just glad for the smile, the gladness did not last long, we soon found out why!

Because of the weather, there were so many students that could not make it back from the holiday and we would be working double shifts in the charity ward. Sister barked out her orders and sent us upstairs to get into our uniforms as quickly as possible, we were glad we had eaten breakfast before leaving our homes. We dressed and ran down the stairs to the basement, sure enough, "The Troll," was there looking up our skirts. We grabbed our skirts close to our legs as well as we could and continued running to the tunnel that led to the Charity Ward. Normally the three of us would not all be working the same shift, but this was an emergency situation. Mother Superior was there barking out orders to the other nuns on call and they in turn were passing orders to the senior nurses.

Red and I were taken to the end of the ward, the first thing we were aware of was a very foul odor coming from behind a screened off area. As we walked around the screen there was the sweetest man lying there in the bed. He looked familiar to me. When he read the pin with my name on it, he smiled. "I know you, your father works with me at the lumberyard, my name is Mr. Alexander, I work out in the yard loading the lumber." Immediately I knew who he was, I had not seen him for quite a while; I did know that his wife had passed away with the influenza a year ago.

The nurse took the metal chart from the end of his bed and read the order of care for Mr. Alexander, we were to clean, apply medication and redress his wounds. I could see no wounds, when his sheet was pulled back, Red fainted dead away and cracked her forehead on the corner of his bed. Yet another wound to take care of, by me, of course. The nurse took Red away and told me to get started on Mr. Alexander immediately; I didn't know where to begin. I started with his chart, he had a severe case of diabetes, he told me that his wife had always taken care of his medications and cared for any open sores that might appear on his feet. Since his wife died, he had not cared for himself; he had taken a leave from work and sat home waiting to die. Finally one of his children was so concerned about him, she traveled from New York City to check on him, she found him in this deplorable state of illness. He was being given medication for pain, but as I took the tweezers and pulled the dead tissue away I could feel him wince. There was one very deep wound in the calf of his leg and when I swabbed it; there were maggots on the gauze square! Needless to say, I came close to joining Red in the infirmary. I placed the tweezers, gauze and maggots in the basin of Lysol solution, covered his legs and walked around the screen. When I cleared his line of vision, I took off at a dead run looking for help!

I found Mother Superior and told her what I had found; we both went running for the nearest doctor we could locate. So many doctors were unable to get to the hospital; the snowstorm had turned into a blizzard. This was not the time of cell phones, it would have been helpful because the only doctor that dealt with this condition was snowed in at home. The doctor gave us orders as best he could over the telephone, each time we ran into a new challenge, we had to call him back. Finally we got Mr. Alexander's wounds cleaned with the help of a little ether being dripped on a gauze mask every few minutes. The pain he had to endure would have sent him into cardiac arrest. Red was back to assist with the ether administration. She sported a large bandage of her own, the cut she had on her head required 15 stitches.

Mr. Alexander's daughter was allowed to come and sit with her father, he would sleep most of the day, and he was given medication to make him as comfortable as possible. We could not tell his daughter how bad his condition was; only a doctor was allowed to inform a patient of this information. We overheard Mother Superior telling another doctor that Mr. Alexander was beyond help; they could not amputate his legs because he had gangrene that had poisoned his blood. I went to the linen closet and cried deep wrenching sobs. I had known Mr. Alexander since I was a small girl; his wife had been one of my mother's dearest friends.

Chapter 20

Death Comes In The Snow

It seemed the whole day was one big mess after another; there was a loud commotion in the hall. A young woman was being carried in by her husband; she was in the last stages of labor. When she was laid on the bed, we could tell she was suffering from hypothermia, her skin was freezing to the touch. Her bloody clothing was frozen to her legs and she was barely conscience. Mother Superior went to find Dr. Lucas Anthony, the head of our gynecologic department. I ushered the young girls husband out into the hall and let him know we would be in touch with him through the whole process that lay ahead. He gave me all the needed information to admit his wife to the maternity ward. Her name was Patricia Kathleen Ryan, she was only 17 years old, and his name was John. He told me he was out of work and they lived in the poorest part of Indianapolis down by the White River. I knew this area well, mother and I used to take Christmas baskets to the downtrodden families that too little money and too many children to care for. I watched him put his head into his hands and sob softly, saying over and over, "It is all my fault."

I returned to the maternity ward, Glenda Faye was there along with Red. They had their bandage scissors in hand and were starting to cut the clothing from Mrs. Ryan's lower half. When Glenda Faye pulled her clothes down, we all gasp with horror! We could see that her baby's head was dangling out of her vagina and was the color of the violets on my mother's teacups.

Dr. Anthony was in attending at this point; he administered medication and sedation to Mrs. Ryan, she was transported to the regular maternity surgery ward on the third floor. We could see Dr. Anthony was visibly shaken by what he had just witnessed, we all knew as he did, that the little Ryan baby was already in the hands of God, now to try and save the mother.

I went out to tell Mr. Ryan what had taken place and that his wife was in surgery, but here again, I could not tell him exactly the whole truth, Dr. Anthony would do that later. Mr. Ryan told me what had happened earlier that day. Patricia Kathleen was due to have the baby three weeks from now, but she noticed blood running down her legs while she was standing at the kitchen sink. He said that she screamed for him, not having a telephone or any kind of transportation, they dressed as warm as they were able and trudged through the knee-deep snow. The bus stop was a little more than a block from their little shack of a home.

With the blizzard still raging, the bus was a half hour late picking them up and there was no heat inside. They were the only passengers on the bus, so he laid Patricia Kathleen, out on the long seat behind the driver. Mr. Ryan said as they neared the hospital, Patricia let out a blood-curdling scream and then went limp in his arms. The driver diverted from his normal route and delivered them to the back door of St. Ann's hospital where the Charity Ward was located. Mr. Ryan told me the driver got out of his seat and came around to help him pick Patricia Kathleen up and get her into the hospital. Mr. Ryan said, he only wished he had remembered to get the drivers name, I told him I could help with that later, I would check the schedule for him and write it down. He sadly looked up at me with tears in his eyes and said, "I do not know how to read." I sat beside him, put my arms around his big shoulders and let him have a good cry with someone who really cared and did not even give one thought about breaking the rules that day.

When the three of us finally finished our double shift, the snow was beginning to let up and other employees were making their way to the hospital. We stopped by the nurses' locker room to run some water over our faces and wash our hands. When we looked into the mirror, we all started to laugh, I know with the horrible things we had witnessed this shift, we felt guilty. It was just that not one of us had our cap on straight and our uniforms were spotted here and there with blood and all kinds of gore you could think of. Here again, another Kodak moment lost in time!

Chapter 21

Welcome Baby New Year 1939

We opened our eyes to the first sunny day in the last week, it was still freezing cold, but we could feel the suns rays streaming through our one little window. Have I forgotten to tell you about Glenda Faye's produce project setting on our window ledge? If not, I will now, you would just had to have known this wonderful person in real life to appreciate her and the quirky little things she did. She decided one night after our parents had taken us to a little Italian joint on College Avenue for supper: that she would grow some produce to replicate the herbs in the sauce. Remember, in two days it will be 1939, even though Red's father operated a green grocery store, the American public had no idea what Basil was, except for a name.

Glenda Faye sent away through a mail order catalog for seeds, she was growing, oregano, basil, parsley and thyme. On one of her late night shifts, she had borrowed a long white enameled instrument basin. She hid the basin under her apron and ran all the way to the dorm. She planted her little seeds in her borrowed basin, these little plants were growing has if they had been touched by the hand of God. Every time I asked her when they would be ready to be cut and put into a sauce on our old hot plate, she would shrug her shoulders, which was my answer. I took it for a, "Never in my lifetime."

We were going to have our New Year's Eve celebration at Mr. and Mrs. Murphy's home this year, we all had the night off, this in its self was a miracle! For a little while I will be calling, Red, Sandra Kay; Mrs. Murphy would never call anyone by a nickname, especially her beloved daughter. Sandra Kay, Glenda Faye and myself were all in Sandra Kay's beautiful bedroom dressing for the party, by now our families realized we were young women and we could wear lip rouge and put our hair up if we pleased. The Murphy's lived in one of the largest homes in Speedway, located on 15th Street. Their home was made of Indiana limestone with wonderful carvings around the covered entrance before entering the main front door. Mr. Murphy had hired help for the evening and had the affair catered, this was due to Mrs. Murphy's nervous condition. As long as Irene Murphy was in her home, she felt comfortable and even jolly in nature. My mother was close to Irene; they talked for hours on the telephone, even though they only lived a few blocks away from each other.

The fearsome threesome came down the winding staircase like three debutants going to the ball. We all had a new dress for the occasion, I can remember feeling as if I were floating down the stairs, my dress was a dark shade of misty blue with a wide satin belt. Mother had taken blue ink and watered it down and dyed my linen peek toe shoes to match my dress. That woman was a wonder at times. Sandra Kay was dressed in a lime green suit with pearl buttons and black patent leather shoes; she wore little pearl earrings that her daddy had given her for Christmas. Glenda Faye wore a dress that was the color of a summer sunset, the rayon material looked like a water color painting in shades of crimson, orange, yellow and light blue all swirled together. There was a little shawl that draped over her shoulders; it seems to me I remember this being on top of their old upright piano at one time! We all make do when times are tough, tomorrow the piano will once again be covered!

My brother James was there with his wife Rachel, along with Joseph and his fiancée, Dorothy. Joseph was still considering joining the army, but daddy would hear none of it, in fact he did not think this war talk would last much longer. That being said, it made you wonder why daddy would sit glued as they say, to the radio overseas broadcast when ever possible? My daddy knew about war, he had so many friends who lost fathers in the First World War. Daddy was a quiet man, but said what he meant and meant what he said!

The New Years Eve party went well, we all had on our funny paper hats once again and blew on the funny little horns that flipped in and out. This year it seemed different, there was an air of unrest with the adults, like they knew something that we three young women did not. Have you ever noticed when things get scary in your family, you lose your feeling of being grown up and all at once you feel like you are playing dress-up in your mother's dress, not yours? You have to look into the mirror to make sure you are not eight years old again; it is a time between girlhood and womanhood that is like a veil of smoke.

Chapter 22

Welcome The Foo's

When daddy left the three of us off early on New Years Day, we were actually sleep walking from being up so late the night before. Thank the saints in heaven we only had academic classes today. We were already dressed in our school uniforms, which were blue skirts and white blouses. Our nursing student uniforms were being cleaned at Yung Foo's Chinese laundry on the far South side of town.

Let me elaborate a little on Mr. Yung Foo and his family, he and Mrs. Foo had a large family like so many others in 1939. They had immigrated to America from China; their first-born son was born in the hull of a large ocean liner. I can only imagine what the conditions were in what they called, "Steerage Passenger Accommodations!" Just the word, steerage, what comes to your mind, yes, a herd of cattle being crowded in a fenced in pen?

Mrs. Foo was a short little lady with a smile that went from ear to ear, I loved to go and sit with her while she mixed the starch for our uniforms. My evenings off were precious to me, but so were Mrs. Foo and her family. I first ate Chinese food at their long table filled on both sides with children seated in order from the oldest to the youngest. My first meal was unrecognizable to me; the dishes prepared by Mrs. Foo had nothing to do with what we called, "Chop Suey." All of their fresh food was planted in a large garden at the back of the property and tended to by the middle-aged children.

When the food platters filled the middle of the table the steam would give you a facial for a few minutes. Mrs. Foo would look at me and say in her broken English, "Eaty up, goo for you, helty." I was treated no different than anyone else at the table; I had to learn the art of using chopsticks. The little girls would smile, just like their mother and hide a giggle, when my food would go flying across the room on to the floor. It did not take me long to master this art, it was either do it or go hungry.

I would watch Mr. Foo gather our laundry up ready to be wrapped in brown paper. What really amazed me was when he would stand in front of a large enameled metal table and peel our caps, collars and cuffs off of the surface of the table. We always wondered how anyone could starch and iron those stiff items of clothing? When Mr. Foo washed the collars and cuffs, he would then dip them in Mrs. Foo's secret starch recipe and spread them on the enamel table. The older children worked in the laundry; they would come behind Mr. Foo and use an ivory tool to scrape over the items and squeeze the starch out of the material. Everything was left to dry on the table, when Mr. Foo peeled a collar, cuff or nurses cap off the table, the underside would be slick and shinning like glass. I cannot remember there ever being the slightest hint of a wrinkle in our clothing, the Foo's were famous for their laundry business. The Foo's catered their business mostly to the wealthy and institutions such as ours.

Mr. and Mrs. Foo had a beautiful young daughter that was away attending a private nursing school in the East. At this time, 1939, Orientals and other minorities were not allowed a graduate nursing degree. Lotus Foo, we called her, "Blossom," as a nickname, was one of my life long friends. Blossom worked in the East until she was allowed to work along with regular doctors here at our hospitals in Indianapolis. Her expertise was research and she was after the host that caused the terrible poliomyelitis disease. One of our presidents, Franklin Roosevelt contracted this dreaded disease. She later sent her research to a famous researcher working on this problem, he told her many years later, if it had not been for one element in her findings, the cure might not have been found.

Chapter 23

Big Changes On The Charity Ward

There, there, I have spoken enough about my special family, the Foo's, back to the fearsome threesome, here we were again standing in front of the cork bulletin board, half semester grades were posted. I don't even have to mention Glenda Faye, the wiz kid, Red did well, but to my surprise I was now an A and B student. Everyone turned and looked at me, all I could say was, "What!" Like I had always been a good student, I bent over, holding my sides and laughed like a fool.

My first day back on the Charity Ward, I went straight to the senior nurse and questioned her about, Patricia Kathleen Ryan. She said, "Go check on her yourself, she is in the third bed next to the window." When I walked around the screen in front of Patricia's bed, she was laying on her side softly sobbing. I went to her and introduced myself; I asked if there was anything I could do to help her feel better? This young girl looked like a 12 year old laying there barely making a dent in the mattress, she rolled over and looked up at me with the bluest eyes I had ever seen. She started to say something and then stopped, she just could not talk, she was suffering from grief and we did not have a cure for that.

I reached for the hairbrush, sat her up and brushed her long blonde hair until it was shinning. I then reached into the pocket of my white starched apron and pulled out a long blue ribbon and tied it into her hair at the end of a long braid. I applied a little lip rouge and rubbed her arms and legs with lotion to help heal the frostbite condition she was suffering from. In this case, I did not tell the patient why there was a blue ribbon in her hair, but normally a woman who had delivered a healthy baby boy would wear this blue ribbon. Patricia was like so many of my other patients I would care for in the years to come, grateful for just a moment of kindness from a stranger passing through their life.

I left the maternity ward and went on about my business with the many patients who had waited until after the holidays to come in for medical care. Glenda Faye and Red were working with Mother Superior in the second floor office where all of the forms and printed materials were made. There was a rush of business going on today, they were ordering the new supplies from the food distributors here in town. Another person was making a stencil that was to be printed and folded into three parts; this was called the, "Menu for the week!" Yes, the word had gotten out immediately on the big changes that were to take place in the care and feeding of the patients in the Charity Ward. Glenda Faye and Red, could hardly contain themselves, they both reached up and rubbed their little gold nursing cap pendants, knowing who was responsible for this big change.

I was changing a bandage on a little girl's arm caused from falling into a wood-burning stove, when I caught a whiff of something wonderful. The carts came rolling in fast and furious; the kitchen staff had hired an additional twenty people to handle the new policy put in place. Instead of watered down oatmeal and a half glass of milk, there was a steaming bowl of thick creamy oatmeal with a little brown sugar to sprinkle on top, buttered toast and a full glass of milk. If a patient wanted coffee or tea, there were two large pots setting on the side of the cart with sugar and cream that could be added, if requested.

I finished the job I was doing and went down the rows of beds, watching the patients smile as they ate their hot breakfast; this was a little more than I could take. I went to the linen closet and cried, this became my favorite spot to fall apart in. All I could think of was why can't all the people of the world treat each other with the respect they give to themselves?

When our shift was over, Glenda Faye and Red could not wait to find me and tell me what was going on in the composing room of the hospital. We walked through the tunnel, thank God; the troll was not on duty! We climbed the stairs not having to worry about holding our skirts tight against our legs. We put our tables together and some of the other students came to eat supper with us, each girl had her own plate and utensils in hand. I had used our biggest pot to boil pasta, I dumped the water off and then through in some canned tomatoes, cheese and a little of Glenda Faye's herbs. I was surprised she did not protest, but then I found out why, she read that the best thing you can do for little herb plants is to constantly keep them clipped. Once again Glenda Faye got the best of me, she just grinned that beautiful grin of hers. We had a wonderful evening; one student brought two loaves of long hard bread. Her father owned a small bakery about a block from St. Ann's and he would drop off bread for the needy, meaning we girls.

We ate our heaping plates of steaming pasta or noodles as we called it back in 1939, and sopped up the sauce with freshly baked hard crusty bread. Red sat back in her chair and rubbed her stomach, she was already in her pajamas, and she kind of leaned sideways and expelled some gas! We all sat wide eyed and started laughing, Red said, "What, you mean none of you girls ever fart?" From that moment on, whenever we thought of it, we would call her, "Farty Tarty." Everyone helped clean up the mess we had made on the table, red sauce, breadcrumbs and spilled wine that had been secreted in by Red.

We fell into bed, exhausted; it seemed like only seconds before we heard the sound of the morning bell calling us to the hospital. We dragged ourselves out of our cots and splashed cold water on our faces, brushed our hair and dressed for the day ahead.

Chapter 24

Summer Is On The Way

Before we knew it spring was once again knocking on our door, we so happy to be able to walk across campus with just a light sweater. The sun was warm against our skin even though there were still little piles of black crusted snow here and there that were not melted from the snowy winter. We were now starting to prepare for our September classes that would take us out of the Charity Ward and upstairs to the regular hospital wards. There was a whole new set of rules to learn when you worked hand and hand with the, "God's of the hospital!" We spent more time in the classroom during our last semester, than in the Charity Ward, being trained in the appropriate manner of dealing with the doctor and the orders given by them to us.

We spent our Easter holiday with our families as usual, but this year we were not all off at the same time, being a regular nursing student, you were given one day off to spend at home over the week-end. This was another big change in our lives that we did not like; growing up was not the thrill ride that we had anticipated. Red and I spent a few hours together at the local soda fountain sharing a banana split, but without Glenda Faye, it just didn't taste the same to either of us. Glenda Faye came by the house early one morning before I was to leave to go back to school in the afternoon. We sat with mother at the kitchen table and drank tea; mother went to her china cabinet and took out one of her precious china cup for Glenda to use. Mother and I used our favorite hand painted teacups that the Great Aunts had given to us. Here again, things were different, we were on a more even level with mother now, and we were three women sitting around a table having tea.

After Glenda Faye left for home to spend some time with her mother and the rest of the family, daddy took me back to St. Ann's, we kissed good-bye and I ran up the steps, stopped to look back as daddy pulled away. I missed my time with my daddy, sitting on his lap while he read to me from the newspaper, smelling his pipe tobacco and the feel of his rough wool sweater on my cheek. Those childhood days had come and gone in a blink of an eye, now I had to look to the future and what lay ahead.

The school year ended in the third week of May, just in time for the big 500-mile race and the carnival coming to town. Once the fearsome threesome got back home and to what you would call normal, we felt so much better, so much younger than we did just a few short days ago. We were so excited this summer; we now had our own transportation! Red received an automobile for her birthday in April, it was not a brand new automobile, but it ran like a top, as my mother would say. I could write a whole book on the fun that went on with our adventures in that old automobile, but what went on in Red's auto stays in Red's auto!

Mother had more volunteer jobs for me to participate in again this year; her pick for this year was helping her with the St. Christopher church festival. Our parish was fairly small, the church was in the front of the building and the priest lived in quarters in the rear. There would someday be more buildings on this large plot of land on the outskirts of Speedway, but for now there was only one, if you did not count the garage.

Mother was as I said earlier, the President of the Ladies Alter Society, she ran the show as some would say. The festival was to raise money for the church building fund and everyone pitched in to do their part, even townsfolk who did not attend the Catholic Church would come to help set everything up. Each church in Indianapolis had a festival. Each year they all tried to out do the church before them, it was kind of a game to the church boards.

My mother's Christian name was, Sarah, but she went by, "Sadie." She was always in charge of cutting the vegetables for her famous Coney sauce. This was a sauce that would be spooned over a hot dog in a warm bun. Mother could cut onions all day long and never shed one tear, believe me there was a lot of onion chopping going on. This year, I had to sit right beside her and dice the green peppers that went into the sauce. It is funny, when I think back on that, mother always called, green peppers, mangos. Even in an old St. Christopher's ladies guild cookbook, they are listed in that manner. She kept her recipe a secret from everyone, until the recipe titled, "Sadie's Coney Sauce," was published in the cookbook.

I will interject into the present at this time, last year I read an article in the Speedway Press giving the history of the St. Christopher's festival and that the Coney sauce recipe was a secret and was kept under lock and key all these years. How wrong can some journalist be, it is right there in the old ladies cookbook, my daughter, Kathleen, has a copy of it all tied up with a pretty blue ribbon.

Back to the drudgework under a big tent erected by my brothers and their friends, this is where all the preparation of food was done. There were several big tents and a few small ones, some had sides and some didn't. My daddy always worked in the small tent where the fish would be brought in packed in ice from the fish market in downtown Indianapolis. The festival was almost as famous for their fish sandwiches as it was for my mother's Coney sauce hot dogs. Daddy would dip the fish in a thin mixture of seasoned milk and eggs, then into cornmeal, back into the milk mixture and back into the crumbs, finally into the huge fryers of boiling hot oil for frying to a golden brown. The men had an assembly line set up and worked like a well oiled machine, it was funny to see these men in white aprons and tall white hats, each with a cigar hanging out of the side of their mouth. I can still hear their laughter and see the smiles on their faces; this was probably the only time anyone of them ever cooked in his lifetime. If you needed a little kitten to take home, there were plenty hanging around my daddy's tent for some unknown reason.

The menu for the festival was the same every year, the women could make the dishes in their sleep if need be. There was macaroni and cheese bake, coleslaw, baked beans and more side dishes I cannot bring to mind. The ladies would all bake their pies at home and bring them to the festival, this was before the food and drug administration deemed this unsanitary. Mrs. Murphy was famous for her mile high lemon pie with mountains of toasted white gooey sweetness. Mother could not be beat in the cherry pie category, but Mrs. Kelly brought a dish called, "Apple Sweetie," it was a baked apple mixture topped with an oatmeal, cinnamon and butter mix. Minerva Bates brought apple boxes filled with jars of her homemade apple butter that would melt on the hot biscuits. The ladies would bake the biscuits in the oven at the priests' residence.

There were pony rides for the smaller children, a ride that had many swings attached to the center pole and it would fly you out in to the air until you thought you were going to fly off the chains. There was a small tent where you could lay down a nickel and they would hand you a fishing pole and you would drop it over the tent, then when you brought it back there would be a little surprise in the basket. The person manning the tent would always say before the basket was dropped over the tent, either this little boy or girl is, "Going Fishing." That would let the person inside the tent know what kind of a prize to put in the basket. It could be a toy soldier or a little tiny doll, depending on what the fishing master called out. The little children would giggle and be so happy, it was like Christmas to them all over again.

Then there were adult games, a big wheel with horses painted on small pie shaped sections of the wheel, there was a heavy leather strap that would flap fast when the wheel was spun. The men would put down their nickels and dimes and hope the leather strap stopped on their horse's number. I don't know what the odds were; I never gambled in my life.

I do remember that when you wanted a cold soda pop, you would pay your nickel, but you had to dig deep into an old metal horse trough filled with ice and water, until you found the flavor you wanted. Glenda Faye, Red and I would walk away with our arms dripping water and burning like hell from the freezing water, pardon my language. The little children would run by and sprinkle everyone with cold water, while chewing on a chunk of ice stolen from the tank.

This event went on for three nights and on the third night; you had to be present, if you had purchased a raffle ticket for a brand new automobile to be given away. Everyone stood so quiet and still holding their breath and hoping their number would be called. God was smiling on the Kelly's this year, they were giving away a brand new station wagon and they had the winning number! This would be a blessing because Mr. Kelly had an old rusted pick-up truck that would sometimes start and every now and then he had to get out, lift the hood and give it a little tinker of some kind or the other.

Red and I grabbed Glenda Faye and twirled her around and around, all the while screaming at the top of our lungs. Mr. and Mrs. Kelly just stood there with their mouths hanging open; they could not believe their luck. Finally, Father Linderman came over and handed them the keys to their new automobile and said, "Do you want to take her for a spin?" Mother Kelly started to cry, she fell to her knees and gave a prayer of gratitude to her God before she spoke or did anything else. Everyone went silent at the sight of this precious woman on her knees just like the saint that she was.

After the drawing everyone went their separate ways, some of the men to play five-card draw poker at one of the long tables in the serving tent. The ladies worked hard cleaning up everything that had to be transported to the dishwashing tent. This is where teenagers were involved against their will, to make many trips back and forth, before being released to run and play. There was no time limit on the last evening of the festival, some years the fun would carry on until dawn, with sleeping children laying on homemade quilts while their parents visited with friends they would not see again until next summer at the festival.

After mass on Sunday, all the men would finish taking down the equipment and pack it away neatly to be stored in a warehouse on the east side of town. A local company called, "The Tent and Awning Company", would pick up the tents. Thank God, one of our parishioners new the president of the company and we always got a good discount on our tent rental.

Chapter 25

Fun and Games

During these three days of work and fun, the fearsome threesome was not idle in the boy department; we met three boys from Cathedral High School. This was a private school for Catholic boys located in the downtown area. Red being the wild child was always holding hands with a boy named, Kenneth, Glenda Faye was shy, but she walked beside a boy named Robert every night after we were released from our duties. My self, I met a handsome you man dressed in his new army uniform, his name was Jan Carl; his parents were from Holland originally. We all thought this was a funny first name for a boy, in Holland it was like Jim or Jerry, very common. We hit it off from the moment our eyes met while I was working in the food serving line. The three nights were fun filled and if the truth were known, I believe we all received our first kiss that last night of the festival.

The rest of the summer was riding in Red's automobile to the swimming club, hanging out at the soda fountain and spending many hours at the Speedway theatre watching movies over and over. By the time September rolled around we were coming back down to reality and getting ready to return to St. Ann's for our second year of the Diploma Program of Nursing.

Red was not allowed to take her automobile, that we called, "Independence," to school with her. So here we were again being dropped off by our parents and with their help setting up our dorm room again. After good-bye kisses and hugs, we stood on the steps and waved until we could no longer see the back of their automobiles. It was a happy moment watching Mr. and Mrs. Kelly pulling away in their brand new station wagon filled with laughing children in the back two seats.

Chapter 26

A surprise For Mother

On our first day of school, we reported to Mother Superior, Sister Theresa Christine, she was a stern woman, but there was always a little hint of a smile behind her eyes. Mother Superior took an instant liking to Sandra Kay, as she was called while working in the hospital by all the staff. Sandra Kay like Mother Superior as well, there was a bond being formed that would soon reveal its self to us. We were to shadow the head of the nursing department in every aspect of nursing for the next two semesters. We kept our mouths shut, unless asked a question, which required an immediate answer, which was the rule. By shadowing, I mean to follow and learn from our instructor.

The first semester had our heads swimming each night when we returned from our rounds at the hospital. We were not allowed to take notes while walking on the wards, but when we hit our door, we all grabbed our black and white notebooks and scribbled down what we could remember. We would compare notes and finally come up with an outline that worked for all three of us.

The work was hard; we experienced every kind of illness or injury that a mind could imagine. We had to watch Red very carefully, she could faint dead away at any moment, we just did not know when this might happen! The time seemed like to fly by, like a clock that had dial hands that whirled around at top speed.

We were walking across the campus and noticed the weather had changed drastically, it was the third week of December, but as the snow started falling it was unexpected. The Fall had been mild, but the Winter came roaring in like a lion. We were all looking forward to going home for the Christmas holiday. Being second year students we were given two days off, we could take either Thanksgiving or Christmas, we all chose Christmas, we remembered the past Christmas when God performed our miracle.

In November of 1939, President Roosevelt declared American neutrality in the war in Europe, but signed an act that allowed the US to send arms and other aid to Britain and France. Needless to say when we arrived at our homes, there was much talk about the war in Europe, our young men were getting nervous.

My father was not happy when on Christmas Eve, my younger brother, Joseph came in with his new wife, and he was sporting an army uniform. Daddy turned, walked to the kitchen and then down to the basement, he stayed there for about an hour. When he returned, you could see that his eyes were red rimmed because he had been shedding tears, not only for his second son, but also for the whole world.

Mother came to the rescue; she cranked up the old phonograph and played our think slate records while daddy went to pick up the Great Aunts. We were all allowed to drink as much homemade wine and mother's famous hot buttered rum. By the time daddy arrived with the Aunts in tow, none of us were feeling any pain. Our house was full of friends and relatives this year, there was a quiet unrest hanging in the background of the festivities this

Christmas Eve, but we went on as usual. Mid-night mass and then home for presents and finally to my own bed, covered up by my mother and father. Each one placing a kiss on my forehead and a low whisper, "We love you, Maggie, dear."

The Great Aunts did not stay the night this year, they other commitments with friends that were also in the clothing business. They did not tell us what it was that they were doing, but later we found they spent all Christmas day, rolling bandages to be sent overseas to the troops fighting the Germans.

Our Christmas Day went on as usual, we had very strict traditions in our family, set down by my mother. We were all seated for our huge Christmas breakfast banquet, the same as last year and the year before that. This year daddy broke tradition, when we had finished our meal and were sitting over our coffee or tea conversing with each other and catching up on the latest happenings in our lives. Daddy got up, went into their bedroom and came back to the table, he laid a small box down in front of mother, and she looked startled as she looked up at daddy. He said, "Well open it for God's sake." Mother opened it slowly, there on the crimson velvet lay a beautiful gold cross made of thin intertwined gold wire, in the middle was a ruby. Mother began to cry, she wondered why now, what had she done to deserve this wonderful present from her quiet husband. Daddy sat down, he looked at mother and said, "The gold was the sign of eternity, never starting or stopping in one spot, the ruby was to signify his heart and his love for his bride." I believe all of our hearts stopped beating for a second; we had never seen mother or daddy share their private feelings for each other before this Christmas morning in 1939.

Chapter 27

Glenda Faye Falls In Love

We all returned to school on a blustery winter day, we would be working through the coming New Year's holiday, but we had planned a little celebration of our own to welcome in baby New Year of 1940. Red's father had delivered wonderful groceries, mother sent one of her cherry pies and Mother Kelly provided paper hats and other decorations made by her small brood of children.

We all sat there in our dorm room looking stupid once again with our paper hats, but as our friends came and went and we left at different times to be on call at the hospital, the holiday was one of the best I remember. That is what is missing in the present, friends that really care and love each other, celebrating each other with love.

As the morning bell rang, we jumped up with a start as usual, dressed and ran down the stairs, forgetting the Troll, he was there looking up or skirts. By this time we did not care one way or the other, in fact Red being the clown that she was, lifted her skirt just a bit and threw her head back and broke into laughter.

As we were waiting for the elevator door opened, Glenda Faye stepped in; she caught the heel of her shoe and fell right into the arms of the most handsome young resident in the hospital. She was flustered and started straightening her cap and skirt to draw attention away from what just happened. We followed Glenda Faye into the elevator, it was so hard not to giggle, but we contained ourselves, the resident introduced himself to us. His name was Donald McAtee, but all of his friends called him, "Scottie." This was due to his Scottish heritage; his grandparents were also immigrants that had come through Ellis Island, like so many others coming to America.

Over the next few months, we could see a romance blossom between Glenda Faye and Scottie. When we would run into Scottie in the hallway, Glenda's face would turn a bright shade of red and he would just give her a big smile. There were many times when we had a night off, that Glenda Faye would slip away from the crowd and return with a contented look about her. She was not fooling anyone; we knew exactly what was going on between these two young lovers.

On Glenda Faye's birthday, Scottie took her to a very expensive restaurant here in downtown Indianapolis, when she came back to the dorm; she was wearing a beautiful diamond engagement ring on her left hand. We were so happy for Glenda Faye; she would never again have to be considered, "Poor Folk." The big dilemma facing Glenda Faye was how to tell her parents; it was not proper to except a ring, without the parents giving you their blessing! We told Glenda Faye, we would stand beside her and Scottie as they went to tell the Kelly's of their plan to wed.

On our next Sunday off we all four drove to the Kelly's house in the country, it was really in a little town called, Clermont. If you blinked your eyes you would pass right by this little spot on the map, but it was farming country with just a tavern and a small general store. We pulled up in front of the Kelly house, this was a two-story building, the paint was peeling and the whole home looked gray to the eye. Mr. Kelly opened the front door, he was surprised to see us and gave Scottie a strange look, but invited us all in from the cold weather. Mother Kelly came out from the kitchen wiping her wet hands on her worn apron, she too wondered who this handsome young man was?

We all sat down around the kitchen table, this was where all-important matters were decided at the Kelly's. Mother Kelly cleared the room of the many little children running around the room. They did not go far, I could see them peeking around the doorframe and trying to hear the latest news. Glenda Faye had a huge lump in her throat and could not speak. Scottie took over, he explained that he had fallen head over heals in love with their daughter and asked for their permission to marry her this coming June?

Mr. and Mrs. Kelly were taken aback, this came as a total surprise to the both of them, but they immediately liked Donald McAtee. Mr. Kelly came around the table and took his daughter's hand and placed it into the hand of Donald McAtee. He told him in no uncertain terms, that he was to love, cherish and care for her, just as he and her mother had done all these years.

Mother Kelly got up and came around to hug and kiss her daughter; she had tears of joy in her eyes. Glenda Faye slipped off her gloves and showed her parents the sparkling diamond on her left hand. There was no holding the waiting brood on the other side of the kitchen wall; they were all over Scottie and Glenda Faye. One shouted, "Another brother to add to our family," Mr. Kelly could not help but break out laughing, that was just what they needed, another person in the family. The ring was showed over and over to each family member, Mother Kelly sat there in her chair and looked down at the empty third finger of her own left hand, but just smiled to herself. She knew it did not take a beautiful diamond ring to make a good marriage work.

On the way back to St. Ann's we stopped at Red's house and my own to introduce Scottie to our families and show off Glenda Faye's new engagement ring. Everyone was so happy for the new couple and gave them their blessings and good wishes for the future.

After the three of us were alone, we realize we had a wedding to plan for and very little time to accomplish this feat. Here I was again, standing on the stool under the wall telephone speaking to my mother, I asked her to help us plan this wedding. She immediately took the reins in hand and told me not to worry about a thing; she would outline the upcoming nuptials down to the very last item.

Not breaking tradition in 1940, it was the bride's family that paid for the wedding, Mother worked with Mrs. Kelly in planning the wedding, the was no money on the brides side of the family for this occasion. Once again, the women of the Alter Society came together as one to make this day special for Glenda Faye and her family. Mother and Mrs. Kelly spent many late nights and week-ends designing Glenda Faye's dress and veil, every part of the dress had once been a piece of another wedding dress donated for the cause. When the dress was completed, all of the ladies stood back with Red and myself as Glenda Faye modeled her white satin gown. She was radiant; the gown had long sleeves that came to a point at the back of her hand. The neckline was dipped in the shape of a heart encrusted with seed pearls and antique lace. The back of her gown had a large satin bow that went from one side of the gown to the other and streamers of ribbon clear to the floor. She was beautiful standing there already looking like a bride, one thing was missing, her veil, one of the Great Aunts stood up with a large white box in her hands and walked up to Glenda Faye. Great Aunt Rose opened the box and lifted out the longest veil any of us had ever seen! The veil was made of French lace attached to a small crown of rhinestones and pearls. This item must have cost a fortune, but Great Aunt Rose had made the veil by hand with the help of her two sisters. Needless to say, there was not a dry eye in the house.

Mr. and Mrs. Murphy were providing the food for the reception that would be held in the side yard of my home. The couple would be married at St. Christopher's church by Father Linderman and then commence to the reception in a large black limousine provided by an unknown donor. We three girls knew exactly who had donated the limousine, the beautiful woman that made our Christmas a miracle, was doing it again.

Mother worked with the other women making our bridesmaids dresses, they were the color of Sandra Kay's beautiful green eyes, we looked like fairy princesses ready for the ball. Only we did not have a prince to hold our arm like Glenda Faye did.

Chapter 28

Two Weddings

We were working long hours at the hospital, there was a late outbreak of influenza this year; the wards were overflowing with patients. We prayed every night that we would stay healthy, this was a deadly strain of the flu and we selfishly had a wedding planned that could not be ruined.

Spring was here and Easter was upon us before we realized it, there was no big celebration for the three of us this year. It was just going to high mass and then on to the hospital to care for our many patients. Scottie and Glenda Faye did not have much time for courting; he was doing his residency in the OBGYN field. There were many babies being born after the long winter months of being shut in, it always worked out this way, remember we had no television in those days. Glenda Faye was going to work along side of her new husband wherever he decided to set up his practice in the future, Mother Superior allowed her to spend most of her semester on the maternity ward.

Glenda Faye and I were walking across the campus enjoying the wonders of spring, the trees were bursting open with fresh blossoms and the birds were building their nests. Little green shoots of flowers were popping up in the flowerbeds around the front of the buildings. We entered our dorm room to find Red with her head on the table crying, we rushed to her side to see what big calamity had come upon her this time? Red lifted her head and said, "Sit down, take my hands and pray." When we asked what we were praying for, she looked at us with those big tear-filled eyes and said, "We are praying for my beautiful red hair!" Glenda Faye and I looked at each other and started laughing; Red let us know immediately it was no laughing matter. Now here is the biggest news of the century, Sandra Kay Murphy, the bad apple of our bunch was going to join the order of the, "Sisters of Charity."

Our Red was going to become a nursing nun, this is where her hair came into play, when you became a novice and received your veil, your hair was cut short as a sacrifice to God, you were to be humble and give up all prideful worldly goods. We had a hard time processing this information, Red was the one who would sneak in liquor and she would sit on her cot and flip cigarette butts into the trashcan across the room.

I thought back to the past few months and the bond Red had with Mother Superior, now I realized just how deep that ran. This was a big decision; Red had already discussed this with her parents, they were proud to have a daughter who would become the, "Bride of Christ." Here we were now, planning two weddings, two completely different ceremonies. This left just me, no plans for my future, except to be a regular registered nurse. All of a sudden I felt lonely sitting here with my two best friends.

I put my worries to rest; we still had our last summer together, even though part of it would be just Red and I after Glenda Faye's wedding. I made my mind up that nothing would take away my happiness, but I soon found myself on the stool under the wall telephone talking to my mother and pouring out my soul felt feelings. Mother always new just what to say to make me feel better, I dried my tears and went back upstairs to my friends.

We finished our second year of the Diploma Program in May, only one more year to go until we were finally registered nurses. My grades improved with each passing semester and I felt pride in the person I was becoming. We left school to return home and get everything ready for the big event, Glenda Faye, Red and I sat at the soda fountain and shared our banana split, this would probably be the last time we did this as single women. Glenda Faye was marrying Scottie and Red was marrying Christ, by becoming a Catholic nun. Red would be wearing a gold wedding band on the third finger of her right hand.

We did not give a thought to the big race or festival this year, it was all about Glenda Faye's wedding and tomorrow was the big day. We spent the night together at my home along with our mothers; only Mrs. Murphy was absent due to her nervous condition. Mrs. Murphy must have called at least three or four times to be filled in on the happenings at the Mann household, mother would fill her in and then come back to join the party. Mother had fixed all of Glenda Faye's favorite treats; we ate, drank a toast to the bride to be and got a little tipsy. The fearsome threesome cuddled in my big feather bed for one last overnight stay together, you could hear each of us let out a little sob along with the ticking of the old clock on the other side of the wall.

The big day, our side yard had been turned into a magical garden; there was a huge white and gold-stripped tent, donated by my daddy's friend, just in case of rain. There were tables covered with white clothes and flowers sat in the middle of each table from my mother's garden. My daddy, with the help of Austin Bates had built an amazing arbor covered over with satin ribbons, netting and roses. The decorations were a gift from the Great Aunts, they decorated the arbor as if it was an Easter bonnet, but done with good taste.

Scotties family had come in by train for the occasion; Scottie's father was a respected physician himself in Dayton, Ohio. Red and I were afraid after our graduation next spring, that Scottie would take Glenda Faye away to another state so far away from us. We were in my bedroom helping Glenda Faye slip into her wedding gown; her mother was given the privilege of placing her wedding veil on her beautiful long auburn hair. Red and I quietly left the room when her father came in wearing a brand new suit, looking stunning, I had never seen Mr. Kelly dressed formally. Glenda Faye later told us her father had tears in his eyes when he saw her in her gown and placed a kiss on her cheek through her wedding veil. Mrs. Kelly wore a cream satin dress my mother had tailored for just this day, her hair was down and curled, pulled up on both sides and tortoiseshell combs with tiny pearls kept it in place.

Everyone was seated as the wedding party came to the end of the aisle of St. Christopher's church; the pews had large white and green bows tied to them. These were a gift from the Alter Society Guild and handmade by them. There was soft music playing as first, the little Kelly girls all dressed in ruffles, carrying baskets of rose petals to throw down on the white strip of cloth leading to the alter. The tune changed as I, the maid of honor walked down the aisle on my brother's arm, then Scottie's brother, Tim, who was his best man, escorted Red.

We all took our places at the alter, the music changed again, this time it was the wedding march, everyone stood up to welcome the bride to be, escorted by her proud father. I could see the tears in Glenda Faye's eyes, even though she was smiling at everyone as she passed them by. When they reached the alter, Father Linderman asked, "Who gives this woman to be married to this man?" Mr. Kelly responded, "Her mother and I do," then he lifted her veil neatly straightening it and kissed his daughter as a single woman for the last time. Mr. Kelly helped Glenda Faye up the two steps and placed her hand into Scottie's and turned and sat down with Mrs. Kelly. What no one witnessed, was when he sat down he slipped a gold wedding band onto Mrs. Kelly third finger of her left hand.

The ceremony seemed to take forever, there was a high mass to sit through before the couple was finally pronounced, man and wife and presented to the congregation as, "Mr. and Mrs. Donald McAtee." We all clapped and cheered as they rushed down the aisle to the waiting limousine, as I passed the last row, I saw the beautiful lady and man sitting there who had presented us with our wonderful Christmas presents that snowy night in December. She reached out and handed me a small package wrapped in a white satin bow, she whispered, this is for our special girl on her special day.

I did not know what exactly to do, I just kept walking, and we were pelted with rice as we walked out of the church to the limousine. When we were seated in the automobile I handed Glenda Faye and Scottie the present and told her who it was from. She asked if it were proper to open it now, of course Red and I both said at the same time, "Yes." Inside were two tickets to Palm Springs for their honeymoon, to be used whenever they had the time to use them. We all just gasped, what a wonderful present, they would really need to use this vacation when we graduated next year, we would all be exhausted. Glenda Faye whispered to Scottie that she would explain the whole story to him later when there was time.

We arrived later than most of the guests, we had taken a side trip downtown to ride around the circle and blow our horn to let everyone know someone had just gotten married. There were streamers flying from the back of the limousine and thanks to my mischievous brothers, tin cans making a clank every time they hit the road behind the automobile.

Everyone was waiting for us; there was a small local band, friends of our families who also donated their time to make this day special for the Kelly's. The men who worked with Mr. Kelly had brought large sheets of plywood from the lumberyard and made a makeshift dance floor. The band struck up a waltz and Glenda Faye and her father had the first dance together, in the middle of the dance, Mr. Kelly handed Glenda Faye off to her new husband. This was really a Kodak moment; I still have the old black and white photo of this moment taken by my mother.

The day was perfect, warm, sunny and filled with wonderful times that would one day be wonderful memories for the fearsome threesome. We ate, danced until our feet were throbbing; even my mother and father took a turn around the dance floor, a first for me to see. Mr. Bates and his son Billy Clyde came from behind the tent, they were carrying a three-tier cake baked by Minerva Bates as a gift to the couple. The cake was beautiful, she had made little white roses with green leaves from cream cheese mixed with powdered sugar and left to dry. There was a china bride and groom on the top tier, made and hand painted by the Great Aunts; they looked just like Glenda Faye and Scottie. The china bride even had a similar wedding gown like Glenda Faye's holding a bouquet of white roses with real green satin ribbons streaming down. There was no holding back our tears at this point, the love that had been put into this special day was over flowing even to perfect strangers passing by. Out of the corner of my eye, I saw a black automobile stopped to see the bride and groom among the crowd of people. I took off at a run to try to stop them and invite them in for cake, but I just got a wave and the automobile pulled away from the curb. I did not tell Glenda Faye about this until many years later.

The cake was cut and passed around, Glenda Faye could not help herself, she had to shove a piece of cake into Scottie's face, this brought a loud applause from all the guests. The sun was starting to set, and things were winding down, we three girls went in the house to help Glenda Faye out of her gown and into a new suit for their short honeymoon. They were staying two days at the Claypool hotel in downtown Indianapolis; they both were expected back at the hospital for work a usual.

I watched my friend pull away with her new husband; I felt my heart breaking, even though I knew I would see her again in two days. The dynamic of our relationship had changed and I did not yet know how to deal with it! Glenda Faye still had to reside at St. Ann's during her next year of school, even though she was married, those were the rules and we had to abide by them.

Chapter 29

Time For Family

After Glenda Faye's wedding I had the rest of the summer of 1940, to my self, I had absolutely no idea how to spend my time without the fearsome threesome. Red was attending a convent out of Indianapolis, where she was being prepared to be a novice with the, "Sisters of Charity." Glenda Faye was staying with her husband in his small efficiency apartment near the hospital, so we did not see much of each other that summer.

Mother and I worked in the garden, times were getting bad, and certain food items were becoming harder to come by. This was due to the war in Europe; we did have a friend in Mr. Murphy, he would set aside what little he could for us and told us he thought in the near future there might even be food rationing.

In the evening, Daddy would sit in his platform rocker, mother in her large wing backed chair and I would sit on the footstool at daddy's feet listening to the latest broadcast concerning the European Campaign. In June Congress passed, The Alien Registration Act, (The Smith Act). This required all aliens to register and be fingerprinted. The Act made it illegal to advocate the overthrow of the US government. I really did not know exactly what this meant, but there was no way it was good, our country was preparing for something in the near future. In July of 1940, President Roosevelt signed the, "Two Ocean Navy Expansion Act." This was the first step in preparing America for war against either Germany or Japan, or both! In August of 1940, President Roosevelt agrees to supply 50 First World War destroyers to Britain in return for the lease of naval bases in the Caribbean. The Congress would pass this in September of 1940. Sitting there on the footstool, I could feel tiny goose bumps stand out all over my body and these would not be the last!

Mother and I put up as many canned goods as we were able from our garden and stocked our basement pantry to full capacity. Daddy made his famous home brewed beer and mother made homemade wine. We had a bumper crop of grapes this year; we had grape jelly, grape butter and grape juice. We even gave grapes away to other families to put up for the coming winter. The one problem was finding enough sugar to do all of the canning of fruits and jelly.

Everyone was getting nervous, as you walked downtown, the passing crowds were talking of nothing, but the war and how long it would be until America was smack dab in the middle of it? I tried to put this to the back of my mind, but it was like an itch you could not scratch, it just bothered me all of the time.

Mr. and Mrs. Kelly came for Sunday dinner in late August, Glenda Faye and Scottie were there too. Mr. Kelly talked about all the changes going on at the Allison plant and some changes he could not talk about that were top secret. You could see the blood drain out of Glenda Faye's face, her husband was a young doctor and would he would answer the call to duty by his Country if there were a need. Scottie was just that kind of a man, he was proud to be born in America. Scottie's family had told horror stories about the First World War; the men who returned were never the same.

After dinner Glenda Faye and I walked in my mother's garden and sat on the lovely arbor bench that daddy had retooled from Glenda's wedding celebration. She commented that daddy was a wizard and absolutely nothing went to waste in either of our households. We sat there skirting the real issue between the two of us, finally here came those famous tears, she laid her head in my lap and we were silent, there was no need for words.

Chapter 30

Sister Mary Johns Explains

We all returned to school in September of 1940, I was the first to arrive; I opened the small window and noticed the long basin with the little herb plants was still there. It contained nothing but hard dried dirt and the hint of brown shriveled stems and leaves that had fallen off of them. I just had to laugh to myself, last year this project was all-important to Glenda Faye and

now she had bigger fish to fry. Life can change on a dime; we really never know what lays in store for us.

Glenda Faye came in followed by Scottie, he was now carrying all of the boxes and suitcases, last year it had been her father. I felt the tears behind my eyes at this change, until all at once, Red burst into the room saying, "Here I am!" She was holding her arms up as she twirled around in an important gesture, we all broke out with smiles, and she was dressed from head to toe in white linen. She was now wearing her novice uniform called, "A Habit." We all glad to see she had not lost her sense of humor while attending the convent all summer, thank God she never did.

There was not much time to get our room in order; the hospital was calling us for duty the next morning. We awoke to the sound of the old school bell ringing, we did not allow for helping Red get into her Habit, this took an extra ten minutes we could ill afford. Finally we went running for the stairs leading to the tunnel, it was raining cats and dogs outside, as some people would say. As we started down the stairs, the Troll was not to be seen, a sigh of relief escaped my throat as I took my next step and caught my shoe on the hem of Red's Habit.

I fell to the concrete, everything was cloudy and the voices seemed to be coming from a far off place. All I could hear was the Troll screaming, "Mommy, Mommy." I could not understand what was going on, Sister Mary Johns came running down the stairs, took the Troll in her arms and said, "It is alright Jimmie, go tell Mother Superior the girls will be late." By this time I was fully conscience, they all helped me up to our dorm room and laid me on my cot. Sister Mary Johns filled the teakettle on the hot plate and sat down beside me, she said, "I think it is time for me to tell you what was going on with Mr. Higgins, but this information is never to go any further than this room."

Sister Mary Johns explained to us why Mr. Higgins always called her, "Mother," we all just figured it was because he was what you would call, "Slow," and was referring to her as Mother Superior.

Sister Mary Johns explained to us what had happened to her when she was 17 years old. She was coming home from the library when she was grabbed, dragged into an alley and raped. This was just a few months before she was to join the order of the, "Sisters of Charity." She found out shortly that she was pregnant, her parents sent her to a home for unwed mothers, but her parents could not give up the baby for adoption. Her mother said, "This little soul came into this world under the most heinous of circumstances, but he is a child of God." Her parents raised, "Little Jimmie," until they passed away, Sister Mary Johns got him the janitor position here at the school. She explained that he was not there at the bottom of the stairs to look up or skirts, he was there to protect us from harm! We were all crying by this time, we loved Sister Mary Johns as much as she loved her little boy living in a grown mans body.

Later she would tell us that he was so upset by what happened, he blamed himself because he had to use the bathroom and was not on duty to protect us. From that point in time, we had great respect for Mr. Higgins and never again referred to him as the, "The Troll." We would bring him little gifts and surprises, he loved airplanes, we gave him a little kit with balsam wood stamped with parts to be cut and built into an airplane. He worked so hard and one day showed us the most amazing airplane, he had painted three girls on the wings of the airplane and wrote under the pictures, "Three Angels." We all gave him a big hug and kiss on the cheek and went on with our lives feeling good about ourselves, but still ashamed of our treatment and assumption about Mr. Higgins.

Chapter 31

Pink and Blue Ribbons

Glenda Faye and I worked in the maternity ward together, but Red chose to work in the Charity Ward doing God's work, as she called it. I loved working with the new mothers and stilled carried the pink and blue ribbons in the pocket of my white starched apron along with the little tubes of lip rouge. There was so much satisfaction in watching the mothers see their faces in the mirror looking fresh and pretty. They had gone through many hours of labor and delivery, just being bathed, powered and having their hair brushed was a luxury for so many of them. I felt in my own heart, like Red, that I was doing God's work in my own way.

Our first semester back went by so fast, Thanksgiving was just a week away and we again chose to have the Christmas holiday off instead of Thanksgiving. We all wanted one more Christmas together with our family and friends before we went out into the world on our own.

President Roosevelt was again elected as President of the USA fir an unprecedented third term with 54% of the popular vote.

He defeated Republican Wendell L. Willke. The frightening declaration was from the Canadian government approving the initiation of mass production of war bacteria! The history of the First World War and the gassing of so many soldiers on both fronts was still fresh in so many minds. We all walked a little softly and were quieter in these troubling times. The unknown was terrifying to the American public.

Thanksgiving at St. Ann's was a big affair; there was a huge donation from an anonymous donor. Produce and meat delivery trucks pulled up and unloaded creates of turkeys to be roasted in the large ovens installed in the new food preparation building. Glenda Faye and I were on the floor as the carts came rolling down the hall at lunchtime, the smell was wonderful and soon our own stomachs were growling from hunger. By the time we were relieved to go to the new cafeteria we were starving, we grabbed a tray and went down the serving line choosing our favorite foods. There was turkey baked to golden brown, mashed potatoes, gravy, green beans, cranberry sauce and pumpkin pie for dessert. When we finished, we had to loosen our apron ties a bit to be more comfortable, we drank a good strong cup of coffee to keep us alert for the rest of our shift. Just as we were leaving, we met Red and Mother Superior entering the cafeteria to partake in the great meal that lay ahead for them. We exchanged a few words of blessing to each other on this really wonderful day of Thanksgiving in 1940.

Chapter 32

A Christmas To Remember

December was a brutal month this year; the flu was once again taking a great toll on our patients. There was also an outbreak of Typhoid fever due to poor sanitation in the poorest section of Indianapolis that was located down by the White river. The water table was contaminated by the huge meat packing facilities located there and dumping their waste in the river. Most people had outdoor toilet facilities and hand pumps that brought this fetid water out of the ground, and into their homes. Here again my mother and her friends got on the band wagon and formed a march in downtown Indianapolis asking for better sanitation laws. These strong women would not be pushed aside and with their signed petitions in hands they got the job done. The city would start working on a new water line connecting these homes to it as soon as the winter thaw would allow.

By the time our Christmas holiday rolled around, the fearsome threesome weary to the bone and needed time off to recoup from the many double shifts we had worked for the past month. Red was allowed to spend the holiday with her parents; she could even take off her Habit and wear the latest fashion of 1940. Her mother had a beautiful dress made for her that matched the color of her beautiful green eyes; the big problem was her short hair. Glenda Faye and I formed a plan Christmas Eve day; we went to the local beauty shop and had our beautiful long hair cut into a short bob. This was hard for us to do, a woman's hair was her crowning glory or so we had always been told. We did not tell anyone of our plan, when the two of us walked out of my room all dressed in our new dresses there was a gasp by all family and friends. Red sat there with tears in her eyes, she knew we had done this just for her, to make her feel comfortable with her short hair. After all was said and done, Glenda Faye and I actually loved our short hair, it was so freeing and did not require much care.

We all ate and caught up on the latest family news, the Great Aunts were there in all of their glory looking like a magazine ad from the 1900. They played the piano and we all sang Christmas carols and had so much fun doing the little things that make a gathering happy. We then bundled up and went to mid-night mass; it was a cold night that froze you to the bone. The church furnace could not keep up with the zero temperature. Father Linderman kept his sermon short and sweet this year; he too was freezing to death, dressed only in his vestments for saying mass. When we arrived at home there was a wrapped Christmas gift setting in front door addressed to our three favorite girls, with love. No signature again being anonymous, of course we knew exactly who had left this package for the three of us. We hurried in and shrugged out of our coats and hats. Red opened the big box and inside was three smaller boxes, each with our names on them. Red passed out the boxes, we told her to open hers first, after all what do you give to a novice nun? She opened the box and inside laid a beautiful rosary with a card attached saying it was made from the polished olive pits from the Mt. of Olives in a far away country. At the end of the rosary hung a solid white gold cross with the body of Christ attached to it. We were all speechless; this must have cost a fortune, but only the best for us by our secret caretakers. Glenda Faye was next; in her box was a small Waterford crystal clock for her and her new husband to sit beside their bed. Her note said, "May you and your husband have the time of your lives during the coming years of your marriage." I was the last to open my box. I did not want to open my gift, I wanted to savor the moment and make it last forever. Everyone insisted, they were on the edge of their seats, I took the lid off my box, there laying on dark green velvet was a 14K round gold nursing pin with a garnet jewel, my birthstone. There was a circle of smooth gold where the garnet was placed and room for many more to be added at a later date. The note read, "This pin will denote the decades you will give to your nursing career in the future. A new jewel for each ten years of service." What confidence these wonderful people had in the three of us women to do what we had set out to do that summer we set up a little table in front of the L.S. Ayres store.

This tops everything, what more can I say about the Christmas of 1940, it was the best ever for the fearsome threesome.

Chapter 33

A Gift For Mr. Higgins

Returning to school the week before New Years was difficult, none of us felt rested with everything that had transpired during our two-day holiday with our families. We returned with a special gift for Mr. Higgins, my daddy had taken up a collection and purchased Mr. Higgins a wood carving set, it was packaged in a polished wood box with a velvet lining and indentation to show where every tool belonged. Daddy also sent along a big box of soft wood for carving, some templates and a little handsaw made especially for woodcarving. Mr. Higgins was beyond himself, his mother, Sister Mary Johns looked at us with so much gratitude in her eyes, and we all shared her wonderful secret.

Every now and then we would find a small wooden carving of an animal, flower or some other creation that Mr. Higgins had thought up in his mind, setting outside of our door. These precious objects now took center stage on our windowsill, the old herb basin had been returned from where it had been borrowed from months ago.

Red was working so many hours in the Charity Ward, that one evening she passed out from exhaustion, she was admitted to the hospital and given fluids and iron to help with her condition. Red was a very small woman as were all of us, we barely reached 5'2" tall, and weighted 100 pounds soaking wet, as my daddy would say. Red was confined against her will for two weeks; she was then placed on light duty until Dr. Lucas Anthony lifted her restrictions.

The New Year, 1941, passed us by this year without a party, we were just too busy and with Red being ill, we did not feel like celebrating. Red's family could be found at almost any time of the day or night in the lounge or cafeteria during the first week of her hospitalization. I believe this was when Mrs. Murphy conquered her nervous condition without even knowing it. From that time on, she could be seen shopping with my mother on Main Street and stopping for an ice cream soda and good conversation.

The war was raging in Europe, in Washington, the US and British military leaders begin secret staff talks regarding co-ordination of a common war policy against Germany. The US Navy is reorganized in to the Atlantic, Pacific and Asiatic fleets and ordered to gradually bring ship crews up to war establishment. My daddy finally gave in to the fact that American was going to be called upon to help fight this war!

Chapter 34

Celebrations and Tears

Spring was bursting forth this year like never before, the weather was mild and sunshine filled the air almost everyday. We were able to walk across campus, but made a few trips through the tunnel to stop and speak with Mr. Higgins. We were all cramming for our final exams, this was do or die time for the three of us, but with our past grades, we just knew we would graduate.

We each spent a day with our family over the Easter holiday, but not all at the same time, mother had our dinner a day early, not only for me, but also for my brother Joseph. He was being sent to Ft. Benning, Georgia for military training in jungle warfare. That was all he was allowed to tell us, we had no idea why he would be fighting in a jungle and where would it be? Needless to say this put a damper on our celebration that year, but we still had our wonderful dinner and daddy and James played checkers on the table my daddy had made many years ago. Joseph and his wife, Dorothy left early to go and see her family so they too could say their good-byes to Joseph. Dorothy had decided to join the women's army core, called the WACS, and she would be given an assignment away from Indianapolis too.

There was already two of the Kelly boys in uniform, Mother Kelly was beside herself, and her health had been failing for some time now. She had a cough that just would not go away. I tried with all of my might, as did Glenda Faye to get her to go to the doctor and be examined. She would not hear of it, she just changed the subject and went on as usual with her life. This did not stop us from worrying about Mother Kelly, we just had to figure out a way to get her help, I would discuss this with my mother, her best friend.

We had our final exams and waited patiently for the results to be posted on the old cork bulletin board. Finally on the last week of April we received our grades, Red once again was a straight A student and elected valedictorian of the class. Glenda Faye graduated with an honors degree in her chosen field, OBGYN, nursing. Myself, I was still an A and B student and was glad to get a regular diploma, but was elected most promising student and the most well thought of by my teachers. I was so proud of myself, being liked and well thought of was as important to me as getting straight A's.

It was time for us to receive our regular white dress nursing uniforms to wear to graduation, Red asked for permission to do the same and it was granted. The big day was here; we all sat in the auditorium sitting through all of the speeches being made by concerned parties. Red gave her speech that had the whole crowd in tears by the time she finished.

The dean of St. Ann's School of Nursing stepped up to the podium, he called out our names in alphabetical order. Glenda Faye was the first of our group to walk across the stage, the dean shook her hand and handed her the coveted diploma, she then proceeded to Mother Superior, Sister Theresa Christine, Sister placed her white nursing cap on her head. It was my turn next, the procedure was repeated and then Red walked proudly across the stage, but when she stood in front of Sister Theresa Christine, you could see the tears both women were shedding as she placed the cap on Sandra Kay Murphy's head. They both knew in one month, the permanent black veil of, "The Sister's of Charity" would replace this white cap. When the last student left the stage, the crowd went wild with applause. The fearsome threesome had finally completed the course set out on so many years ago.

The crowd filed out first, but as I was passing the last row, I saw the beautiful lady and man that had played such a big part of our getting to where we were today. I stopped right in front of them, they had no where to go and had to sit in place. They knew exactly who I was, I bent over and gave the lady a big hug and shook her husband's hand. I told them there was only one person missing that would have made the day complete. This was Mr. Ayres, he had passed away in 1940, they agreed with me, but they had kept him informed all through the years on our progress. I finally had to ask the question all of us wanted to know? Who are you people, what is your name, the lady looked up at me as she was getting to her feet and said, "All I will tell you, is every time you open your canned goods, think of us." I let them pass with a wave, I knew immediately they had to be the, "Stokely's."

For years to come, every time I opened a can of pork and beans, green beans, etc., the beautiful woman and her husband would come to my mind. I would never forget that snowy Christmas night we first met outside my family home.

Chapter 35

Graduation Party For The Fearsome Threesome
(With Pink and Blue Ribbons)

We all gathered for a big celebration at my family home, once again there was a big stripped tent set up, Mr. and Mrs. Murphy provided all of the food, except for all of the desserts brought by almost every woman in the town of Speedway. Minerva Bates baked one of her beautiful cakes, this time instead of a bride and groom on the top tier, there were three little nurses in white uniforms with tiny white caps, but most important on one little statute she still had a, "White Starched Apron," tied around her waist. Minerva knew about my pink and blue ribbon therapy for my maternity patients, she honored me that day with replicating my secret.

There were many people that asked about the one nurse statue with the apron and Minerva answered, "I must have made a mistake, but too late now." I loved this woman, she knew how to handle people and send them on their way with a smile.

The fearsome threesome wore our white uniforms all day; we were so pleased with ourselves that we never wanted to take them off. I was disappointed my brother Joseph and his wife were unable to be here, but this Kodak moment was not lost in time, mother was all over the yard, taking on photo after the other.

Glenda Faye and her husband Scottie broke the news to us that after they attended the ceremony at St. John's Cathedral for Sandra Kay Murphy, taking her final vows, they would be moving to Dayton, Ohio. This was what I was afraid of all along when they married. That was not the worse news of the day; Red informed all of us that she would be doing missionary work in the Philippine Islands. My daddy's ears perked up at this news, he never raised his voice or voiced an opinion concerning someone else's business. He stood up and walked over to Red and put his arm around her shoulders, he advised her to change her mind in no uncertain terms! She looked astonished by this, he went on to tell her about what was going on with the war and she was putting herself in great danger! Being Red, she just smiled and said, "They would never send me anywhere there was danger to my life." Little did we all know what was in store for the Philippine Islands?

The party started to break up and everyone packed up and went on their way around sunset. Glenda Faye, Red and I wondered off alone to talk over our last four years together and how hard it had been, but then again all the fun we had doing it together as friends of the heart. Red stated, "We are the sisters of St. Ann's, maybe not by blood, but by friendship. This was so true; a heart knows no bounds or has no limits.

Chapter 36

Sandra "Red" Kay Murphy, Takes Her Vows

Sandra Kay Murphy was to take her final vows as a, "Sister of Charity," today at St. John's Cathedral in downtown Indianapolis. It was her choice of where she wanted the ceremony held, she had fond memories of our school days there together and that was where it was to be held. When a novice takes her final vows, she wears a regular wedding dress, just as Glenda Faye had when she married Scottie McAtee.

My mother and the whole Alter Society came together as one and worked on making Sandra Kay's wedding dress, no one was to see it until she walked down the aisle of St. John's.

We all dressed in our best clothes, the church was overflowing with friends, family and classmates. It seemed to me the whole of Indianapolis was in attendance that wonderful day, Sandra Kay's special day. Sandra Kay had told us in secret, that she had chosen her new name as a Sister of Charity. She would be called, "Sister Margaret Faye, she would carry our names as hers for the rest of her life. This was the best gift I ever received and Glenda Faye felt the same.

We were all seated in the pews of the church when the choir started singing Ava Maria, the organ sounded softly in the background. We turned to see our friend standing at the end of the church. She was holding her father's arm, her dress was unbelievable. No one had ever seen a dress like hers before; I cannot imagine the hours that went into the making the dress.

Her veil was layers of the finest tulle held in place by a crown of white roses intertwined with satin ribbon. The dress had a high-banded neckline covered with antique Irish lace, I knew at once this came from a spool coveted by my mother and kept in her treasure closet. The lace was covered with hundreds of tiny seed pearls; the bodice of her dress fitted her like a glove showing off her 18" waist. The skirt of the dress was an underlay of heavy white satin covered with so many layers of fine tulle that matched her veil. On the top layer of tulle, the women had lace cutouts of white lilies covered with seed pearls. The sleeves where puffed at the shoulders and tapered down to her wrists and banded to match the neckline. She looked like the fairy princess in, "The Wizard of Oz."

Sandra Kay had the four needed items of a bride, something old, the pearl earrings given to her by her father many years ago. Something new, the beautiful gown sewn by the ladies. Something borrowed, a contract signed in our own blood to promise to always remain friends. We were loaning this to her on this special day. She tucked the small pouch in the undergarment of her clothes. Something blue, she wore a tiny rosary necklace that was made of bezel set small diamonds with a blue topaz at the five stations of the rosary with a white gold cross set with diamonds. This necklace was so dainty, it had to have been special made just for her, and it was stamped, "Tiffany," on the back of the cross. We knew who had given that present to her, our wonderful benefactor of so many years.

Glenda and her father proceeded down the aisle slowly, when they reached the alter; Mr. Murphy kissed his daughter for the last time as a single woman. He turned and took his place next to his wife in the first pew along with the rest of the family, meaning all of the families.

Two nuns came to help Sandra Kay kneel down on the white cloth that had been spread out for this occasion. She then was laid down face against the cloth and her arms spread out to signify a cross. The bishop said all the vows and Sandra Kay answered in turn, she was lifted up and the bishop made the sign of the cross on her forehead, eyes and lips. He then placed a gold wedding band on the third finger of her right hand. Sandra Kay was now the bride of God, devoted forever in her love for Him.

Sandra Kay was led out of the church accompanied by at least twenty nuns and taken to the auditorium. We had to wait for about 15 minutes before we could join her, when we walked in, Sandra Kay was dressed from head to toe in black with a huge white starched head piece. There was a large rosary bead belt around her waist. We did not know how to react to her now, but she broke the ice in just a few seconds as she rushed towards us with her arms outstretched. We were not given much time to say good-bye to our friend; there were so many people who wanted to congratulate her. Sister Margaret Faye, as she was now called, pulled us aside, she handed us a little box, and it contained the three of the four items she wore for good luck with her dress. She explained that she could not take any worldly goods with her on her new journey as a nun.

Red as I will always think of her, handed me the box, and said, "I hope one day one of your daughters will wear my earrings and the beautiful rosary could be carried at their first communions. We told her we would cherish these gifts and share them with our children as they came along in the future. She said her mother could not give up the beautiful dress; she would wrap it and save it in her cedar closet the rest of her life.

Then in the wink of an eye it was over and Sister Margaret Faye was whisk away from the crowd of people left there weeping and heartbroken. Glenda Faye and I walked to the front of the church; there standing with her husband was the beautiful lady.

She was drying her eyes with a lace handkerchief, we hugged her and then she was gone again.

When I returned home, I loaded Glenda Faye and Scottie into, "The Independence," our old automobile and dropped them at the train station. They would be going to their new home in Dayton, Ohio, where Scottie was joining a new practice in OBGYN.

As I drove home I was all alone for the first time in my life, I had decided in the last two weeks that I would stay on at St. Ann's, until I could make up my mind on what I wanted to do with the rest of my career.

Chapter 37

Maggie's Story Is Finished For Now

As I opened my eyes, I realized that I had drifted off to sleep while telling my granddaughter, Lil the story she had requested. At that moment the young in blue pajamas came to take me to my scan, Lil went with me and it was over quickly. She helped me dress and bundled me up like we were going out into a blizzard; she took such good care of me.

When we arrived at my home, she got me undressed and into my pajamas and propped me up on two big fluffy pillows. She brought me a nice hot cup of tea, served in my hand painted cup given to my mother by the Great Aunts. As we shared our tea, I asked her to pull the little wooden cedar chest that sat in the corner, over to the side of the bed. I asked her to open it for me, as the lid opened the hinges squeaked from being closed for so many years. Lil looked inside, there were two blue and white striped student nursing dresses, two sets of collars and cuffs, yellowed from time, three nursing caps, each with a different color stripe denoting the year I was in at the time. One plain white nursing cap with a round 14K gold pin, this pin was set with five different jewels one for every decade of my nursing career. Then she lifted out a package carefully wrapped in white tissue paper, my most precious item. It was a, "White Starched Apron," the pockets still contained pink and blue ribbons and little tubes of lip rouge, that I had given to my maternity patients those many years ago.

I smiled as I lay back on my pillows thinking of, "The True Friends of my Heart, The Three Sisters of Ann's."

AKNOWLEDGEMENT

I would like to thank my family and friends who believed in my writing and story telling abilities. Without their help and God's hands this book would never have been completed like so many other projects that still lay in a closet half finished.

I asked God for the time to finish this book and He allowed me that time, now this is a big one, I am going back to God a second time! If God grants my wish for a little more time you will be able to read and enjoy, part two of the, "White Starched Apron."

"THE THREE SISTERS OF ST. ANN'S"

PART TWO OF "THE WHITE STARCHED APRON"

PART TWO

THE THREE SISTERS' OF ST. ANN'S

I will continue the saga of these three, "Friends of the Heart," on their journey into their future. There will be twists and turns that you cannot imagine, their adventures are like a piece of string that is knotted and slowly untangles at the end of the book.

Clara Margaret "Maggie," Mann is returning to St. Ann's as an OBGYN surgical nurse, she has just said good-bye to her two best friends. Glenda Faye Kelly, now Mrs. Donald McAtee M.D., they are traveling by train to Dayton, Ohio, where he will set up his own, OBGYN practice. Sandra Kay (Red) Murphy, now Sister Margaret Faye, is on her way to the Philippine Islands, to work as a missionary nurse deep in the jungles, almost beyond contact with the outside world!

Does this sound interesting to you, it does to me, I cannot wait to get started, in fact, I believe I will do that right now. The Three Sisters of St. Ann's are in danger and they need a helping hand! Come along we need you.

Love and blessings to my gentle readers of the heart,
Saragene Stamm Adkins
April 4, 2009

DEDICATION

I dedicate my second book, the continuing adventures of, "The True Friends of My Heart," which I have named, "The Three Sisters of St. Ann's," to my readers that had the faith to buy the first book, "The White Starched Apron."

To my family and friends that have been loved well by me during my lifetime, I may not be here to see this published, but that does not matter to me. I wrote these two books for my own purpose and by God's hand and giving me the time to complete them. Thank you God, you have never failed me, I have made my own mistakes, and You just helped me up and guided me back on track during my life.

Saragene Stamm Adkins
April 2009

Special Dedication

I have never seen an angel in a business suit, have you? I know I have one and his name is, Rich Cancilla, he is the owner of :

Shade Tree Greeting Cards
704 S. Clinton Ave.
Rochester, N.Y. 14620
1-800-836-4206
info@stgreetings.com

The above information is how I came to know Rich; he is an "Archangel," not just a regular angel. I found one of his greeting cards, while looking for a birthday card for my friend, Glenda Faye. I had started writing, "The Three Sister's of St. Ann's," when I saw this card with three little girls on the front cover; I knew I had the cover of my book! I bought two of the cards, one for Glenda Faye and one for contact information for the use of this card for my purpose.

I called the 1-800, number, a sweet lady named, Sue, put me through to Rich's voice mail. This amazing man not only returned my call, but also donated the artwork for my cover picture.

Now here is the kicker, I am playing, "Beat The Clock, writing this book, I have lung cancer and passed my expiration date in January of 2009. When I spoke to Rich, and relayed my personal story, he told me that he had just been to a fundraiser for Cancer Research the night before. What are the odds? Guess I should buy a lottery ticket.

I would love to meet Rich in person, give him a big hug and thank him, this probably will not happen. I have him imprinted in my heart, I know what he looks like, "An angel in a business suit."

Rich, you helped make my dream come true, "The Three Sister's of St. Ann's", thank you too. Your kindness in giving me the cover for my book brought the three girls to life and kept me living, writing their story.

Thank you, Mr. Rich Cancilla, "True Friend of My Heart."
Saragene

FOREWORD

I am not going into a long drawn out foreword in this second book of my series. I wrote a three page foreword for my first book, "The White Starched Apron." I explained that I am a Cancer patient, I don't believe in doctors giving you expiration dates, but according to the powers that be, I passed mine in January of 2009. It is now the end of May 2009; I finished this book on May 15th, 2009.

When I wrote the first book, that was going to be it, I just asked God for the time to finish the book, "The White Starched Apron." God answered my prayer and then I found myself with time left over. I grew to love my characters; the three main characters are based on real people. Even though I put them in a different time period, I am Maggie, along for the ride are my two best friends in real life, Glenda Faye Kelly and Sandra Kay. Sandra Kay passed away in 2007, from the same dreaded disease so many people and I are suffering from.

My first idea for a book, came to me while sorting old pictures, when time gets short, you sort. I found a photograph taken in the late 1930's, of my real mother, Clara Margaret Mann. She was standing with her other friends in front of their school of nursing. They all had on their uniforms and white starched aprons. When I saw that photograph, I had my story, first and last chapters, all I had to do was fill in the empty spaces.

I am repeating myself with words taken from the foreword of my first book. This book is a total work of fiction, if you are a faultfinder, fact checker or you like to naysay, then this book is not for you. Even my actual facts are a little shaky; remember I have been working under pressure, in a tight time frame. This is not a history book, the characters just happened to fall into that time period, due to the photo of my mother. If you want to know the exact facts of historical accounts from 1937 to 1941, Google it!

To the, "Readers of My Heart," that read my first book; I love you, thank you for coming on this journey with me. You have a surprise in store, there is more, the girls have done it again, you will cry, laugh and remember them for the rest of your lives.

Saragene Stamm Adkins
May 15, 2009

Chapter 1

"Maggie Looks Back In Time"

I just celebrated my 90th birthday, on January 22, 2009, my granddaughter; Lil has taken a Family Leave from St. Ann's hospital to take charge of my care. That sounds so odd to me, I have been in charge of my own life for ninety years. All of the medical tests I have been put through for the past two months showed that I am basically healthy for my age. The problem is due to being an old woman; my body is worn out from the years of service to my career and my family.

The weather is warming, but the air is still crisp, even with all of the beautiful days we have been given this April. Lil and I are sitting together in my kitchen, the kitchen where I grew up and sat for many hours with my own mother. When my parents passed away, there was always a member of our family living in our family home. Thirty years ago, I had the opportunity to buy my family home; the house that held all of my memories. I have been happy and content living here. I feel as if I had never left home those many years ago.

My daughter, Saragene, and I spent many weeks searching thrift shops and used furniture stores for just the right furniture to recreate my mother's home. We even found a little white wooden table and chairs that could very well have been the one my father made those many years ago for my mother. We were able to replicate almost all of the furniture and found reproduced wallpaper for the living and dining room walls. When we finished, this was once again my home, where, "Maggie," grew up!

Lil pours steaming hot tea into our antique hand painted cups with the little violets and green stems, given to my mother by my Great Aunts over 100 years ago. All of a sudden Patti, my other granddaughter, comes bursting through the back door bring in a gush of wind with her. She is here to spend the weekend and check on my vital signs and fill my little pillbox for the coming week.

Patti flings off her scarf and light jacket as she sits down at the table with Lil and I. Lil tells her she will have to have her tea in another mug, that there are only two little china teacups left from the set made by the great aunts so many years ago. Patti looks at her and says, "As if I did not already know that, just make my tea hot and strong!" The girls and I sit and talk about the latest happenings at St. Ann's where Patti is still working as a research nurse.

Lil asks me if I will continue my story about my days as a nurse at St. Ann's and the adventures with my friends, Glenda Faye and Sandra Kay, nicknamed, "Red?" I think to myself as I sip my tea from the fragile little hand painted teacup, there is another back-story I would like to tell the girls today. I asked them if they remembered, "The Great Aunts, Lena, Beana and Rose Kelly?" They both shook their heads, meaning they did and then they had to laugh, because their memories were of three, odd, old spinster ladies who were dead long before they were born. Patti and Lil's only connection to these ladies were these lovely teacups and an old vase the Great Aunts, had left to my mother over a hundred years ago.

Chapter 2

"The Great Aunts Story"

There is a story I need to tell you about these three ladies that were far ahead of their time, not only socially, but also politically. Lena, Beana and Rose came to America with their older brother, Patrick Joseph Kelly. After the death of their parents during a flu epidemic, their small estate was sold and each one of the Kelly children were given a small sum of money. A family meeting was called and the four Kelly's decided to immigrate to America for a new start in life. They all contributed a portion of their money to their trip fund; they found a sponsor in America, located in New York City. This sponsor was procured for a sum of money; he was not a relative of any sorts. This was becoming a standard practice for many immigrants that wanted to make the long voyage to a better life in America.

After all their business was settled in Ireland, their meager belongings packed and created, they began their journey to Dublin, Ireland, their port of call. The four Kelly's booked passage as, "Steerage Passengers," meaning low class citizens, who had to remember their station in life at all times. The three sisters despised this label, and never forgot it for the rest of their lives!

I would imagine you are picturing three grown women, but Lena, Beana and Rose Kelly, ranged in age from 14 to 16, with Lena being the oldest of the three girls; and Patrick Joseph Kelly was only 18 years of age. Can you imagine children of our day embarking on a journey of this kind; we won't even let our children go on Spring break by themselves.

The Kelly girls stood on the deck of the huge ship, looking up at the upper class passengers. They were strolling along with their beautiful gowns, hats and parasols, Lena said, "One day we will be outfitted like those beautiful women." Not to say the Kelly girls were not beautiful, they were what my mother would call, "Real Irish beauties." The girls all had the coal black curling hair, they were not the red headed Irish, like my friend, Sandra Kay. All three girls had green eyes with little flecks of gold, my mother always said, "I believe the Kelly girls had a touch of gypsy in them from some where back in our family history."

All of the young gentlemen passengers in the steerage compartment had their eyes on the Kelly sisters. Their brother, Patrick Joseph, was their protector, sometimes against their will, which could be very strong at times. The Kelley's loved to join in on any celebrating going on during the long voyage, which reminded me of the recent movie, "The Titanic." The Great Aunts would tell me stories about the sickness on the ocean liner and the passengers' fears if they were found to be ill. They knew they would be returned to their country of origin, if the illness escalated, before they were processed through Ellis Island.

When the Kelly's disembarked from the great ship and walked down the gangplank into the throngs of people, they were overwhelmed. Everyone was looking for someone just as they were. They caught sight of a gentleman holding up a sign with their names scribbled on it. The man holding the sign was unseemly and looked as if he could not be trusted with holding your dog, much less your life in his hands.

Their sponsor took the Kelly children to Ellis Island to be processed and then to procure housing for the four Kelly's. He found a boarding house for the young women where he left the girls to fend for themselves. He then escorted Patrick Joseph to a run down tenement building that was a make shift hotel for the many immigrant male workers flooding into New York.

The three Kelly girls were in luck; there were few other women who had a whole room to themselves. This was only due to the fact that they had sewn their money into the hem of their skirts and could pay the extra penny per week. Patrick did not fare so well, his room was filled with shabbily constructed beds stacked one on top of the other. These beds reached clear to the ceiling. There were mattresses stuffed with straw and crawling with lice and God only knew what else! Patrick was as tight as a tick, as my mother would always say. He braved the lice, he was saving his money to start his own tailor shop, which was his occupational training from the time he was a small boy in Ireland.

As the weeks and months passed, Lena, Beana and Rose found work in a, "Shirt Waist," factory, now days we would call these garments, blouses. Their workday could sometimes be as long as 18 hours, with just a break for lunch and other bodily functions. They worked for a tyrant called, Mr. Rosinga, he was from Holland and spoke broken English to the point of misunderstanding most of what he said. There was one point he could get across loud and clear to every woman in the shop, if she would follow his orders, her load could be lightened. They all knew exactly what he meant by this, he discussed not only the Kelly girls, but also every other woman in the shop. He would lean over their shoulders and his fetid breath would make them gag to the point of actually vomiting at their station. A rejection of Mr. Rosinga's affection could cause a worker to lose her employment or she could be slapped off of her stool. These brave young women had no recourse against this treatment; there were no unions for garment workers at this time in history. Mr. Rosinga would then eye someone else to be his object of torture for the rest of the day.

Patrick procured a job in the garment district too, he worked nights sweeping the scraps and filth from the floors of several sweat shops that stood as legitimate businesses for the wealthy owners. The whole time Patrick worked his bitterness for this business grew stronger and stronger, until it consumed him.

On the way home from Sunday mass, Sunday being their only day off, the four Kelly's stopped for an ice cream and held another family meeting. The girls had a plan; they would dig into their savings and fund the trip for Patrick Joseph to travel to Indiana. They had contacted a relative there who was willing to give Patrick employment in his tailor shop. Patrick pondered this over in his mind and his manhood was really taking a beating. He did not like the idea of his little sisters taking care of him. It was almost more than he could comprehend. Finally there was no other way, it was settled, when the Kelly girls set out to do something, they usually got their way.

Patrick Joseph would work hard to set up a tailoring business of his own in Indiana, and then send for Lena, Beana and Rose to join him in his tailoring shop. The four Kelly's worked until their fingers actually bled, long hours, odd jobs that the lowest human would not do, to save for their future endeavor. Little did they know at this time, it would take four years before the trip to Indianapolis, Indiana would come to fruition?

Lena, Beana and Rose Kelly, dabbled in many occupations while still working in the tailor shop with their brother. They finally decided to strike out on their own as wig makers and milliners, the making of hats as their main occupation. After working for Mr. Rosinga, they had made a pact that the Kelly women would never marry; no man would ever lay their hands on them again. This was a choice not many women had the right to make at that time in history.

It was many years later while sitting with my mother over these same two little hand painted teacups that I learned the whole truth about the Kelly sisters making their pact and why. Great Aunt Lena had forgotten her purse where she had left it at her workstation in the factory. When she went back to retrieve it, Mr. Rosinga was there, he grabbed her by the hair and dragged her into the filthy janitor closet. There he beat and raped her repeatedly, until she was unrecognizable. This was never mentioned and Mr. Rosinga reported her absence to the other workers that she had come down with the flu! The girls never returned to the Shirtwaist factory and made their pact that they kept till their dying days.

This is why these little teacups hold the story of three brave, beautiful young girls who took their own journey into our lives. They made this little tea set and painted the little violets with green leaves and stems, but due to a dramatic unexpected cat accident, the only remaining pieces were these two china cups and saucers.

This is just a little back story to let you know when you see an old, odd and somewhat senile lady sitting at a piano singing to her hearts content an old Irish ballad, remember she too has a story to tell.

Patti and Lil both agreed that I needed to take what I called, "A Lay Down," or a rest, we had the whole weekend together. The great grandchildren were all away, Jacob Adam was in Germany, Bailey Ann was out and about and Lucas was with his father.

Chapter 3

"Maggie Brings Her Friends Back From The Past"

Sunday morning was another beautiful day, still warmer than Saturday had been, Lil and Patti, bundled me up for mass, we were still attending St. Christopher's parish, now 5,000 strong in parishioners. I had grown tired of the way our church had changed over the past 40 years, nothing was the same, and I liked tradition. When we arrived home from church, Lil started preparing our traditional Sunday dinner. Patti was a little nervous, when I asked her what was going on with her, she looked down and then up at me, she said, "Grammie, I want more," I laughed, more of what? The girls, your friends, "The Three Sisters of St. Ann's." I said, "That is a lot to ask of an old woman, my memory is not as good as it once was." Patti looked me straight in the eye and said, "Who are you kidding, your memory is as sharp as a tack!" Lil laughed so hard, just like Glenda Faye, many years ago had shot ice cream out of her nose from laughing so hard. Today as Lil laughed she shot diet coke right out of her nose all over the stove.

I told Lil and Patti, I would try to remember where I thought I had left off. This was in the early summer of 1941; we had graduated from St. Ann's School of Nursing. Glenda Faye Kelly, no relation to our Kelly's, had married the man of her dreams, Donald McAtee, MD, they were on their way to Dayton, Ohio by train to set up his OBGYN practice. I had decided to remain living at home with my parents and return to St. Ann's as an OBGYN, surgical nurse. Sandra Kay, "Red," Murphy, had finalized her vows as a Sister of Charity and now she had taken the name of Sister Margaret Faye. She would carry one of each of our names with her for the rest of her life as a nursing missionary nun. Immediately after her veiling and the taking of her vows, Sister Margaret Faye was whisked away to serve as a nurse in the jungles of the Philippine Islands. God only knew where she was going and what she would go through!

This is where I want to start, with Sister Margaret Faye, on her way to a brand new adventure. She was alone for the first time in her life, without, "The Friends of Her Heart," beside her. Lil and Patti were practically on the edge of their seats, leaning in, trying not to miss a word of what I was about to relate to them. They had loved my friend, "Red," Sister Margaret Faye, as long as I had through the telling of my stories.

I will try to call, "Red," Sister Margaret Faye, this will be hard for me, so if I refer to her in that vernacular, please excuse me. Now this is her story, I will just be narrating it in part, joined in by her at crucial times, then I will fade into the background until I am once again called forth.

Chapter 4

"Sister Margaret Faye"
"Red"

Standing on the metal deck of the huge naval ship, Sister Margaret Faye looked out over the vast ocean that surrounded her; it was beyond anything she could imagine. Her other three companion nuns were below, sea sick in their bunks, but the rolling of the ocean did not bother her, she loved the feeling, it calmed her. She was thinking of her friends left behind, Maggie and Glenda Faye, she hoped they would find the happiness she had found choosing to be a nursing missionary nun. She had always been the fearless, in, "The Fearsome Threesome," our old school name for one another.

Sister Margaret Faye watched the waves roll by and she wondered to herself where the past four years had gone to so quickly? It seemed just yesterday, she, Sandra Kay, "Red," Murphy, Clara Margaret, "Maggie, Mann and Glenda Faye Kelly had just graduated from St. John's Academy for young Catholic girls.

We had all grown up in the small town of, Speedway City, Indiana, our mothers and fathers were all best friends. It was a time when friendship meant something holy and forever, we were, "True friends of the heart," as Maggie always said. You could not separate one from the other, we were a pretty package, and three girls all wrapped up and tied with a pretty bow of friendship.

How afraid the three of us were that first day entering nurses training at St. Ann's School of Nursing. Those four years were full of fun, hard work and heartache at times. Every semester we would stand in front of an old corkboard checking our grades and then let out a sigh of relief finding we all had passed on to the next semester. Isn't it funny what you remember from the past, Sister Margaret thought to herself?

Sister Margaret thought back to the third year when Maggie and Glenda Faye came into the dorm room and found her weeping. She remembered saying to them, "Sit down, join hands and pray." Maggie asked, "What are we praying for?" I answered, "My Hair," Maggie and Glenda Faye burst out laughing, "I told them it was not funny!" I related to them that I had decided to take my novice vows to become a nun of The Sister's of Charity. This meant having to have all of my beautiful long red hair sheared off! What a time that had been for the three of us, now it seems so small and not worth a mention, but at the time for me it was a life or death situation.

Sister Margaret remembered the day her friend, Glenda Faye, had caught her heel stepping into the elevator and fell into the arms of the most handsome doctor at St. Ann's. Then, just this summer Glenda Faye Kelly became Mrs. Donald McAtee M.D., and they were now in Dayton, Ohio, where they worked together in an OBGYN practice.

Then when Sister Margaret brought her friend Maggie to mind, she felt warm tears running down her cheeks. She and Maggie had a special relationship, in fact, everyone who knew Maggie, felt special just knowing her. Both Glenda Faye and I had seemed to have our dreams come true and our vocations fulfilled, but thinking back on the past, she really did not know Maggie's dream for her own future.

Our final good-bye was at the taking of my final vows as a bride of Christ, dressed in the fairy tale bride dress. Mother Kelly, Mrs. Mann and my own mother worked on my dress for months to my day special and one I would remember forever. When my father, Joseph Murphy, walked beside me to the alter of St. John's Church, there was not a dry eye to be found. I knew my mother was thinking that there should be a groom waiting for me to say my wedding vows. She had doubts that I had made the right decision and maybe too quickly without enough thought put into my future.

Sister Margaret could hardly remember her last words of good-bye to her two best friends; before being redressed and whisked away to join her sister nuns. She had given her two friends her most cherished gifts of, something old, new, borrowed and blue, that she had carried down the aisle. There was an amazing necklace made of tiny diamonds and blue sapphires with a white gold cross. This was really a tiny rosary given to her by the anonymous benefactors that had helped them the previous four years. There was their oath as friends forever, written in their own blood, dug up from Mrs. Mann's rose garden and taken out of a Mason jar, which she carried in a little satin pouch placed in the bodice of her dress. Then there were her pearl earrings given to her by her father, not really that old, but so dear to her heart. The only item she could not give to Maggie and Glenda Faye was the beautiful dress; Mrs. Murphy could not part with the last piece of her daughter's belongings. It was all Mr. and Mrs. Murphy could do to hold themselves together on this, Sandra Kay's, special day. Sister Margaret Faye, as she was now called, was their only child and now she was going half way around the world from them.

Maggie had slipped a little note into Sister Margaret's hand as she kissed her good-bye. When Sister Margaret read the note, she giggled, it was so like Maggie to have a plan, an outline, just like the old days at school. Maggie told her she was going to go back to St. Ann's and work as an OBGYN surgical nurse. She had bigger and better plans in the works, but for now she needed a break in her life to just relax, do her job and enjoy her family. Family, meaning sharing herself between, not only her immediate family, but also Mr. and Mrs. Murphy and Mother Kelly, her other seven children and her husband Frank. They would be missing their daughters and Maggie was really a daughter of their hearts and would help fill the emptiness left by their own daughters' absence.

Sister Margaret was so excited she could hardly contain herself; it was such a short time ago that she and her friends, Maggie and Glenda Faye would be out searching for boys. Wouldn't you know it, now handsome young men of all sorts surrounded her on all sides, you could have your pick. It was so hard for Sister Margaret to remember she was a nun, a holy woman, with that she burst out in laughter. This would take some getting used to and learning to be pious and humble at all times, if you knew Sister Margaret, you would be smiling too.

Chapter 5

"The Nuns Arrive At Pearl Harbor

The government had stopped almost all ocean travel for pleasure to European countries and the South Pacific, the United States was doing everything they could to sign a peace agreement with Japan. So many of our air force pilots were already in Great Britain teaching air fighting techniques to the RAF. The British airplanes were very old and outdated, compared to the ones being manufactured in the United States. Many factories were being refitted to make parts for anything needed pertaining to the war to help win the war in Europe, that would most likely to involve America.

The long voyage with Sister Margaret Faye and her three companion nuns was taking a toll on them. They had not properly prepared for this journey; there was nothing for them to do to keep themselves occupied. All of their books and hand sewing implements were stored in the hold of the ship and unattainable to them. The sailors got wind of this problem and together they made a suggestion to the senior nun, Sister Susan Marie. They asked if the nuns would like to help them with the many mending projects needed by the sailors? The nuns were so happy to have busy work to keep their minds off of what was to come in the future; because they had no idea where they were to be stationed after stopping in Hawaii.

The magnificent ship, The Arizona, was docked at Pearl Harbor; this was their first port of call in Honolulu, Hawaii. From there they would be flown to an unknown island in the South Pacific where a small American airstrip had been constructed. This airstrip would allow small aircraft and cargo planes to unload and load supplies needed for other islands. The air base also was used for refueling planes and transporting wounded military, if the case should arrive. The nuns would travel deeper into the jungle to work at a small village school and clinic built for the natives of the island.

The sun was rising as the four nuns came onto the deck of the ship; it was so beautiful that it brought tears to Sister Margaret Faye's eyes. She wished her two best friends were here to share this moment with her. The ship was entering the bay, coming around Diamond Head, an inactive volcano; there were no words to describe the beauty of the island stretching out in front of them. The miles of white sand beaches, palm trees swaying in the breeze, the fragrance of millions of different flowers in the wind, this was really paradise!

As the ship was towed to the dock, there was a big welcome waiting for them from all the sailors and other military personnel waiting to help unload the cargo. The nuns were introduced all around, by now Sister Margaret felt the crew had adopted her as a little sister, like the ones they left behind in American or the mainland as they called it.

Sister Margaret Faye soon realized they would have a little layover to rest and recover before flying on to their destination. She really did not know what to do with her self; she had always had Maggie and Glenda Faye to show her the way. Now she felt loneliness for the first time in her life, she sat on a high outcropping of lava rock watching the waves burst against the shore and then pull out over and over. She lifted her face to the sun and prayed to God to help her cope with her new vocation and to show her she had not made the biggest mistake of her life.

The next few days were spent sight seeing and attending classes on jungle medical care, watching retched films of oozing jungle rot and festering sores. There were lessons on the caring of patients that contracted the many jungle fevers that lurked in every drop of water on the island. Sister Margaret decided to take the opportunity to contact her family and her, "Friends of the Heart," while she still had the wireless communication telephone service on Pearl Harbor. When the connection was set up, everyone had gathered at Maggie's house to speak to Sister Margaret Faye, or as they called her, "Red." Mrs. Murphy broke into tears immediately and could hardly be understood, the telephone was passed around to all the remaining family and friends. When Maggie took the telephone, there was silence on both ends of the line, they could not speak, finally Maggie started the conversation. They missed each other so intensely it took their breath away, Red felt the same about Maggie, she wanted to crawl through the telephone line and hug and kiss her friend. Finally Sister Margaret Faye, composed herself and told them to be sure and write to her in care of the postal service at Pearl Harbor. The military would in turn deliver her mail to her on the next flight to her island. Good-bye was all Sister Margaret Faye could squeak out, and then the connection was broken.

Chapter 6

"First Flight For Sister Margaret Faye"

When the nuns awoke it was a morning that the people on the island called, white hot, steaming and just breathing was difficult. The four nuns were waiting on the pilot and crew to load all of the cargo destined for their island, the nuns had huge crates of medicine and books for the school and the clinic. They had never seen an airplane as big as the one that was going to transport them to their destination. The back loading door of the cargo plane was slowly dropped down to the tarmac and there was enough space to drive a jeep or other vehicles into the body of the cargo hold. Finally the nuns were told to approach the ramp and take a seat up front behind the pilot and the flight engineer and buckle up for the ride. As Sister Margaret Faye looked from one end of the plane to the other, she could not believe her eyes, there were bunks fastened on the sides of the plane that could be dropped down to transport wounded military. It was finally hitting her smack dab in the face how real and how dangerous this mission was going to be!

Chapter 7

"Maggie Starts Her Own Journey"

When the overseas connection was broken on the other side of the world, everyone who had gathered at the Mann household was in tears. My mother came to me and asked if I would console Mrs. Murphy, she said, "Maggie, you are Red's best friend and like another daughter to Mrs. Murphy." It was true; I felt in my heart that I had three mothers. I sat next to Mrs. Murphy, put my arms around her and drew her close to me and kissed her on the cheek, she was sobbing and inconsolable at this point. I knew we were thinking the same thing, but afraid to say it out loud. The dangerous location Red was locating to be getting worse by the day according to the overseas broadcasting station. Every night when I sat and listened to the news with my daddy, we knew the world was in dire straights.

I didn't quite know what to do with myself, like my two friends, I was now alone for the first time. I took two weeks off work before returning to St. Ann's to start working as an OBGYN surgical nurse. I spent a lot of my time at Mother Kelley's; she missed Glenda Faye so much. She said, "It doesn't matter how many children you have, when one is gone you grieve for them."

Maggie thought to herself when she was sitting with, Mother Kelly, that she was getting thinner each time she saw her. Knowing Mrs. Kelly, she had not a pound to spare. The hard life she was given raising eight children had taken a toll on this wonderful saint of a person I was proud to call, "Mother." We sat at the long kitchen table where so many family decisions had been made over they years, there were too many empty seats now. With two girls married and two boys in uniform, your voice seemed to echo in the emptiness of the room.

Maggie stood up and kissed Mother Kelly on the cheek and told her she would be back again before returning to work at St. Ann's. Here again were Mother Kelly's large hard working hands holding Maggie across her back; loving hands that knew how to embrace you, until once again you came together. This was a memory Maggie would carry with her for the rest of her life, the little moments of time you pull out, when times are rough and you need a loving thought to make you feel better.

Maggie thought to herself as she drove home in, "The Old Independence," the car that Red had turned over to her when she became a nun, I needed to talk to my mother about Mother Kelly's health. Being a nurse she was concerned and she knew her mother would know how to handle the situation.

The two-week vacation was quickly coming to an end; Maggie took an afternoon to stop at the green grocery to talk to Mr. Murphy. The store had a quite air without, Red, spinning around dancing to the radio as she pretended to be working. She was now on her way to an unknown island as a missionary nun, not that happy-go-lucky young girl working in her father's store. Mrs. Murphy sat by the old potbelly stove, now cool and shut down for the summer months. She was knitting, the needles clacking to the rhythm of the music playing on the radio, or so it seemed. Mr. Murphy was arranging vegetables on the display table in neat little rows as he had done everyday since Maggie could remember.

When the Murphy's saw Maggie come through the door, they broke into broad smiles of happiness. Mrs. Murphy soon started to cry, she seemed to get Maggie mixed up with her own daughter, Sandra Kay, or Sister Margaret Faye as she was now called. Here again, was reason for worry, Mr. Murphy gave Maggie a big hug and whispered into her ear, don't pay any attention, mother is having another one of her spells. After the birth of Sandra Kay, Mrs. Murphy was never quite the same; she had three miscarriages before Sandra Kay's birth. We all just referred to Mrs. Murphy as having a nervous disposition.

I could tell this was more serious than in the past, for one thing, Mrs. Murphy almost never came to the store, but Mr. Murphy said, "I am able to keep an eye on her and she feels safe here with me." All I could think, is my own mother going to fall ill to some unknown disease, like my other two mothers of the heart? The three of us had a nice quiet visit; there was no news from Sister Margaret Faye since the transatlantic phone call. Mr. Murphy said this was to be expected with all that was going on in the world right now; personal mail was way down on the priority list of the governments to do list. I picked up a few items that I knew my mother needed for supper, as I watched Mr. Murphy's hands wrap the brown paper around the chuck roast and tie it with butchers twine, I wondered how many times he had done that same maneuver over the last thirty years? Those wonderful bony hands that could hold a little hand with such gentleness and give the child a peppermint stick to suck on?

I pulled my old rust bucket of a car up in front of our family home, I sat there for a few minutes taking a long look at what I had taken for granted all of my life. There was my daddy sitting on the porch reading the evening newspaper and smoking his cigar and mother was snapping green beans into a bowl sitting in her lap. Everything was so normal, but I felt a chill go up my spine, what would it be like to be living in Great Britain at this point in time? I tried to imagine what it would be like with air raid sirens going off, having to take shelter huddled in our basement, all the while praying for our safety and the safety of our neighbors. Finally my daddy's voice yelling to me, brought me back to reality, "Maggie, are you going to sit there all night, or are you coming in?"

Chapter 8

"Sister Margaret Faye's Fearful Flight!"

Sister Margaret Faye could feel her hands shaking; she quickly put one hand over the other so no one would see how nervous she really was. When she looked at the other nuns, she knew she was not alone in her fear; they were not hiding the shivers over taking their own bodies at this point. One of the military personnel came by passing out small wads of pliable material that reminded Sister Margaret of the putty her father used when he replaced windowpanes. The young man told the nuns to mold this and put it into their ears, they all looked at each other and then back at him. He laughed and said, "When we start up these engines you will think you are coming straight out of hell its self!" The nuns laughed this time, and then they looked out of the window and saw the props start to turn, first slowly with a sputter, then a whine, finally the engines went full force. The noise was ear splitting, even with the soft material stuffed in their ears, they could not imagine how it would sound standing outside of the plane.

The pilot was speaking to the tower through his headset, they could only see his lips moving, he turned around the small wall that separated them from each other and said, "Hold on to your hats ladies, we are about to take off for the wild blue yonder!" Sister Margaret grabbed hold of the little pull down seat with both hands, she did not know what to expect, and she had never been on a plane before. The huge engines were now at full speed, she could see the pilot reach for the throttle and push it forward, and he revved the engines until she thought they would explode. Slowly they started to move down the runway, then with a burst of speed as the throttle was fully forward they could feel a kind of floating motion. The plane cleared the runway and headed out over the ocean, Sister Margaret wondered just how long it would be before she stepped out onto solid earth again or if she ever would?

After they had been in flight for a few hours, the pilot told them the air currents were very calm and if they wanted to unbuckle and walk around the small area, to feel free to do so. Sister Margaret didn't realize how tense she had been until she stood up; the other three nuns took her lead and also stood up. Sister Ann Francis whispered to Sister Margaret, I have to use the ladies room, Sister Margaret laughed out loud. She could not help herself, this was her old self-coming out, and she was once again, "Red," the jokester. Without wanting to embarrass Sister Ann, she asked one of the men if they had made accommodations to take care of a ladies needs? The answer to her question was, "Yes, follow me," he led them to a very large wooden packing crate standing on end. He opened a small door that had been cut out, hinges attached and a small knob applied. Inside was a wooden seat with a hole cut out in the middle and a large metal container placed under the hole with a small amount of water in it. Sister Margaret thought, my friend Glenda Faye would be right at home here, she used an outside toilet most of her life.

It seemed to the four nuns that they had been traveling for days, not hours. As the sun was setting, the young man pulled down a few cots from the walls, he told the nuns they had better try to get some rest while the weather held in a calm pattern. Sister Margaret and her companions lay down and pulled the middle strap over their bodies, just for safety sake. Soon all you could hear was the even breathing of Sister Margaret and the other nuns.

Chapter 9

"Glenda Faye Adjusts To Her New Life"

Glenda Faye Kelly, now Mrs. Donald McAtee, was having a hard time adjusting to married life, she loved her husband, but she missed her friends immensely. Glenda thought to herself, I am not used to a man telling me what I can and cannot do; being one of eight children you always knew what to do.

Donald was not at all what Glenda Faye thought he would be; there was no period of adjustment for the newly married couple. It was straight to Dayton, Ohio, "Scottie's," hometown, once again he went by his nickname, being of Scottish heritage.

Scottie's father, like his grandfather before him had all been doctors; Scottie was the first to specialize in only one kind of medical practice. He was an OBGYN, doctor, a new field of medicine, taking care of the maternity patients and then delivering them when their time was due. He also dealt with every kind of women's medical problem known to the medical world at this point in time.

Glenda did not like Scottie's mother from the first time they met, Glenda found her to be bossy and spoiled. Mrs. McAtee thought Glenda was some kind of white trash that her son had picked up off the street. Glenda tried her best to keep out of the way when it came to Mrs. McAtee, but every Sunday it was not an invitation to dinner, it was a command performance.

After Attending mass, Glenda Faye and Scottie would drive out to the McAtee mansion, there was a huge iron gate that opened on to a drive lined with tall pine trees, then all at once you were in front of the mansion. The first time Glenda Faye came to the mansion, her knees were knocking and her palms were sweating. She stood for a moment looking from the pavement up to the fourth floor of the mansion, she would one day be shown all the treasures stored there in the attic.

Glenda Faye recalled when the maid asked her, "May I take your coat Mrs. McAtee," Glenda Faye looked around for Mrs. McAtee, Scottie's mother. Scottie gave Glenda Faye a little nudge, meaning, she was now Mrs. McAtee too. Glenda Faye knew her face must have been as red as a lobster, she felt the heat rise from her feet to the top of her head, she could not recall another time when she had suffered such embarrassment! Scottie gave her a look of contempt, this was new for Glenda Faye, no one had ever treated her in such a manner, and she wondered if this marriage had been a mistake?

Driving with Scottie, out to the mansion this Sunday was almost painful; it was such a hot day. By now Glenda Faye was used to being invisible in Scottie's mother's eyes and her life in general. She no longer feared Mrs. AcAtee; she just avoided her when ever possible. Glenda Faye was glad to be out of the city, for July, it was unbearably hot. This weather was more like what Maggie's mother would call, "August, The Dog Days of Summer." The mansion was encompassed by many acres of ground that bordered on a large lake. There was a long dock beside a boathouse and further down the waters edge the McAtee's put in truck loads of wonderful fine sand for a swimming beach. It reminded Glenda Faye of her days spent with Maggie and Red at the Westlake Beach Club, where Maggie's brother was a lifeguard.

This beach was so different; no one ever went there, it was never used, until Glenda Faye came on the scene.

Glenda Faye sat at the elaborate dining table with Scottie seated to her left, his mother always sat at the head of the table; she was the matriarch of this family. Today was special, Scottie's brother was home from medical school in the east and he had brought his fiancée, Lillian Claire. Mrs. McAtee was fawning over Lillian; she was a proper young lady and had just graduated from a finishing school for young ladies in Switzerland. Lillian's family lived across the street from Central Park in New York City; her father was in real estate of some kind. Glenda Faye really did not pay much attention to the details being talked about having to do with, "Miss Wonderful Lillian!"

When the meal was finished and the family moved to the summer porch for cocktails and more chatter, Glenda excused herself and grabbed her straw bag filled with her items for the beach. Scottie gave Glenda a look that almost looked to her like relief, that her leaving would make everyone more comfortable with her being absent. Glenda Faye strolled slowly down to the boathouse; she would not let them spoil this beautiful day for her. She stepped into the boathouse and changed out of her Sunday dress and shoes and into her brand new bathing suit. Glenda unpinned her long wavy hair, it fell down to the middle of her back, to anyone else's eyes, and she would have looked like a movie star. Glenda Faye had a long lean body, beautiful legs that went on forever, the legs that every woman longed for, but did not have.

Glenda walked the short way to the beach; she pulled the rubber bathing cap from her straw bag, looked at it and then put it back in the bag. Today she wanted to feel the cool water all over her body from head to toe. Glenda was in a playful mood, she thought, what would her friend Maggie do? Glenda Faye waded a little further into the water, slipped out of her bathing suit and threw it up on the beach. She then did a little jumping dive into the water and came up sputtering as she blew water from her face. Glenda Faye leaned backward and dipped her hair in the water to clear it from her face. When she brought her head back up, she was staring into the most beautiful blue eyes she had ever seen! Standing in front of her was a stranger with a smile on his full sensuous lips. His hair was black as jet, combed straight back with just a hint of a wave; he had deep set dimples on each side of his mouth.

Glenda Faye could not speak, but the stranger spoke first, he said, "Hello, beautiful lady of the lake! I am Josh Wakefield, I live the next house over from the McAtee's, and Scottie and I grew up together." Glenda Faye was beside herself, finally, she answered Josh, and said, "I am Scottie's wife, Glenda Faye Kelly." Once again, she forgot she was a married woman with a change of her last name. Josh just smiled at her, he was standing leaning against a pillar, he had on leg crossed over the other with the toe of his brown and white shoe stuck in the sand. To Glenda Faye he looked like he should be a statue in a museum somewhere, she could not keep her heart from racing and started to shiver and it was not from the water temperature!

Glenda Faye came to her senses, she asked Josh if he would be kind enough to throw her swimming suit to her, he instantly did as requested, but not without a small hint of a laugh. Glenda Faye turned her back to Josh when she thought to herself, this man has already seen all there was to see of her whole body. Now, how do I handle this situation, instantly she remembered her friend, Red, and her wonderful way of dealing with odd situations with humor?

Josh thought to himself as he watched Glenda Faye walk out of the water that she was the most composed and beautiful woman he had ever met. She did not have that false beauty that comes with too much make-up and the best clothing money could buy. Here she was totally natural shinning in his eyes, all he could think was, "I only wish that I had met her first!"

Chapter 10

"Glenda Faye Fights Temptation"

After meeting Josh Wakefield and introductions were made, Glenda Faye felt so at ease being with him here on the beach. Glenda Faye spread out a large towel on the beach for them to sit on; she pulled another out and started to dry her auburn hair. The lake water was shinning like little miniature diamonds all over her body. Josh could not help staring at Glenda Faye; he knew if he could not control these new feelings for her, she would start to feel uncomfortable. Just at that moment, Glenda looked up at Josh and smiled, any tension that might have been between Josh and Glenda Faye melted away like ice on hot pavement, gone just that quickly. Josh felt that he had known Glenda Faye all of his life, she made what could have been an uncomfortable situation a pleasure for him. Josh explained that he was home for a visit with his family before being shipped overseas.

Glenda thought after Josh told her he had enlisted in the Navy, wow, I would love to see him in his white Navy uniform. She wished that Maggie and Red could have been here to witness what had just taken place. A perfect stranger had done more for Glenda's self-esteem in a few minutes, more than Scottie or his family was capable of doing if they really tried. She and Josh talked about everything, laughing, just having an easy wonderful afternoon. Josh filled her in on so much hidden history between the McAtee and the Wakefield's; it explained so much that had puzzled Glenda Faye about the family she had married into.

Josh and Glenda Faye sat close together, talking for what seemed liked hours and in reality it was, all of a sudden Glenda Faye realized the sun was slowly setting. Josh did not want to, but reluctantly he looked at his wristwatch and told her what time it was. Glenda and Josh had been at the beach for three hours. Glenda thought to herself that Scottie might have at least come to check in on her being gone for so long.

Glenda Faye did not want to say good-bye to Josh Wakefield. Something amazing had connected them instantly, he knew this also, and felt as she did. Josh asked her if she had a fountain pen and some paper in her bag? Glenda Faye went digging in her straw bag and came up with a stub of an old pencil and an envelope from a bill she had paid. " Will this do," she asked Josh, he took the envelope and pencil, wrote his military address down and handed it back to her. Glenda put the pencil and envelope deep down into her straw bag. Josh helped her up; together they shook the sand from the towels, getting each other covered with a light spray of sand. Laughing they folded the large towel, bringing their hands together at he corners. They both could feel the electricity pass between their hands. They said nothing to each other while Glenda finished packing the beach items back into her straw bag.

Josh Wakefield stood facing Glenda Faye face to face, she had a bit of a tear starting, he touched the corner of her eye and then gently put his arms around her and gave her the lightest kiss. Glenda Faye thought she was going to melt right into the sand, his lips were so soft, and his breath was sweet on her cheek. Josh did not say good-bye; he turned and started walking down the waters edge. Josh then stopped, turned back, and said, "Maybe when you empty your bag, you might think of me and write to me if that would be possible?" Glenda could not speak; she just nodded her head up and down. Glenda then wiped away a tear that Josh could no longer reach to wipe away for her.

Glenda Faye hurried up the beach to the boathouse, at the boathouse she changed back into her Sunday dress and pinned her hair up as good as she could under the circumstances. Strolling up the path to the mansion, she wondered if what had just taken place on the beach, was real or a dream? As she walked into the mansion, she heard the piano playing and Lillian Claire was singing. Lillian Claire had the voice of a recording star, was there anything this darned girl could not do? Glenda Faye made a feeble excuse for being gone for so long at the beach, stumbling over her words. Mrs. McAtee made a smart remark to let Glenda Faye know that she was not missed at all. Glenda Faye looked across the room at Scottie to see if he was angry with her. Glenda Faye was taken aback, Scottie was smiling and laughing over the checkerboard with his brother, he looked up and asked, "Did you have a good swim?" Glenda was angry and elated at the same time, she wouldn't change her time at the beach with Josh Wakefield for one minute with this bunch of, "Stick in the muds," as Maggie would have called them. Glenda Faye was silent and smiling on the trip home to their city apartment, she was holding her straw swimming bag close to her heart.

Chapter 11

"Sister Margaret Faye Meets Her Fate"
(She also refers to herself as, "Red.")

Sister Margaret Faye was awakened by the bumping turbulence of the cargo plane, she knew that she had not been asleep for very long, but still felt refreshed. As she started to unbuckle the belt that held her onto the fold down cot, she realized she was literally dripping with perspiration. When she stood up she felt little rivulets of sweat running down her legs and arms. Before the nuns had boarded the cargo plane, she had suggested that they exchange their heavy black habits for their lighter weight white summer habits. She thought to herself, I wonder who ever named their uniforms, habits, in the first place? It seemed quite odd to her, but the Catholic religion was never questioned or was any senior to your junior status. The other three nuns all thought her suggestion out of the question, but in Pearl Harbor the heat was just starting to kick in and she knew it would only be worse in the jungle.

Sister Margaret Faye looked around for something to wipe away the sweat that was pouring down her face, her white starched headdress was hanging limp on her shoulders. She started to laugh out loud, the other three nuns gave her a look of distain, they were already up and sitting on their little fold down seats and buckled up. To Sister Margaret Faye, they looked like three drowned penguins; she had to stifle a laugh. She thought to herself, I must look a fright too. I would love to pull this headdress off and strip down to my slip, Maggie would do that, I know she would, I wish she were here.

Sister Margaret Faye paid a visit to the ladies room to relieve her discomfort for waiting so long to take care of personal business. Sister Margaret stifled a cry of instant pain, she had her first injury to take care of; a small splinter removal in a private part of her body. Sister Margaret Faye returned and took her place beside the other nuns and buckled up. The pilot turned around and in a loud voice, told them to look out of the window, they all looked out over the ocean. In the distance there was a very large island, Sister Margaret said, "It is shaped like a cigar." From that moment, they all referred to their island as the, "Cigar Island." The nuns were never told the real name of the island, which was top secret. There could be no slip up with someone mentioning the islands name in correspondence that might fall into the wrong hands.

All of this secrecy very mysterious to Sister Margaret Faye, but she had no idea what was going on in various parts of the world. She thought the perils of war were in Europe, not in the Philippine Islands. The big cargo planes engines were revved even louder if that was possible as far as the nuns were concerned. The plane circled the island and then they started their descent, this was frightful, the airstrip was surrounded on all sides by jungle forest. It was in reality a fifty-fifty chance of running out of runway on landing or taking off.

Their descent was steep with a quick leveling off just as the wheels skidded onto the runway, the four nuns braced themselves as best they could. The pilot pulled the throttle back quickly and pushed the braking system to the limit. There was a trail of white smoke trailing behind the plane from the burning of the rubber tires on the tarmac. Sister Margaret Faye was glad she could not see in front of the plane, all she could see was the jungle passing by at a high rate of speed. The plane slowed, the pilot started turning a hard right and idling to the little air base. Sister Margaret Faye could see that this little base had been hastily constructed for one purpose only, that being for landing, unloading and taking off again, by many airplanes.

No one realized that this whole time they had all been holding their breath until the plane came to a stop. There was cheering all round from the crew and the bedraggled nuns with frightened eyes as big a headlights. The pilot shut down the big engines and finished flipping the many switches and knobs on the dashboard of his plane. He came around and introduced himself personally to the four nuns and then helped them to a small side door for them to deplane from. When the door was opened the base personnel were there with a large ramp of stairs for them to walk down to the tarmac, needless to say this was done on very unstable legs.

Sister Margaret Faye walked to the check-in building with the other three nuns; there they were directed to what they called, "The Chow Tent." Never could Sister Margaret Faye call to memory, being so grateful for a cold glass of water and canned meat served with crackers. What she would give for a slice of Mother Kelly's homemade bread straight out of her wood-burning oven. Her bread never tasted as good after she was given a gas range for cooking, but just the same she was a master baker. Sister Margaret Faye bowed her head and asked God to forgive her for thinking this thought, but she could not help herself.

Sister Margaret excused herself and got up from the table she took her cool water with her outside of the building. She stood looking at the jungle surrounding her and even with the steaming hot temperature, there was that chill again, going up her spine. Sister Margaret bowed her head and started talking to God. She was really not praying in the way nuns were supposed to pray with memorized prayers from a Sunday missal. Sister Margaret Faye said, "God, this is, Red, right now I am not speaking as a nun, but as myself and I do not think I can do this, can You forgive me?" Red did not expect an answer, but she knew God heard her and she would get a reply in His time, not in hers.

Chapter 12

"Maggie finds an Ace in the hole!"

Maggie was dreaming that she and her two best friends, Red and Glenda Faye, were eating together at the diner on Main Street, laughing and giggling about boys. Maggie opened her eyes only to realize that the wonderful smell of her mother's fresh brewed coffee and sizzling bacon in her old iron skillet had brought her out of her dream and into the reality of a new day.

Maggie sat on the side of her bed, she pulled her nightgown away from her body; even the nights were unbearable this July. The little black steel fan that sat on her table in front of the window did little to cool off her bedroom. She slipped her feet into her house slippers and shuffled off to the bathroom. Maggie refreshed herself with cool water overflowing into her cupped hands; she splashed the water over her face and neck, not caring if her clothing got wet in the process. Her thin nightgown was already plastered with sweat against her skin. Maggie decided to slip out of her nightgown and rinse her whole body and change her clothes. She went back into her bedroom and put on a freshly ironed sundress. Maggie then joined her daddy and mother for breakfast.

Mother was standing in front of the stove and daddy was sitting at the kitchen table smoking his cigar and reading the morning paper. Maggie stopped in the doorway for a few seconds taking in this moment, for some reason seeing her parents this morning, tugged at her heart. Nothing was different this morning, except that Maggie was observing her parents in a different aspect. She just could not get the war in Europe out of her mind and this picture of her parents brought it home to her and how dear they were to her heart.

Daddy looked up and said, "Well, Miss Maggie, good morning, come sit down next to me." Daddy was getting ready to leave for his supervisor position at the Speedway City Lumber Company. He only had to walk a block each day to work, which he loved; he got to see each neighbor on his way to and from work. Maggie's throat tightened and she could feel tears in back of her eyes, she loved her daddy and mother so much, not like other young people. She did not want to leave home, but she knew one day she would be kissing daddy and mother and moving to her own home.

Maggie's daddy left for work, only stopping to give her mother a peck on the cheek, mother smiled up at him and then down at her teacup. Maggie spoke up asking mother, "What were you thinking right at the moment, when daddy kissed you good-bye?" Mother jerked her head up and met my eyes, what I had asked her hit her square in the heart. She looked at me with her crystal blue Irish eyes and said, "I have never taken the love your daddy and I have for granted, you asked what was I thinking? I was not really thinking, I was saying a soft prayer for the man God had sent to me those many long years ago." That was all it took, Maggie's held back tears came bursting out and running down her cheeks. Mother said, "There, there, Maggie my girl, one day you will have what I have with your daddy, just wait for God's plan, not yours."

It was Maggie's day off from St. Ann's Hospital, and she did not know what to do with the day, she missed her friends so dear to her heart. Maggie asked her mother if there was anything she could do to help in her in her flower or vegetable garden? Mother put her finger beside her cheek, a habit she always had when deep thinking was needed. She said, "Maggie you know your daddy and his co-worker, Austin Bates have been doing volunteer work on Saturday afternoons?" I answered that I did know daddy was doing something, but I did not know any of the details. Mother told me, they had totally refurbished an old freight house down on Wabash Street. This project was accomplished with the help of many volunteers also donating their time. I asked mother what that had to do with me? She told me they had opened the first USO club, I asked what the stood for? Mother told me it was initials for, United Service Organization, the Army, Navy and Marine Servicemen's club.

Here I was again, being volunteered by my mother, at least I did not have to work the St. Christopher's Festival this year, but I did miss helping in the kitchen tent with all of the older women. I loved to just listen to their stories of the, "Good Old Days," these ladies taught me useful things that one day I too would put to use in my life. I was on a swing shift at the hospital and could not work in the festival this year. Mother told me to go down and sign up to join what was called, "The Cadettes," these were young women who volunteered their time to help at the USO club. Their function was to help serve Sunday Dinner and snacks seven days a week for our servicemen. I know, being a Catholic we were to refrain from any work on Sunday, it was after all the Lord's Day. Here again, things were starting to change in my world, Maggie thought to herself, the war is coming closer to my country!

I gave my mother a kiss and a stronger hug than normal from me, she just hugged me back tighter, we broke apart laughing, I loved my mother's laugh. I will one day hear that same laugh coming from my own daughter; I just know God would not let it go to waste. I grabbed my purse and slipped on my cool sandals and wide brimmed straw hat, inherited from my friend, Red, now Sister Margaret Faye. I walked down the front steps and got into, "The Old Independence," yet another inheritance from my friend, Red. Her father had given the automobile to her as a surprise so she could chuffer all three of us around town. It was a running heap of rust with wheels, but daddy and Mr. Murphy kept it going, they loved their girls more than life its self.

Driving out of Speedway City always felt odd, like going to another state, even when I went to work at St. Ann's, the same feeling came over me. Speedway City was my safe place, I knew absolutely everyone in our little town and they in turn knew me by my first name. Mother had given me a crude map of directions on how to get to Wabash Street; it was in an industrial part of Indianapolis. I pulled into the parking lot and sat for a moment, there was a huge banner hanging from the top of the building all printed in large Red, White and Blue letters, USO CLUB. I knew I was in the right location, I just could not take it all in, people were everywhere working on one task or the other. The club had opened at the end of May 1941, but there were still many finishing touches to be completed.

I got out of my automobile and felt a little nervous walking into the massive sliding front doors. A young man stopped me, he said use the little door on the right, and we do not open the big steel doors until there is a function with a large crowd. I thought to myself this would be to cool off all the people attending a party during this oppressive heat wave. I entered the small door and it looked like I was stepping into a hive of bees, but organized chaos. A kindly woman named, Dorothy F. Buschmann, introduced herself to me as the temporary director. Dorothy would later that year become the first full-time Director of the USO in Indianapolis, Indiana. She treated me as if she had known me all of her life, I told her I would like to volunteer, but had to work around my schedule at St. Ann's Hospital. Dorothy said it would be nice to have a nurse around just incase some of the military wounded would have a problem. I was overwhelmed at this point, but Dorothy soon put me at ease and signed me up to be one of her many, "Cadettes," in training.

Dorothy showed me all around the club, there were many rooms for different purposes. There was a game room, library, and café, but most important to the military was the dance hall, where they could get up close and personal with the beautiful young Cadettes for dancing partners. I was getting excited, I had been so lonely since my friends left me, and this could be just what I needed to ease the emptiness in my heart!

After leaving the USO Club, I came flying through the front door and almost knocking my mother flat on her bottom, she was coming out to water her flowers on the front porch. She did this every afternoon; sitting in her wooden rocker daddy had made for her. Mother would just sit with the hose and water as far as the water would spray and say a prayer for the rest of the foliage that had to wait for rain. I ran to the kitchen for a cool drink, I really wanted a soda, but daddy only dispensed his sodas on special occasions. I was opening the cool water bottle out of the icebox when I heard my mother yell, bring me a soda pop, I think this will end up being a special occasion! How can this wonderful woman read my mind, it was kind of creepy, but on the other hand I liked it, she kept me in line with her special gift. I brought our cold drinks out to the front porch on a small tray. I placed napkins under the glasses to catch the moisture already forming and running down the sides of the glasses. I had chipped away a few pieces of ice from our precious block of ice, this normally would not have been allowed, but mother did not reprimand me today.

We sat together and I told her all about the USO club, she could tell that I was excited and this pleased her, she knew how lonely I was with my friends so far away. Letters just were not the same as one on one visits and excursions in the, "Old Independence." When daddy came walking up the front steps, mother could not help herself; she had a bit of an Irish imp in her. She gave daddy a quick spray of the hose, but not so as to really get him wet. Daddy pulled the wet cigar out of his mouth and roared with laughter, you could just see these two older folks turning back the clock with one another. I repeated everything I had related to mother, to daddy, he was glad too that I had something to do with my idle hours. Daddy would also be at the USO on occasion when needed to build or repair any items in need of his services as a carpenter. I loved those afternoons spent with him and Austin Bates, at the USO Club.

I looked in the mirror; it was late Saturday afternoon, I was getting ready for my first USO dance. I had my dark brown hair pulled up on the sides and fastened in place with the pretty tortoise shell combs my mother had given me for my birthday. This was the fashion in 1941, I wore a little bit of a thin bang across my forehead, but the back of my hair fell to my waist. Daddy thought it was my best feature, I had to agree with him when I held a hand mirror up to look at the back of my hair. My hair fell in large soft waves and curled at the ends, I would fight my curly hair for the rest of my life. I said, "Good-bye," to mother and daddy, with a hug and a kiss. I ran out of the front door, my yellow see through dress with the satin under slip blowing in the breeze. Mother had purchased a new pair of white peek toe pumps for me when she was downtown at the L.S. Ayres Department Store, to go with my dress. Just thinking about that department store brought back beautiful memories from four years ago. No time for looking back now, I was on my own mission.

Believe or not, I was so nervous when I walked into the USO, they had the two big sliding doors open, because of the heat wave that was over taking the whole city. I could not believe how many people were in attendance, there must have been over five hundred people here already and it was only six o'clock. Dorothy came running up to me and asked if I could fill in for one of the volunteers who had called in sick. I was not on the schedule to work this evening, but I was glad for the transition, from guest to volunteer. I did not feel out of place or have people think I was, "Boy Hunting," as my two best friends would have said.

There was a long table lined with many cups for punch, and at great expense, and long metal trough filled with chunks of ice. I remembered that Dorothy had told me everything was donated one way or the other. Maybe the Ice Plant had done their part for the war effort tonight by providing our ice. I put on my apron and started filling a dozen cups with small chunks of ice and using a large ladle, filled the cups with punch.

I had the perfect opportunity to look over the crowd. Almost all of the young men were in uniform, except a handsome young man in civilian clothes standing against an iron upright with his hand in his pocket. I checked him out from time to time. He never moved or talked to the many women moving all around him, he was always looking straight at me. I could not stand it one more minute, when my relief volunteer came behind the table; I took off my apron and handed it to her. I saw the young man break into a smile, first his eyes widened, then when he smiled he showed wonderful white teeth. I felt no fear in walking straight up to the young man and introducing myself to him, I said, "Hello, my name is Maggie, what is your name." There was that smile, shyly, he said, "Just call me, "Ace."

Chapter 13

"Glenda Faye Deals With Devastating News"

Glenda Faye and Scottie worked together side-by-side everyday in his luxury OBGYN practice, which was bought and paid for by his father. His practice was one of the few starting to spring up across the United States, there few doctors specializing only one field of medicine in 1941. Glenda Faye was bored by all the rich patients, the only people who could afford to come to a specialist for no other reason than to be cared for because they were pregnant. She thought back to the many times she helped her own mother bring yet another, Kelly, child into this world. There was no doctor, only other women along with Glenda who had delivered their own children in their own family homes.

Scottie's patients were spoiled rich socialites, dripping in jewelry and tailor made clothing to try to conceal their condition, which was an embarrassment to some high born women. Glenda Faye was always dress in her white starched nurses uniform, white from head to toe, the ladies paid no attention to her, like she could have been a maid in their own homes, for all intense purposes. On the other hand, they treated her husband with the respect that Glenda Faye would have awarded to the Pope of the Catholic Church. He was a god in their eyes and could do no wrong as far as they were concerned.

There were days when Glenda Faye thought she would lose her mind, she was so unhappy with her marriage and the treatment of her, by her husband's family. Glenda was home alone in their small apartment, Scottie was at the hospital delivering a baby, she was glad for the solitude. Glenda fixed herself a light dinner and sat at the small writing desk and penned a letter to her friend Maggie. She poured her heart out about her marriage and how unhappy she was being here in Dayton, Ohio, all alone without a friend to talk to.

Glenda Faye stopped; she had a favor to ask of Maggie, but was reluctant to do so, but she knew Maggie would understand and be her staunch supporter in what ever she decided to do. Glenda Faye was not an impulsive person and Maggie would know she had given this idea a great deal of thought before writing to her. Glenda Faye explained all about the three hours she had spent with Josh Wakefield on the beach that wonderful Sunday afternoon in July. Glenda asked Maggie, if she were to write to Josh Wakefield, could he write back to her in care of Maggie's address? Maggie would in turn put the letter in another envelope and mail it on to Glenda Faye and Scottie would not be any wiser. Glenda Faye almost tore up her letter, but she had nothing to lose, except her respect, if she were found out. It would just confirm to Scottie's mother that she really was white trash that Scottie had picked up in Indianapolis, Indiana. Glenda Faye quickly licked the envelope, stamped it and left the apartment for the post box on the corner. Glenda Faye stood there holding the metal flap down in the position to receive her correspondence to Maggie in Speedway City. Glenda Faye said a prayer of forgiveness and slid the letter into the post box and closed the metal flap. No going back now, the deed was done, Glenda walked for a while thinking, the weather had finally broken, the heat wave had subsided and it was mild that evening in early August of 1941.

Scottie and Glenda Faye came in from work, he stopped to pick up their mail, he handed her a letter from Maggie, her best friend. Scottie said, "Maybe this will cheer you up, I don't seem to be able to do that!" Glenda Faye thought to her self, you are so right, you never even try. Glenda waited until Scottie went to their bedroom to check through his medical charts from that day at his practice, to open the letter from Maggie. Her hands were shaking as she cleanly opened the letter with the silver letter opener they had received as a wedding present.

Maggie's letter started, "To my dear friend of my heart," and read as follows: Glenda Faye, I miss you every moment of my day, I wanted so much for your marriage to work out with Scottie. I had doubts about him when his parents excused themselves from coming to your wedding, due to a pre-planned trip. That did not bode well with me, but you were so happy and who was I to rain on your parade. When I dropped the two of you off at the railroad station, I cried all the way home. Not for the missing of you, but because I knew one day I would receive the letter you had just sent to me.

Maggie told Glenda Faye to remember that, men come and go, but friends last forever. This was a bold statement for 1941, but how it has come to pass over the years to be so true. When the letter came to an end, all said and done, Maggie was willing to do as her friend had requested of her. Glenda Faye held the letter to her heart as the tears rolled down her face onto the paper blurring the ink on to her pajamas.

When Glenda Faye and Scottie awoke on Sunday morning, Scottie jumped out of bed and headed for the bathroom, Glenda Faye slowly drug herself up and went into their galley kitchen and put the coffee pot on. Being Catholic, she not to eat or drink anything before attending Mass and taking the Holy Sacrament. Glenda Faye thought that her Sunday's had turned into anything but Holy, she sat and poured her self a cup of coffee; she had decided not to attend Mass today. Scottie came in adjusting his tie; he leaned over her and told her she should not put so much sugar in her coffee. She looked up at him and added another spoonful of sugar, when she took a sip; she almost gagged, but swallowed it in one gulp. Glenda Faye told Scottie she did not feel well and thought she would stay home from not only Mass today, but also from the McAtee Sunday dinner. Scottie kissed her on the top of her head and walked out of the room and then out of the front door. Glenda only wished Scottie's departure was for the rest of their lives, not just this one day. She was really on edge, being a Catholic, she could not divorce Scottie, according to the church she would go, as Maggie used to say, "To hell in a handbag!"

Glenda Faye went to the closet and got out her big straw bag, grabbed her box of notebook paper, fountain pen and a pencil. She changed into her street clothes, a cool pair of shorts and a new yellow blouse she had bought for her honeymoon, which was yet to come. She walked to the local park and found a nice spot under a shade tree; she spread out her blanket and wrote her first letter to, Josh Wakefield.

Chapter 14

"Sister Margaret Faye Has Doubts"

Sister Margaret Faye and her sister nuns spent two days at the small air force base before beginning their journey into the depths of the jungle. They were all glad for the chance to rest and adjust to the steamy atmosphere that took your breath away at times. Sister Ann Francis asked Sister Margaret if something was bothering her, Sister Margaret Faye seemed so distant? Sister Margaret was so much younger than the other three seasoned missionary nuns who were in their late 30's to 40's. She felt as if she could easily be one of their children, should they have chosen to marry instead of taking the veil and devoting their lives to God's work. Sister Margaret gave Sister Ann Francis an off handed excuse that it was do to all the travel and exhaustion, she assured her she would be better once they were settled.

The nuns were waiting for their jungle guides to bring their little donkey pack animals and lead them to the small village where the school and clinic were located. Sister Margaret Faye saw this little band of short dark skinned men coming out of the jungle leading their animals with ropes made from the braiding of jungle vines. She wondered to herself, just how primitive this village would be, will it be just past the Stone Age? Sister Margaret Faye asked Sister Christine Rose if the villagers spoke any English, she told her she would give her a short history lesson on the way to the village. Their main guide introduces himself to them in English, a little broken, but very easily understood by all of them. His name was Philippe Miguel; Sister Margaret thought to herself that he had a kindness about him that reminded her of her own father.

There was a fairly decent path through the jungle to the village, but Philippe warned the nuns to never leave the path, the foliage could swallow you up and take away your sense of direction in no time at all. Sister Margaret Faye put that advice to memory immediately; anything she needed to survive this ordeal was helpful. On the walk Sister Christine started her history lesson, she told Sister Margaret that until 1897, the Philippine Islands were ruled by the feudal Spanish governance. America took control of the islands and ended 400 years of oppression by the Spanish rulers. The American government provided the training and goods to make the Philippine Islands what it is today. The native people are good, honest, hard working English speaking citizens. General Arthur MacArthur, the father of one of our own leading generals, Douglas MacArthur, was the third U.S. Military Governor of the Philippines. He instituted all the programs that are in place today, the native people of the Philippines are grateful to this day for his belief in them. Sister Margaret Faye had no idea, where was she when this was taught in school or was it taught; some history is swept under the rug to always be politically correct.

With what was about to break lose with Japan and unknown to the nuns; they would be glad the Philippine people would be there to befriend them in their time of need. Little did they know just how great this need would be in the months to follow!

It seemed to the nuns that they had walked for at least twenty miles, but Philippe just laughed with them, not at them, he assured them it was only about three miles to the village. There was quite a large pack train following behind the guide and the four nuns. The nuns had brought much needed supplies to the school and the clinic. These two properties had been setting vacant for about a year, the previous occupants, a missionary priest and a doctor, had contracted a jungle fever and passed away. The two were now resting in the small graveyard beside the little chapel. This news did nothing to ease Sister Margaret Faye's fears; they had been inoculated for just about everything you could think of before setting out on this journey.

Philippe turned and yelled back to his friends that the village was just around the corner, more for the nuns' sake than theirs. These men knew the jungle inside and out, they were born here and would die here. Some men lived in the large village where the nuns were going to reside and others lived further up in the hills. Philippe spent his time between the large village and his family home in the hills. Later, Philippe would become what Maggie's daddy would call, "Our Chief Cook and Bottle Washer."

Sister Margaret Faye and the other nuns were worn out, they were not yet used to the climate of the jungle. With orders from Sister Susan Marie, their charge nun, they were still dressed in their black wool habits. Sister Margaret Faye could see the white rings formed under the arms of the nuns from perspiration drying there. She didn't have to check to know how bad she smelled, there is nothing that smells worse than wet wool mixed with sweat. She could not wait to take a bath and change into a fresh starched white summer habit, which was made from the finest cotton.

Philippe led them into the village, Sister Margaret Faye looked around at her surroundings, there were many open-air huts, a small make shift Chapel and two joined stucco buildings. She thought to herself, and this is the large village, what must the other villages consist of? All of a sudden native people came streaming from every direction, there must have been at least thirty people in all. The nuns were overwhelmed; the little children grabbed their knees and smiled up at them. Some children had little gaps between their front teeth where their baby teeth had been lost to age. Philippe was trying to quite the villagers in his gentle way, and they soon calmed down. Introductions were given, the villagers lined up and kissed each nun on the topside of their right hand. Sister Margaret Faye did not know what to make of this action, but she would find out later from Sister Ann Francis. The villagers were paying reverence to the nuns; they were brides of Christ according to the Catholic religion. Most of the Philippine Islands were Catholic, because of all the missionary work done by the priests appointed by the Pope in Rome many years ago.

Things settled down and the nuns went to explore their new home, clinic and school. When Sister Margaret Faye walked into the first building, she almost fainted, the smell took her breath away, and it was just as the former residents had left it. No one had cleaned away the spoiled food, dirty bedding, and some animals had taken over and made high corners and crossbeams their home. Sister Ann Francis looked at the other three nuns and said, "I believe we had better roll up our sleeves, we have a lot of work to do here." Sister Margaret Faye thought back to how over worked she had felt when she and Maggie helped her father in his grocery store, if they could see what lay in front of her now!

Chapter 15

"Maggie Gets Serious"

Maggie knew the minute she looked into the eyes of her new friend, who by the way would not disclose his real name, that she was already in love. When Ace took Maggie in his arms for their first dance, she noticed he had a bandage on his right hand. Ace had kept his hand in his pocket until they started to dance; he explained it was a slight war injury, but not enough to keep him from flying. He could no longer fly the fighter planes he was trained in and later trained pilots in the RAF. Flying was his greatest passion, even as a small child he had airplanes all over his room built from little wooden kits. Maggie thought of the kind Mr. Higgins that worked at St. Ann's School of Nursing. The girls had given him a little airplane building kit, and for Christmas a beautiful wood carving set, which he put to good use. The girls all had tiny miniatures from Mr. Higgins imagination, he was a little boy in a mans body. Maggie brought her thoughts back to the present when Ace asked her if she had heard him, guiltily, she lowered her head and said, "No, I was thinking of a friend who also built little airplanes in his basement."

Ace and Maggie were made for each other, they spent every minute together that her schedule would allow. Between the hospital and the USO, that was not much, but Ace would come every night or day when Maggie was volunteering. In 1941, your word was your bond; Maggie would never have thought to quit her job as a volunteer. Love or no love, you did your duty to God and your country come what may. A little wisdom from Maggie's mother, she was a staunch supporter of the aid to Europe. She had a little paper hanging in her front window, showing that she too had a son in uniform.

Maggie and Ace spent a lot of their spare time driving around and visiting with her friends and she loved showing him off. Mother Kelly was the first to meet Ace, Maggie had not yet figured out to introduce him to her own mother. Her mother would want details, like maybe, a full name and family history. Maggie knew Mother Kelly would never ask any embarrassing questions like that. Mother Kelly, Ace and Maggie sat at the long Kelly kitchen table and talked over the latest news. Maggie new more that Mother Kelly did, she knew Glenda Faye was very unhappy in her marriage, but Glenda Faye never said a word of this to her mother. Both Maggie and Glenda Faye knew Mother Kelly was not well, each time Maggie would visit; she would find her to be a little thinner. Ace loved Mother Kelly at once, she took him in her arms and patted his back, and Maggie loved her hands and the feel of them on her own back. She had what my mother called, "Honest, hard working and baby holding hands." Lord knows she held enough babies in her day, she had eight children, and there were a few outside at the old water pump playing today.

One of their best days was on a trip to visit the Foo's; they lived on the Southside of Indianapolis, the family and the surname intrigued Ace. Maggie explained all about the family, how they ran a large laundry that catered mostly to hospital uniforms and only the wealthiest people sent their fine laundry there for Mrs. Foo to process. As Maggie was driving, Ace, brought to memory something that was still kind of vague, his own mother sent her fine laundry out to be done by professionals. He wondered if Mrs. Foo could actually be the person who made his mother look so beautiful in her suits and dresses?

When Maggie pulled into the driveway of the Foo residence, a beautiful young Chinese woman came running out and grabbed Maggie right out of the automobile. Ace grabbed the gearshift and put the automobile in the parking gear and shut off the engine. He got out of the passenger side and walked around to where Maggie and her friend were standing. Maggie introduced her friend, "Blossom," yet again another nickname, with her real name being Lotus. As they walked inside, Blossom told Maggie she was at a different research center, still working on the poliomyelitis problem and finding a cure before all of the children were infected. Blossom knew in her mind that would really be many years down the line, and too late for her little brother, but it would remain her life's work.

Mr. and Mrs. Foo insisted that Ace and Maggie stay for dinner, Maggie was used to the table fare, but Ace stated that he had never seen food that was so green! Everyone at the table roared with laughter, the littlest Foo child actually had an accident and had to change her underwear. She was so shy and upon her return to the table, Maggie picked her up and sat her on her lap for the rest of the meal. First feeding little Pearl a bite with her chopsticks and then a bite for herself. The Foo's took pity on Ace and gave him a fork and a knife; there was no time to train him in the fancy art of using the chopsticks.

Ace pushed back a little from the table, he let his eyes scan around each and everyone of the Foo's, and then he stopped on Maggie and little Pearl. Ace saw his future sitting right here in front of him; he could imagine Maggie holding their little girl on her lap one day. He was staring for so long that Maggie finally felt his eyes on her and little Pearl. She just looked at him with so much love in her smile, it washed over him like a wave at the beach, but did not pull away and go out to sea. The feeling was real, it stuck and now Ace knew exactly what he had to do and this would be done as soon as possible. The time was getting late and Maggie was scheduled for the third shift at St. Ann's Hospital. There were many hugs and kisses exchanged between the whole Foo family, Ace and Maggie. Little Pearl clung to Ace; he picked her up and gave her a kiss on the forehead. Mrs. Foo thought to herself, this was my change of life child, but so dear to my heart and she keeps us all on our toes.

On the drive back to the USO club, where Ace had left his borrowed car parked, she turned to Ace and they embraced each other not wanting to let go. Maggie loved the feel of Ace's lips on hers; it was like they became one person. She did not know anything about sexual love between a man and a woman, but she could only imagine with just kissing Ace. They finally separated reluctantly, Ace watched Maggie pull out of the parking lot with a plan already in place. Ace was so excited, as he drove home; he spent the drive fine-tuning his plan of action.

Chapter 16

Glenda Faye
"Josh lifts her hopes and dreams"

Glenda Faye was working in the private practice with her husband, she detested the work she was doing, but tried to keep up a good attitude for his patients. She wondered if she would ever receive an answer to her letter she had mailed to Josh Wakefield in July, it was now the middle of August. The military took its own sweet time in forwarding mail to the armed forces as far as she was concerned.

When Glenda Faye and Scottie returned home, there was a letter from Maggie, Scottie handed it to Glenda and went on sorting through the normal mail containing mostly bills. Glenda Faye's heart was beating; she and Maggie had a code, if the letter was from Josh. Maggie would place a little heart on the point of the envelope where it was resealed. Glenda Faye slowly turned the envelope over and sure enough there was a tiny red heart, her own heart skipped a beat. What if that day on the beach was a fluke, a one-time encounter that really meant nothing to Josh Wakefield?

Scottie sat on the couch listening to the latest news on the war raging in Europe; Glenda Faye was in the galley kitchen fixing them a light supper. Scottie was a stickler for healthy food, Glenda Faye thought to herself, what I wouldn't give for a nice pot of ham, beans and cornbread! She was a country girl at heart, but Scottie had never even been in their kitchen in the mansion. The family was served by maids with a ring of a tiny china bell that sat at the right hand of Mrs. McAtee. Glenda put together a summer salad with baked chicken slices, tomatoes, cucumbers and hard-boiled eggs. The salad looked so pretty when she sat it on the table along with hot rolls from the bakery down the street, all Scottie could say was, "Where is the butter?"

After Scottie went to his desk to check his charts for the day, Glenda Faye told Scottie she was going to go outside and sit on the steps. He gave her a smirk, but said nothing; she hurried downstairs with her letter tucked in her apron pocket. She sat close to the main door, if Scottie came down, she would be able to hear him and put the letter back in her pocket. As Glenda carefully opened the letter, she pulled the second envelope out written in Josh's precise handwriting. Glenda's hands were shaking as she slipped her index finger under the flap of the second envelope. She pulled out the three pages, hesitated, she had never been so afraid to read a letter in her life. Immediately, Josh put her mind to rest, he addressed her as his dear, "Lady of the Lake." "I was so happy to hear from you, I never thought that day on the beach at the McAtee mansion that you would reciprocate my request to write to me. Be sure to thank your friend, Maggie, for being a go between for our writing to each other. I want you to understand, I am not the kind of man who would in any way want to come between a husband and wife. I think of marriage as a holy vow, being a Catholic myself, I feel so much guilt, even putting pen to paper and writing to you. After receiving your letter explaining the pain you are going through in your marriage, it broke my heart. I wanted to get on my white steed and ride up and sweep you off your feet and take you back to my castle. We could live

The White Starched Apron

happily ever after, you would always be a princess in my eyes, I would worship you for being the person I know you are."

Glenda Faye went on reading the pages over and over; Josh had nothing but wonderful things to say to her and about her. All this from just three hours on a beach, she let her mind wander to what could be if they had the rest of their lives together? Josh told her he was still in the United States, but was being shipped out in just a couple of weeks. He could not tell her where he was bound for or which ship he would be assigned to.

Glenda Faye kept up on all the latest news on the problems going on in the Pacific, she knew her friend, Sister Margaret Faye, was somewhere in the Philippine Islands. She was more worried about the Japanese conflict than that of the Germans in Europe. She prayed every night for God to keep, "Red," safe, she still could not get used to calling her friend by her new name as a nun.

Now she felt, with Josh being in the Navy, she had two people to worry and pray for God to keep them safe. She folded the letter and was putting it into her pocket when she heard someone coming down the steps in their apartment building. Glenda Faye hurriedly pushed the letter deep in her apron pocket as Scottie stepped out of the main door. She smiled up at him, he asked her how Maggie was, she gulped, and said she was fine and sent her best to him. Scottie told Glenda Faye he going to meet a friend for a drink, lately she noticed he had been drinking way too much and she was starting to be concerned about this problem. Then she smiled and thought of Josh, Scottie would also be concerned about her writing to him.

Chapter 17

Sister Margaret Faye
"Red" gets a reality check!

The first month after landing on, "The Cigar," which was what everyone now called their island, Sister Margaret Faye, could hardly recognize herself in the small cracked mirror hanging over the hand-washing basin. The nuns had little to work with, but Philippe Miguel was indeed a reincarnation of Maggie's daddy, he could construct anything out of a palm tree and a few long vines. They had taken the two stucco buildings and added on a separate quarters for the nuns to sleep and take care of their daily cleanliness routine. There was no running water; every drop was carried from a small well in the center of the village, until Philippe found a use for a large roll of rubber tubing left over from the previous tenants. He buried the tubing under ground from the well to the hospital and attached it to a small hand-siphoning pump. How this marvelous man was able to do all of this for the nuns, none of them could figure it out. They were just glad to have him, now they could pump their own water into the large pots for boiling. The military had given them more than enough metal five-gallon containers for their drinking water. They also kept canteens filled with drinking water hanging on hooks in every room, each nun was in charge of her own canteen and making sure it was filled with boiled water at all of the time.

Sister Margaret Faye was taking her turn in their makeshift bathroom, which consisted of a waist high cabinet with a large metal basin and pitcher of water for washing. Today she was completely naked standing in the basin, she poured some water over the top of her head, grabbed the foul smelling homemade soap. She then lathered her body from the top of her head down to her feet. She was groping for the handle of the pitcher again, feeling her way to the washstand. The soap was stinging her eyes, but finally her hand touched the handle of the pitcher, she immediately poured the water into her eyes and then all over her body. When she finished, she still felt sticky from the soap; she forgot to bring extra water with her today to get a good rinse. Oh well, the way her chopped off red hair looked and her skin that was starting to look like tanned leather, who would really cared?

Sister Margaret Faye walked out into the bright sunshine to greet the day, having a full washing of her body, made her feel so much better. She was now dressing in the white habit of summer, Sister Susan Marie, would not give up her black, hot wool habit under any circumstances. She said that people respected nuns that looked like nuns and that was that as far as she was concerned! The other nuns followed Sister Susan Marie, I believe out of suffering her wrath, she could be frightening at times. Sister Margaret Faye wondered what Sister Susan Marie's life was like before she took the veil; she would never find this out. The nuns never spoke of their lives before their vows were taken. Red thought this was funny, excused her self to God for her mistake in using her nickname. God, this is Sister Margaret Faye, the heck with it, I will call myself what ever I want to in my mind when I talk to my God.

There were only a handful of students coming to the school, it was harvest time and anyone who could work, did. The schoolroom was so nice, Red was talented, and she helped

Philippe whitewash the walls, which ruined one of her two black wool habits. She painted little cartoon people and animals on the walls; across the top of the chalkboard she painted the alphabet in different colors. She was so glad she had insisted on being able to bring her paints, Red was a great artist in her own right. The children loved her from the very first time they met her, even looking like a drowned penguin. Red decided today they would just play some games and tell stories since so many other students were working on the harvest. The children all cheered and loved to tell stories, that was how they kept most of their family history going from one generation to the next.

Sister Ann Francis had awakened with a throbbing headache and her throat felt raw, she started to get out of her cot and collapsed on the dirt floor in her nightgown. Sister Christine Rose found her lying there, face down on the hard packed earth, when she turned her over, she could see a trickle of bloody foam coming from the corner of her mouth. Sister Christine Rose was hysterical, yelling for help of any kind, she did not have the slightest idea what to do. Red could hear her yelling with only three walls separating them; she immediately dismissed the children for the day. She went running; pulling her long dress up above her knees, she saw that Sister Susan Marie had just arrived. The senior nun reprimanded Sister Margaret Faye for her unlady like behavior; this was indeed Red coming back at her senior nun, not sister Margaret Faye. Red said, "You can take your manners and lady like behavior and stick them where the sun does not shine, now you get out of my way!"

Red was a graduated nurse, she knew death when she saw and smelled it, and Sister Ann Francis was not long for this earthly world. With the help of the other two nuns, they place her back on her cot after the linens were changed. Her temperature was raging, Red had no idea what kind of fever she had or where she had gotten it from, they were so careful with their food and water. Red turned around and saw, Luli, standing in the doorway, her eyes were as big as saucers and she had her finger resting on her two front bottom teeth. Red walked over to Luli, just as Philippe grabbed Luli around the waist, she was his granddaughter. Philippe apologized for her presence. Red stopped him, she told Philippe to put the little girl down, and she looked up at the nun with tears starting to run down her face. Red assured Luli that this was not her fault, Luli said, "It is my fault," Red asked her how that could be possible?

Luli asked the nun if she remembered that Sister Ann would take them on nature hikes, they would explain what all the plants were and what they used them for. Sister Ann would draw the plants in her notebook and write their uses for various medications and cooking properties. Luli told her that yesterday they went to the hills and Sister Ann was so happy to find a berry that grew in Michigan, the part of America where she was from. The children told her not to eat it, but she loved blueberries and had been raised on them in her home state. She ate quite a few, but said they did not taste the same; they were not sweet like the blueberries she was used to eating. The children did not want to offend Sister Ann, so they said nothing more, they knew that their parents had told them from a very young age never to eat these berries!

Philippe immediately went white, he knew exactly which berry Sister Ann had eaten and it was a deadly poison to humans. Red thanked them and reassured Luli that it was in no way her fault and to never think that again. She kissed the girl and sent her home to her grandmother for consolation, she could tell how upset Luli was and Philippe too. Red returned to the other three nuns and relayed the story to them; she said all we can do is keep her cool and comfortable. Sister Ann had lost consciousness, the bloody froth was pouring from her nose and mouth. The nuns propped her up and kept her as clean as possible, they knelt beside her bed and prayed the rosary as she took her last gasping breath. Sister Ann's body was quickly prepared for burial, with the heat of the jungle, burial was immediate. She was given the last rights of the Catholic Church and the villagers gathered in the small graveyard to pay their respects to Sister Ann Francis.

Chapter 18

Maggie
"Ace Works His Plan"

Ace had made a date with Maggie for Sunday, he was picking her up at the USO club, and she was on the schedule to help serve Sunday dinner to the military personnel. When Ace walked into the long dining room with its many rows of tables, it was hard to sort out where Maggie was working. Finally he saw her coming out of the kitchen with a large pan of piping hot mashed potatoes, he ran over to her and grabbed the pan just before she dropped it on the floor. Ace helped Maggie set the pan on the table, now he had two injured hands, one from a bullet and this burn from a pan of mashed potatoes. Maggie was so sorry, he just laughed, who in their right mind holds a steaming hot pan. Maggie gave a giggle, and said, "You."

Ace thought to himself, I hope this is not the way our whole day will be going, my plan has just got to work. He had worked out every detail in his mind; if his plan fell through he would be devastated. Everything depended on Maggie from now on and he knew in his heart she would not let him down. Maggie finished her shift and grabbed her sweater, it was September and the evenings could surprise you and turn very cool. When they walked out into the parking lot she headed for, "The Old Independence," but Ace stopped her, we will take my car. Maggie did not know Ace had a car, much less the one he helped her into, it was beautiful, with caramel colored leather inside. He just winked at her and said; "I just thought I would take you in style this afternoon." Maggie did not quite know how to take all of this, she just liked having Ace take charge for a while, and she was tired.

They drove out of the city to the north side of town; there was one huge estate after another, Maggie said, "I love to take a Sunday drive, daddy, mother and I used to do that on a regular basis." Ace just smiled to himself, as they rounded a bend in the road, Ace turned into a wide drive that led to the biggest house that Maggie had ever been this close to. She was getting very nervous, she looked to Ace, and he was smiling, she could tell he was causal and relaxed. He turned off the motor and came around and helped Maggie out of the car, they walked the ten or so steps to the front door. Ace reached for the chain that rang the front door bell, the family maid answered the door. The maid was all smiles, she said, "Mr. Ace," your parents are expecting you. They are in the sun porch for a late afternoon tea," Ace put his arms around the older woman and gave her a big hug. The maid just smiled and turned around to hang up Maggie's sweater. Now Maggie was really puzzled, Ace took Maggie by the hand and led her through the huge entrance room. This room led to many other rooms and a parlor that she could see leading off of it. They walked straight back and took a left turn, there were two white French doors standing open facing the sun porch and you could feel the breeze coming in from the open fields behind the house.

Ace squeezed Maggie's hand to reassure her everything was going to be fine, he walked through the door first and gave a greeting to his parents. Then he turned to look at Maggie who was standing behind him and then to his parents and said, "Mother, father this is Clara Margaret Mann, who I hope will except my proposal of marriage." Ace took Maggie by the shoulders and turned her to face him, she still could not see his parents. Ace knelt down and pulled a velvet box from his pocket, he opened it for Maggie to see. Ace explained to her that the ring was given to his grandmother when his grandfather had purposed to her. He then slipped it on the third finger of Maggie's left hand and said, "Would you give me the honor of becoming my wife?" All the while, Maggie had her back to Ace's parents. All at once it came to Maggie how rude Ace was in purposing this way. Maggie burst into tears when she finally turned to face Ace's parents, when she saw his mother and his mother saw Maggie, full faced in front of her, his mother stood up and dropped her teacup, which went crashing to the floor!

Ace had no idea what had just taken place; surely his mother would not be that rude, after all she didn't even know Maggie. Maggie went over and grabbed Ace's mother before answering his question of marriage. His mother pulled away from Maggie and Ace thought, oh boy, what have I gotten Maggie into? Ace started to explain to his mother, but his mother took over, I believe introductions are in order for Miss Maggie. Ace's mother started with Clara Margaret Mann, nice to finally know your full name, Maggie. My son's full name is, Leo John Van Camp Jr., she laughed and so did Maggie. We are Mr. and Mrs. Leo Van Camp, not the Stokley's or the Pork and Bean Van Camps. Maggie looked puzzled, but you said to me, "When you open your canned goods think of me." "I know dear, I had to keep you girls guessing, we wanted to remain anonymous, not that we are not wealthy, we are, but not in the canned goods business." Ace was scratching his head; he sat down and poured himself a stiff shot of bourbon with a water chaser.

Ace's father reached over and patted him on the knee; we have a lot to fill you in on. Your mother and I have known Maggie and her two best friends since they set up a little flag stand in front of Mr. Ayres' department store many years ago. These young girls were in need and over the years we helped them with their problems, but never told them who we were.

Ace's father explained to him, that when he was no more than an infant, he fell ill with a raging fever. We took you to St. Ann's Hospital in the middle of the night for care. A young doctor at St. Ann's hospital worked through the night, and all the next day to save your life. Our friend, Mr. Ayres called and related the story of the three young women he had helped with a problem one summer day in front of his department store. Mr. Ayres was now asking for a very large favor, which we were glad to contribute to. When it came to St. Ann's Hospital, we felt we had a debt even larger than his request, to pay for the saving of your life. Ace knew Mr. Ayres well, he could feel stinging behind his eyes, Mr. Ayres was no longer with them and was sorely missed by so many. Ace could not believe the coincidence that had just taken place, what were the chances of he and Maggie meeting and falling in love?

Ace stood up, and said, "We have some unfinished business here, and I asked this lovely young lady to become my bride, now I would like an answer?" Maggie walked over to Ace and put her hands on his cheeks and kissed him on the mouth, "There is your answer," she said, looking at the sparkle on her third finger. The rest of Ace's plan went well, there was no more plan to go wrong. His parents already loved Maggie, maybe even more than he did, who wouldn't love this beautiful, sweet, funny bundle of happiness?

On the drive home, Maggie told Ace that there was a whole lot more to face and they had to do it soon. He was shipping out to what the flyers called, "The Pearl," meaning Pearl Harbor. He would now be flying other styles of airplanes, his days of flying fighter planes were over, but he was happy to just be in the air. Maggie was happy too, feeling he would be in less danger than before. He agreed with her on what they had yet to face, Maggie's parents had never met Ace; they heard bits and pieces here and there. Maggie knew her mother was not a fool and could tell her daughter was in love, but being cautious, she wanted a man just like her father and would settle for nothing less!

Chapter 19

"Scottie Secret Surprise"

Glenda Faye could feel the tension between she and her husband growing stronger by the day. Finally she could not take it one moment longer, she walked into their small eating area off of the galley kitchen and sat down at the table. Scottie never even lifted his head from his reading of the morning newspaper, to say good morning to his wife. Glenda pushed her plate away and sat her coffee cup at the edge of the table in front of her, while she stirred in two teaspoons of sugar. Once again, Scottie must have caught this action out of the corner of his eye and reprimanded her for her over use of sugar. This was all she could stand, it was her breaking point, Glenda looked up and said to Scottie, "Be honest with me, why did you marry me, I have come to find out over these past months, that you and your family have no use for me?" Scottie hesitated before answering her, finally he said, "I am sorry, I have serious issues with my family, especially with my mother. It was not fair of me to marry you for the selfish reason that I did." Glenda remained silent, just as she suspected there was a hurtful story behind their marriage. Scottie continued relating to Glenda Faye his purpose for marring her, he said, "These will be harsh words for you to hear, but do not take it personally, it is not about you, but you were the one who ended up suffering the brunt of it all. My mother had hand picked my bride, a high-class young woman who could have been the exact replica of my mother in her younger days. Number one, I did not want to get marred to this woman, and I hated my life and the way I had been raised by a nanny, not my mother. My mother would dress me and my younger brother up and show us off and then put us back in a neat little box, until she needed us again for her own personal reasons." Glenda Faye was wiping away the tears running down her face with her napkin, Scottie came around the table and gave her a hug, grabbed his hat and left the apartment.

Glenda Faye remained seated at the table trying to figure out what to do, Scottie didn't really finish the question she had asked him. It seemed to her he had stopped right in the middle of his explanation, maybe he needed some time to himself. When he returned, she would ask him to continue, there had to be more to it than just him picking his own bride, someone he really wanted to marry. Glenda cleared away the breakfast table, washed the dishes and cleaned the kitchen to keep herself busy waiting for Scottie's return.

Glenda Faye was getting restless waiting for Scottie to return to their apartment, she remembered she owed Maggie a response to her last letter. She sat at the small writing desk and penned a letter to Maggie, she poured out her heart to her friend, relaying what had taken place at the breakfast table. Glenda disliked complaining so much to Maggie, she knew Maggie would take on Glenda's problems as if they were her own. It seemed that every letter she sent to Maggie lately, had one or two tear stained blotches here and there on the pages. She did not forget to thank Maggie for her help in forwarding Josh's letters on to her; this was against everything that both girls believed in being raised as proper Catholics. Glenda signed the letter with her beautiful penmanship and added a tiny heart drawn in red pencil.

The sun was starting to set over the city, this evening the sunset was spectacular, and there were all shades of pink, blue and green streaking across the skyline. Glenda was seated with her head resting on the back of couch, she watched the sunset until the sun went down past the building across the street. Glenda heard Scottie turn his key in the lock. She thought to herself, thank God he is safe; she had really been worried with so much time passing. Instantly Glenda knew that Scottie was rip roaring drunk, as her father would say. He came over to Glenda and said, "All of your and my mother's troubles are solved. I have enlisted in the Army, you will no longer have to put up with my black moods and I will not have to dance to my mother's tune any more!" Glenda started to weep, deep racking sobs, this is not what she wanted, she knew Scottie's mother would have no part of his decision. Scottie staggered into the bedroom, fell across the bed and passed out; Glenda was left trying to figure out their future together.

Chapter 20

Sister Margaret Faye
"Red comes to the surface of Sister Margaret's Life"

Life in the jungle village had taken on another dimension after the death of Sister Ann Francis; Sister Margaret had all but disappeared. Not in the literal sense, but to Sandra Kay "Red" Murphy, she no longer considered herself a nun in her mind. Even with the tragedy of death, her senior nun, Sister Susan Marie, could not let go of Sister Margaret's behavior on that day. She called Sister Margaret to account, belittling her in front of the other two nuns in attendance. She lectured her on the etiquette of not only being a lady, but the status of being a nun. Sister Margaret was silent; she would not give this senior nun the satisfaction that she so greatly wanted by embarrassing her in this manner.

Sister Susan Marie waited for an apology from Sister Margaret, but none came. The young nun just stood in front of her, head bowed, staring at the earthen floor. Sister Susan Marie took this as Sister Margaret being sorry for her actions, she was so wrong in her assumption! Sister Margaret was so angry; her Irish temper was reaching the boiling point. Just as Sister Margaret was about to defend her actions, Sister Susan Marie, dismissed her.

It was final in Sister Margaret's mind, she was no longer a nun, she would do her duties without complaint, but her future would be forever changed. Now she thought to herself, I am, "Red," I will find my wonderful humor and spirit, these qualities I will pass on to the people I care for here in my village. Red walked out of the little school where she left the other two nuns whispering among themselves, she gave not a thought to their discussion. For the first time since she had arrived here on, "The Cigar," island, she felt light and free. Come to think of it, what could they do to her, send her home on the next flight, I doubt that, they need me, but it would be nice?

Red walked through the village smiling, stopping to speak with the village venders selling their fresh jungle fruit. She picked two fully ripe bananas and walked down the path to a large rock. She climbed around the rock until she could comfortably sit down on a flat spot that overlooked the village. No one knew of her secret spot, she had happened upon the rock by accident herself. She loved to stroll around the village, but hardly ever strayed off of the path, remembering Philippe's warning. Today there was a rare breeze blowing across the island, Red untied the headdress that weighed down her head and laid it next to her on the rock. She let the warm breeze caress her head; she could feel her hair moving for the first time in almost two years.

Red stayed in her secret place for about an hour and then she returned to the nuns' quarters. Standing there was Sister Susan Marie, with her arms crossed and tapping the toe of her shoe on the hard packed earthen floor. Red started to open her mouth, but was not given that opportunity, Sister Susan Marie shouted out orders to Red. She was giving Red the worse chores that everyone of the nuns tried to avoid doing. Normally they would take turns attending to these chores so no one would feel less than their sister nuns. Red took hold of both sides of her skirt and did a little curtsy in front of Sister Susan Marie, told her she would be proud to take care of these chores, as ordered. She could tell Sister Susan Marie was once again, out bested by Red, and she was fuming mad!

So many times Red would run up to Philippe when he returned from the air base to check for incoming mail, only to be disappointed. This did not stop her from writing every week to her family, who would then relay the details of her life on to her friends. She always wrote a separate letter to Glenda Faye, because she was in Dayton, Ohio, with her new husband. Red knew when her family in Speedway City, received her mail, it would turn into an occasion for a party. Mr. Murphy invited everyone who knew her and they would all listen as he read her news from the Philippines. Mrs. Mann and Mother Kelly would provide baked goods and Maggie would make her world famous coffee and tea. Maggie had perfected this art by watching her mentor at the USO club. Mrs. Murphy would sit next to her husband and softly cry into one of her beautiful lace handkerchiefs.

There was always something to do in the village, the children were returning from the harvest work at their farms located higher up in the hills. Red loved teaching; Sister Christine Rose had no talent or tolerance to teach the children. Really all she was good for was complaining, you would think at her age she would have gotten used to being a missionary nun by now. The one talent Sister Christine did excel in was cleaning and organizing absolutely everything. Sometimes this drove Red right up the whitewashed walls, but she was a loveable sort, so unlike Sister Susan Marie. Today Red was letting the village children give her a history lesson about their island; there were smiles from all the children, they were from proud stock.

Chapter 21

Maggie
"Ace and Maggie break the big news!"

Maggie had asked her mother if she could ask her new boyfriend to have Sunday dinner with them? Mother was surprised by the request, but she was excited, it was about time her daughter found some happiness in her personal life. Mother wanted to plan a special meal, but Maggie insisted they have their normal Sunday dinner, fried chicken, mashed potatoes, green beans, corn and biscuits with her mother's wonderful cream gravy. Daddy overheard the conversation; he was smiling as he puffed on his cigar, he already new who the new boyfriend was. He and Ace had been introduced at the USO club just a few weeks ago; Mr. Mann instantly liked this young man. Maggie was so nervous sitting through the long Sunday service at St. Christopher's Church, she felt guilty wanting mass to be over. On the way home Maggie was quiet, mother turned and asked her if she was feeling all right? Maggie smiled back at her mother and assured her she was just fine.

When they arrived at the house, mother changed out of her Sunday dress and put on a freshly ironed cotton dress and tied an apron around her waist. She headed straight for the kitchen to start their meal; Maggie was in charge of peeling the potatoes and breaking the fresh green beans. Time seemed to drag by, mother was humming a hymn that they had sung in church earlier and Maggie joined in with her. Watching her mother cook today was the same as it had been for the past twenty some odd years, but today she looked especially pretty. Daddy was listening to the overseas broad cast as usual; this was his Sunday afternoon ritual. Maggie's daddy wanted to relate some of the most recent news to mother and Maggie, but decided to wait until later.

Today they were eating in the formal dining room; Maggie had laid out her mother's best china and stemware for the occasion. She checked and double-checked to make sure the table was just perfect; after all, Ace came from a very wealthy family. He was used to the best that money could buy, when it came to home furnishings, but you would never guess this with his casual attitude. Maggie had done everything that she could do and now all she could do was wait for Ace; just then there was a knock on the front door. Daddy got up and went to greet Ace, he invited Ace into their home and said with a bit of a laugh, and said "I believe the women are prepared for your arrival." Daddy asked Ace to take a seat on the sofa and make himself at home, Maggie came rushing into the living room with a big smile on her face. Mother followed behind Maggie, Ace immediately stood up out of respect for the two women standing in front of him. Mother told everyone to sit down, she said, "We do not stand on formality in our home, everyone is welcome." Mother said that dinner would be ready in about fifteen minutes, she had just put her famous biscuits in the oven, Ace took in all of the amazing aromas drifting from the kitchen and his stomach started growling. He was embarrassed by this noise, Maggie could not help but giggle, and mother corrected her with a small giggle herself.

Maggie stood up and Ace followed her lead, Maggie looked first at her daddy and then at her mother, she said, "We have something to tell you and ask you for your blessing." Daddy looked at mother and back to the young couple, he said, "Continue, I believe I know what is coming." Ace took Maggie's hand in his and asked, "I would like your permission to marry your daughter, if this is all right with the two of you?" Mother spoke first, she looked at her own husband with thoughts of long ago, when he first asked for her hand in marriage, she knew how nervous the young couple was. "Daddy and I have already discussed this proposal that we knew was coming, we are both in agreement that you are perfect for each other and you have our blessing." Maggie ran to her parents with tears of joy spilling down her cheeks, she hugged her mother, while Ace shook her daddy's hand. They then exchanged places; Ace gave Mrs. Mann a hug and a kiss on the cheek to seal the deal.

The four future family members sat down to their first Sunday dinner together, it would be one of many more to come over the years with God's blessing and protection. With dinner over, the two men went out on the front porch, daddy put his old wool sweater on, September was coming to an end and there was a nip in the air. Mr. Mann lit up a cigar and asked Ace if he had heard or read about President Roosevelt's speech on September 27th? Ace was embarrassed to say he hadn't, daddy told him they had dubbed this day as, "Liberty Fleet Day, and launched the first 14 Liberty ships. President Roosevelt cited Patrick Henry's famed speech and stated that the ships would bring liberty to Europe. Mr. Kaiser who built the Bay Bridge and the Hoover dam pioneered new techniques for the building of these Liberty ships. Ace wondered if Maggie's friend Glenda Faye had heard this news, Ace new all about Josh Wakefield and that he was in the Navy, would Josh be assigned to one of the new Liberty ships? He would speak to Maggie about this at a more proper time in private.

The men returned from their long conversation on the front porch just in time. Mrs. Mann was setting a steaming hot cherry pie on a trivet in the middle of the kitchen table, this was much more cozy for conversation, she thought. Maggie was coming in the back door with fresh frozen vanilla ice cream from the corner drugstore. Ace did not know that Maggie had left the house. Mother said, "Sit down you two men, enough with all the standing and waiting for us ladies to be seated first." The two men just looked at each other, daddy said, "You better get used to this, it will now be your way of life, Maggie is just like her mother," That was a great compliment, if you knew Mrs. Mann, she was a saint of a woman, nothing was too much trouble for her. In some respect, Mrs. Mann wore the pants in the family, but her husband never suspected this in any way.

When everyone pushed away from the kitchen table, so full they could hardly move, Maggie got up and went into her room. There in her little cedar jewelry box that her daddy had made for her, she retrieved the velvet box with the magnificent diamond engagement ring. It was all she could do to keep this a secret from her mother since the day Ace had slipped it on her finger at his parent's home. She walked back into the kitchen where Ace was talking non-stop to her parents; she asked if she might interrupt them for a moment? They stopped their conversation and gave Maggie their full attention; she sat down and laid the velvet box in front of her mother. Mother looked at the box, Maggie said, "Well for the love of God, open it." Mrs. Mann picked up the box and slowly opened it, there in front of her was the largest diamond she had ever seen, surrounded all around with smaller stones. Mrs. Mann gasped as she took it out of the box, she could not say a word and for her this was a brand new happening. Ace reached over and asked Mrs. Mann, if he may have the ring? Mrs. Mann handed Ace the ring, which he then properly placed on the third finger of Maggie's left hand. Maggie related the history of the beautiful ring and how it had belonged to his grandmother. His mother had made him promise to save not only this ring, but also his undying love, for the true love of his heart!

Chapter 22

Glenda Faye
"Glenda Faye is set free"

Scottie had returned late in the evening on Saturday, but Glenda was not given an opportunity to talk over their problems, as she had planned. When Scottie finally staggered drunkenly into their apartment, Glenda could tell there would be no conversation tonight. He did take just a moment to stop in front of Glenda on his way to the bedroom. Scottie informed her that now, not only her problems, but also his mother's problems with him were solved. Scottie stated that he had enlisted in the United States Army, they were in dire need of doctors and he fit the bill!

When Glenda opened her eyes, she was starring at the living room ceiling; she had fallen asleep on the couch. All of a sudden, what happened yesterday came rushing in on her like a tidal wave, she even felt as if she might drown in her sorrow. Glenda sat up and tried to clear her mind, she could smell coffee brewing on the stove, she wondered if she were still dreaming? She pulled herself up from the couch and shuffled into the kitchen, Scottie was already bathed and dressed, and then she realized it was Sunday.

Oh God, not Sunday, I don't think I can bear going to Mass and the farce of a happy family dinner at the McAtee mansion.

Scottie asked Glenda to sit down and handed her a steaming cup of coffee, she thanked him and started to take a sip of her coffee, but hesitated. Scottie told her to go ahead and taste her coffee, he had added just the right amount of sugar, and it was just the way she liked it. Glenda was totally confused at this point; she almost felt as if she were standing outside of her body watching a scene in a play. Scottie had never entered their kitchen except to grab a beer from the icebox or get a drink of cold water. She had no idea he knew how to brew coffee, she looked up and gave him her best smile. She thought to herself there might still be hope for the two of them.

This thought of hope by Glenda, was soon dashed when Scottie sat down with her at their small dining table. She told him she had to hurry or they would be late for Mass, but he reached across the table and took her hand in his. Scottie had tears in his eyes when Glenda gave him her full attention, he told her they would be skipping Mass today, but they did have to go to the mansion. Glenda felt her teeth grating together as she tried to hold her tongue about going to the mansion and playing happy for Mrs. McAtee. Scottie was a different person, she had never seen this side of him before, and the gentleness with the way he held her hand in his.

Scottie patted Glenda's hand and got up from the table, he went to the bedroom and came back with a document in his hand and sat back down at the table. Scottie said, "I guess for the first time, the trust left to me by my grandfather is being used for a good purpose. Yesterday, when I left you, I went to see Monsignor McFarland, he is in charge of all the parishes in Ohio." Glenda had never heard this man's name before, but what else is new when it came to the McAtee's? Scottie went on explaining what had transpired between the monsignor and himself. How he felt trapped by his mother and that he had hurt the most wonderful woman in his world. Scottie then handed

Glenda the document, she was reluctant to read the words that were now only a blur on the page. The tears in her blue eyes were falling on the front page lying in front of her.

Scottie said, "Let me make this as easy as possible for you, with enough money, you can make anything happen in your own time without having to wait for approval from a higher power. You know that my family built the new wing on our local parish, you have seen the huge plaque stating, donated by, The McAtee Foundation." Glenda could not speak at this point, but she just whispered, "Yes, I do know that." Scottie informed her that the document she was holding was an official annulment of their marriage. He said, "I am giving you back your life. The life I took from you under false pretenses. I want you to be able to find happiness, have a real husband and many children like your mother." Scottie told Glenda that he knew about Josh Wakefield, his boyhood friend, Glenda dropped her coffee cup and the coffee spilled all over the table. Scottie got up and grabbed a towel from the kitchen; he wiped up the spill and poured Glenda another cup of coffee with just the right amount of sugar.

Glenda was shocked, how did Scottie know about Josh, she was very careful to keep his letters hidden in the bottom drawer of their writing desk. Scottie looked at Glenda with love, not accusation, he told her he was happy for her and knew she would be in good hands with Josh. Glenda asked Scottie how he found out about Josh, he replied, "It really does not matter, but I will tell you anyway since you asked. I was searching for our marriage license to take with me, for my meeting with the monsignor, when I found the little bundle of letters tied with a blue ribbon. When I saw the first letter addressed, "To My Lady of the Lake," I went no further with my reading. It just made my load a little lighter, knowing you had someone who loved you the way I never could."

Glenda looked at Scottie, for the first time she knew what unconditional love was, it was too bad that Scottie did not realize he was giving that to her for the first in his life. Why now, what had kept Scottie so cold and aloof during the past months of their marriage? She realized that Scottie was broken, his mother had manipulated him for his whole life, she wondered if he could ever be normal? Glenda got up and came around the table and sat on Scottie's lap, she took his face in her hands and kissed him. It was a sweet kiss, "Saying, thank you for being a decent human being. She wanted that kiss to relate the forgiveness she had for him and the forgiveness he had for her."

On the drive to the McAtee mansion Scottie told Glenda that just knowing she was by his side it made what he had to relate to his mother bearable. Glenda reached over and squeezed his hand, letting him know she was there for him, as she had always been, he just did not realize this. Scottie pulled the automobile up in front of the mansion, he hesitated, but then he took a deep breath and opened the driver's side door. He went around and helped Glenda out of the automobile; hand in hand they entered the mansion. Scottie's mother was there to greet her son, she was taken back seeing Scottie and Glenda holding hands and smiling at each other. Mrs. McAtee immediately scolded Scottie for being ten minutes late for dinner. She started to lead them to the dining room, when Scottie took hold of his mother's arm and said, "Call father and meet us in the parlor, we have an urgent matter to discuss." Mrs. McAtee was not used to being given orders in such a manner, especially from her son! She turned on her high-heeled shoes and went clacking down the hall to find her husband.

When Mr. and Mrs. McAtee entered the parlor; they saw Scottie and Glenda seated by the fireplace. Scottie asked his parents to sit down, Mrs. McAtee started to say something, but her son stopped her half way through her sentence. Scottie stood up and looked his mother straight in the eye and said, "Mother, I am sorry to tell you that I have had my marriage to Glenda Faye, annulled." Mrs. McAtee could not hide the happiness she was feeling hearing this news from her son. She stood up and started to tell Scottie that it was finally time that he had come to his senses, but here again, Scottie stopped her cold! Scottie asked her to be seated and went on with his news, he said, "You don't understand the love I feel for this wonderful woman, I am so very sorry that I ruined her life out of spite. Mother, I wanted to make you unhappy, I knew you would never accept Glenda Faye, you would think she was so far beneath our status. You did not disappointment me, you treated her like one of your maids, maybe not even that well. I am ashamed of my behavior, but more ashamed of yours! I guess you taught me well how not to be a man and stand up for what I really wanted for myself."

Mr. McAtee did not utter one word; Mrs. McAtee too had emasculated him many years ago. Their own marriage was one of convenience, arranged by their parents. Mrs. McAtee's family held most of the wealth brought to their union; Mr. McAtee brought to the marriage his highborn family history. He wondered how he had put up with this beautiful woman, which was now ugly to his eyes, for so many years? Glenda realized that Mr. McAtee was being silent through this whole ordeal, but when their eyes met, he smiled at Glenda with love in his eyes.

Mrs. McAtee stood up and said, "Well, I guess that is that, everyone can go on with life as usual." Scottie thought to himself, his mother would sweep this under the rug, in a manner of speaking, as if it had never happened. She was an expert at this kind of behavior; Scottie felt that he had spent most of his young life, swept under one rug or the other. Scottie once again stopped his mother and said, "I have released Glenda Faye from a life in hell and I have released myself from you, by enlisting in the United States Army Medical Core." There was pure silence in the room; the clock on the mantel even seemed to stop ticking. Mrs. McAtee looked at her son, took a deep breath and fell to the floor, she lay there unconscious, and Glenda Faye jumped up, ran to Mrs. McAtee and yelled for Mr. McAtee to call for an ambulance.

Chapter 23

Sister Margaret Faye
"Red feels free from her situation"

Sister Susan Marie was relentless with Sister Margaret Faye, she ordered her around like a maidservant, most of the time. She had no idea who she was dealing with; it was as if Sister Margaret Faye was leading a double life. She obeyed Sister Susan Marie, but she carried out her duties as, "Red," the good-humored, high-spirited lovely person that she had left back in Speedway City. The villagers loved Red, and she loved them back, she thought of the small children as little brothers and sisters, that she never had. There was nothing going on in the little hospital clinic at the present time, so she spent a lot of her time, teaching and playing games with the children.

Sister Susan Marie was beside herself, she knew disliking Sister Margaret Faye, was a sin in God's eyes, but she couldn't help herself. She confessed her sin over and over, but would not repent in a sincere way that excused her sin. Sister Christine Rose stayed out of the way and you hardly knew she was around most of the time. She did as she was told, but envied Sister

Margaret Faye's tenacity when it came to Sister Susan Marie. She liked this young girl and knew in her heart that she had made a mistake taking her vows at such an early age.

Red was on laundry duty at the open-air hut where all the other village ladies did their laundry. There were two long troughs filled with water, one was for washing with a harsh lye based soap made in the village. The other trough was to rinse the clothing, two women would hold on to each end of the bedding or clothing and twist the water out. They would then hang the laundry out to dry in the sun. Red loved doing laundry and having fun with the ladies, it reminded her of the days spent at Mother Kelly's on washday. She longed to see Mother Kelly and like Maggie, to feel Mother Kelly's wet hands hugging her, not caring if her blouse got wet with the loving hug. Red was constantly pushing the starched headdress back on her head, it hung limp in the jungle heat most of the time. One of the ladies addressed this problem for her when she noticed Red constantly pushing the headdress back over and over again. Lanita asked if she might help Red with this problem, Red was quick to answer, "Yes." Lanita removed the limp headdress from Red's head; she could not help but let out a giggle that was contagious with the other women. Red's hair was plastered to her scalp in a hundred different lengths; they could tell that at one point in time, this nun must have had beautiful hair. The women of the village had long shinning jet-black hair braided down the middle of their backs.

Lanita told Red that she would be right back, she ran across the square and came back with a large square of white material. Lanita folded the square into a triangle, and laid it aside; she rinsed Red's hair with clear cool water and dried it in the sun. Red loved the way her head felt being bare. She knew Sister Susan Marie would have her head on a platter if she could see her in this state of undress. Lanita then showed Red how to cover her head with the triangle of white cotton and fold it at the side of her head and tie it at the back of her neck. Red could not contain her joy, she felt freed from the heavy headdress, but yet still her head was covered like the other nuns. She kissed Lanita and thanked her profusely. Red was now comfortable, she finished the laundry for the nuns. She washed her old headdress, and hung it to dry. She would never wear this part of her habit again while stationed in the jungle!

Red gathered her dried laundry from the clotheslines, folded each item carefully and placed them in her large woven basket. She knew there would be hell to pay when Sister Susan Marie caught sight of her new headdress, but she just smiled. Red was placing the laundry in the closets of each one of the nuns when Sister Susan walked in; she grabbed Red by the head and pulled her new headdress off. This action knocked Red off her feet and she ended up seated on the earthen floor. Red looked up at the red-faced nun standing over her. It took Red a minute to figure out what had just taken place; she had taken quite a jolt falling on the floor. She pulled herself up and stood in front of Sister Susan Marie, she could see strands of her own red hair clenched in the nun's fingers.

Sister Susan Marie let her know in no uncertain terms this would not be allowed! Red looked her straight in the eyes and said, "If you don't like my new headdress, then send me home, I don't care one way or the other, I am wearing my new headdress!" Sister Susan Marie was speechless, no one had ever dared to address her in this manner and this was the second time for Sister Margaret Faye. Red reached over and took the headdress from Sister Susan Marie, turned and walked to the hospital clinic. There she stood in front of the cracked mirror and reapplied her white head covering in the manner taught to her by Lanita.

Chapter 24

Maggie
"Maggie says, good-bye to Ace"

Ace picked Maggie up after her shift at St. Ann's Hospital, he sat in the automobile watching her walking down the front steps, and she was arm in arm with an older man. They were looking at each other, laughing and they seemed to know each other very well, Ace wondered if he had reason for worry? Maggie and the gentleman walked up to the drivers' side of his automobile, Maggie gestured for Ace to roll his window down, which he did. Laughing at a comment the gentleman had said to Maggie, she looked at Ace and said, "This is my, Mr. Higgins, he works maintenance at the nursing school. The two of you have a lot in common, you both build little airplanes." Ace, smiled up at the man, he had heard the story from start to finish concerning, Mr. Higgins, without thinking, he asked Maggie and Mr. Higgins to hop in the automobile. All at once, Mr. Higgins had a worried look on his face, Maggie reached over and told him they would stop by the school and let his mother know where he would be for an hour. After that, Mr. Higgins was happy again; he hardly ever got the opportunity to leave the campus for a night of fun. He came out of the school with his mother, she smiled at her wonderful Maggie and blew her a kiss, and they both knew what this meant to her son. Ace introduced himself to Mr. Higgins, the man in the backseat said, "Just call me Jimmy, that is what my mommy calls me, but it is a secret. How sad, Ace thought, a young girl getting raped, just as she was entering the order of the Sister's of Charity. When this violent crime leads to a pregnancy, her parents raised her mentally challenged son and loved him. Now his own mother, who is the nun in charge of the St. Ann's Nursing School, was taking care of her son in secret.

Maggie, Jimmy and Ace had a great night together. They took Jimmy to a local burger joint; he was thrilled with the burger and chocolate milk shake. Jimmy told Ace about the day one of the girls fell down the basement stairs and how scared he was. It was as if Jimmy could not stop talking, in his little boy mind, he was so very happy being with Ace and Maggie. They were his friends; he loved them as he did his own mother. Little did Maggie and Ace know that this happiness would be short lived for Jimmy and his mother? Jimmy's heart gave out one day while working in the school; when he was standing on a stepladder. It was not the hard fall from the stepladder that killed Jimmy Higgins, but his unknown heart condition. The doctors all said, he was just worn out, his heart had never developed properly, just like his brain. The funeral service for James Higgins, filled the church to overflowing, this was the largest funeral Maggie and Ace had ever attended. Not many people knew the true story about how James Higgins came into the world, but now everyone knew how admired he was when God took him home. Jimmy's mother sat in the front pews with all of the other nuns from St. Ann's, but Sister Mary Johns, was weeping. Very few in attendance knew the true story of James Higgins and his real mother, even at a time like this, she had to keep her secret.

Every flower shop in Indianapolis had emptied their stores with orders to be sent to the church for Jimmy's funeral. Everyone felt sad that Glenda Faye and Red were not in attendance, Glenda Faye tried to make it, but her mother-in law had suffered a severe stroke and was bedridden. Her husband, Scottie had been shipped overseas to help the British with their wounded soldiers and civilians. Ace and Maggie met Sister Mary Johns outside the church and consoled her as best they could, without drawing attention by the other church personnel. Maggie promised to come by for tea and a long visit soon, Sister Mary Johns, gave them both a hug and a look of gratitude.

On the ride home to the Mann's residence, Maggie thought to herself, so much sadness, what had happened to the happy-go-lucky days of young adulthood? She looked at the side profile of her soon to be husband. He was so handsome with his square jaw and large deep-set eyes. She wondered what their children would look like? Maggie stopped herself and tried to stay in the present, no matter how bleak it was at this time.

When Ace pulled his automobile to a stop in front of Maggie's house, he turned to her and took her hands in his. "No, no, don't say it, I don't think I am able to bear what you are about to tell me," said Maggie. Ace said, "Hey, where is my, "Little Magpie, always chirping happily?" Maggie was in no mood for fun and games and Ace soon realized this. He laid it straight out on the line, he was shipping out next week; the doctors had checked his wounded hand. They had given him a clean bill of health, but no flying fighter planes for this brave young man. Maggie asked where he would be stationed. Ace looked at her and told her that was, "Top Secret," like everything else connected with the war that would soon involve America. The only thing that gave her a hint was when he said, "Put this to mind, I love the pearl earrings that you are wearing tonight. You are good at puzzles you will figure this out in no time at all. Remember your friend Red, and where she is at this very moment."

Ace and Maggie sat in the front seat of his automobile for a very long time, they were kissing and really wanting more, but that was out of the question with Maggie. The windows were all covered with steam; Ace took his index finger and drew a large heart on the window. In the middle of the heart he wrote Ace loves Maggie and drew an arrow on both sides. They laughed together like teenagers, this was fun, and this was real, what it meant to really be in love. Times like this, Maggie would remember forever and one day teach her own children, the innocence of real love.

Chapter 25

Glenda Faye Kelly
"Glenda Faye's short lived freedom"

The ambulance arrived with sirens blazing as the driver pulled to a quick stop in front of the McAtee mansion. The maid was already holding the large front door open for the medical team to enter and be shown to the parlor. The McAtee family doctor was right behind the ambulance team, they all rushed through the parlor door at once. Glenda Faye was holding Mrs. McAtee's head in her lap and smoothing her hair away from her forehead with a gentle touch.

Dr. Edelman knelt down beside Glenda Faye and opened his black leather bag, he checked Mrs. McAtee's vital signs, and he looked at Glenda Faye and shook his head. Mr. McAtee, himself a retired doctor, thought Dr. Edelman was silently saying that his wife had passed away. Scottie rushed to his mother's side crying out, "I did not mean it, I did not mean it, please forgive me, mother." Dr. Edelman stood up and gave instructions to the ambulance team to bring in their gurney and prepare to take Mrs. McAtee to the hospital. He then sat down with the McAtee's and explained to them that Mrs. McAtee had suffered a severe stroke and he did not hold out too much hope for her.

Mr. McAtee rode in the ambulance with his wife, she was not conscience, but he held her hand and spoke softly to her. "Why did our life have to be like this, it could have been so different, you of all people should have had compassion for others in more dire straights than yourself!" The medical team could hear his words, but had no idea what he meant by this statement to their patient. The ambulance pulled into the emergency entrance of the hospital, followed by Dr. Edelman, Scottie and Glenda Faye. Mrs. McAtee was admitted and taken to a posh hospital suite, donated by the McAtee Foundation.

It was a touch and go situation for a few days with Mrs. McAtee; she finally opened her eyes, but was barely able to utter a sound that could be understood. Dr. Edelman took her hand and consoled her; he explained her situation to her as easy as he could without exciting her too much. He had cared for the McAtee family for over twenty years; he knew that Angela McAtee could be a very difficult to deal with most of the time. When Dr. Edelman mentioned the word severe stroke, he could see the fright in Angela's eyes. He had no idea that Angela's own mother had suffered a stroke when Angela was only eight years old and her mother had lingered for three long years. Angela tried her best to make her words heard and understood, but when the words came out of her mouth, no one could understand what she was saying. Scottie had not left his mother's bedside except to clean up and change his clothes. He was so happy when his mother regained consciousness; he was mistaken when he thought everything would be fine with her. Glenda stood behind Scottie, he was sitting beside his mother's bed, and she was sleeping. Glenda whispered to Scottie, so as not to disturb his mother, come with me to the cafeteria.

Glenda and Scottie took a tray and walked down the food line, she was really hungry and knew that Scottie needed to eat something. She selected a few items and put them on his tray and did the same for herself. They put their trays on the table, Glenda went to the small coffee and tea station, and she poured them both a cup of coffee. When she returned to the table, she was glad to see that Scottie already tasted his food, he stood up and pulled the chair out for her to sit down. Glenda began eating her meal, she was famished, but felt guilty because she was not grieving like Scottie and his father. Glenda had a standard as a nurse, where there is life there is hope. Glenda did not quite know how to approach Scottie with her decision on their future plans.

Scottie spoke up first; he said his father had talked to Dr. Edelman about hiring a live in nurse to care for his mother when she was stable and could be released. It was as if Scottie had read her mind, she told her now ex/nerver was husband, and she did not know what to call him now; that she had a plan. Glenda knew Scottie was shipping out in a week, he had no choice, he was not an only son and the Army had rules on family leave. Glenda took Scottie by the hand, looked him straight in the eye and stated, "I am going to take care of your mother, full time, day and night. I will not take, "No," for an answer!" Scottie sat there with his mouth hanging open, then he realized his food must have been falling out onto the table and quickly shut his mouth. "Glenda, how are you able to do this for a person who treated you like something she scraped off of the bottom of her shoe," said Scottie?

Glenda told Scottie that she did not like his mother's treatment of her, but she did not take it personally. She had seen Angela treat everyone in the same manner, except Scottie's younger brother and his fiancée, Lillian Claire. Angela did play favorites, and she knew Lillian Claire and Thomas was a good match. Her plan had nothing to do with love, Lillian's family were what Angela referred to as, "Filthy Rich."

Mr. McAtee entered the cafeteria, poured a cup of coffee and sat down to join his son and Glenda Faye. Mr. McAtee had a different air about him today, he seemed almost happy; Glenda had never even seen him break a smile before. His father's demeanor also surprised Scottie today. Glenda was so happy to see Scottie and his father laughing and carrying on an actual conversation together. It amazed her that when you took one person out of the equation, how the family dynamics changed for everyone else!

Scottie said to his father, "Glenda Faye would like to stay on at the mansion when I leave for my overseas assignment." Mr. McAtee had a startled look on his face, but remained silent and let his son continue. Scottie told him that Glenda Faye had volunteered to care for his mother. It was her choice to do so, until Mrs. McAtee no longer needed her. Mr. McAtee, put his face into his hands and began to sob, right there in the cafeteria. Scottie got up and helped his father to his feet and escorted him to a more private room. Glenda Faye sat at the table; alone again, she had not had a spare moment to think of Josh Wakefield. He was now somewhere outside of the United States, she had not a clue to where he actually was stationed. He could be on a large ship of one sort or the other; then again he could be on dry land. She really could not wait to give Josh an account of all that had transpired here in her world.

Chapter 26

Sister Margaret Faye
"Red was now in charge, she had her life back"

Red was helping Sister Christine Rose in the clinic, they seemed to be having a population explosion, and every female patient was pregnant. Philippe explained that most of the women they were checking and treating for various pregnancy related problems came to the clinic from the upper hills. The women stayed in the hill country until the harvest was finished, just like the older children that were returning to the little schoolroom. Red did not mind, but she knew soon her job would be to go from one patient to the other catching babies that were being born. Red thought if only, Glenda Faye and Maggie were here, they would have great fun caring for these wonderful women.

Sister Susan Marie was standing in a hidden part of the jungle, not far from the path, but where she could not be seen. She had started a ritual of flaying her back in repentance for her sins. She would strip to her waist and smack her back with braided palm fronds. The blood would trickle slowly out of the swollen red stripes on her back; where the palm braids left crisscrossed stripes. Sister Susan Marie was imitating what she thought Jesus went through to repent for our human sins before His walk to Calvary. In reality Sister Susan Marie was losing her mind here in the steaming jungle. No one knew of this practice, everyone tried to stay out of her way as much as possible.

Sister Christine Rose was coming out of her shyness slowly; this was due in part to the love she received from Sister Margaret Faye and Philippe. She loved the village people and their happiness was contagious. These villagers were always celebrating one thing or the other, anything to throw a party. Philippe and his family were down from the hills and living in their little hut until the next planting time. There were three seasons here on the island and each season had a crop of its own. They kept their soil rotated by a different crop to insure its viability, this was taught to them by missionary priests that had studied agriculture.

Tonight there was to be a huge party with music and dancing. The villagers had killed a hog for the occasion and the aroma was floating all over the village. The small boys took turns turning the large handle that was attached to a spit, while the men basted the hog with a mixture of vinegar and salt water. Red and Sister Christine were in the outdoor area where the women were preparing all of the local side dishes to go with the roasted hog. The two nuns were getting a real lesson on how to prepare vegetables and fruits from the jungle, everything smelled delicious bubbling in the clay pots. They were hungry for the tasty treats in front of them, they could feel and hear their stomachs growling and started laughing at the sound.

Sister Susan Marie had cleaned her wounds and covered her back with layers of white muslin to collect any blood that might ooze through her habit. Sister Susan had not seen the other two nuns for some time; she went in search of them, looking in each room. The nuns were nowhere to be found in the hospital or the schoolroom. This infuriated her, she could feel the anger welling up inside of her and she needed an outlet for this. Sister Susan went out into the village, she could smell the food roasting and cooking over the open fires of the village kitchen. What she would not give to be able to sit down and enjoy a wonderful meal. She kept the nuns on a strict bland diet, this was what she called, "Suffering for Christ."

Red and Sister Christine were sitting at a long table helping to scrub a local root vegetable to be baked and sweetened with honey before being served. Sister Susan Marie stomped up to the table and grabbed the utensils out of the nuns' hands and through them to the ground. She ordered both nuns back to their quarters. The local women were stunned by this behavior, they normally had no dealings with the senior nun, and they had no idea of her cruelty. The two nuns got up from the table, excused themselves, and followed Sister Susan Marie back to their quarters as ordered.

Needless to say, Red was fuming; she would not let this crazy old woman order her around. Little did Red know how right she was in her assessment of Sister Susan Marie, being crazy? Sister Susan informed the two nuns that they were not to leave their quarters; they would have their normal supper as usual. Sister Christine Rose could no longer contain her hurt; she started to cry and reached for her handkerchief. Sister Susan reached out and slapped Sister Christine across the face and told her to get a grip on her emotions. Red stood up and grabbed Sister Susan's arm before she could strike Sister Christine again. This surprised Sister Susan Marie, she was stunned that this young girl thought she could out best her. Red stepped back and told the older nun that she was out of order and if she did not change her outlook on their lives here in the jungle, she would report her to the Mother House in the United States. Red went on to tell her that if she did not start right here and now, she would get some men to help restrain her until she could be shipped home. Sister Susan Marie felt as if she was about to explode, her face turned a bright red from the embarrassment by Sister Margaret Faye's statement.

Red went over to the sink and wet a soft cloth and held it to Sister Christine's cheek and consoled her. When they looked around Sister Susan Marie was nowhere in sight, they both sighed with relief. Red told Sister Christine to go lay down for a bit, they were going to go the party later in the evening. When the two nuns left for the party, Sister Christine was now also wearing her white habit with a triangle head covering. She was happy for the first time since they landed on this Jungle Island. The party was a huge success; the nuns ate, danced and had the best time of their life that night.

The next morning Sister Susan Marie was missing, she never returned to their quarters the night before. Red was worried, she found Philippe and asked if he could send out some scouts to try and find a trace of Sister Susan Marie. He gladly complied; he rounded up some of the best trackers on the island and they mounted a search.

The two nuns waited all day and sat up all night waiting for word of Sister Susan Marie. Around noon, the search party came into the village with a pack donkey; there was a body strapped across the animals back. The two nuns went running to meet the search party; Red pulled the cloth away from the body, and it was Sister Susan Marie. On closer examination, they could see she had her throat slit from ear to ear. Red looked at Philippe, he said, "We have heard rumors that the Japanese are invading other small islands, trying to set up camps of their own." He went on to explain they had found a small knife, he showed it to Sister Margaret Faye, and the writing on the handle was in Japanese!

Chapter 27

Maggie
"Maggie holds down the home front"

Maggie was working long hours at St. Ann's Hospital and still volunteering at the USO club. She and her mother spent much of their spare time tiding up her flower garden for the winter months quickly approaching. Late October was cool with some cold nights that left a thin layer of frost on the windshield of her automobile.

Maggie was upset when she received the telephone call from Glenda Faye relating everything that had happened in her life. Not just one thing, but multiple sorrows all at once, all Maggie could think was no one deserved this treatment, but especially mild mannered, Glenda Faye. She was the kind of person that could never even step on an insect as a child; in fact, Maggie could not bring to memory Glenda Faye ever being cruel in any manner.

Mrs. Mann, Maggie's mother asked her if she would take her out to see her best friend, Mother Kelly? Maggie said, "Of course, I had the same idea, she must be so worried about her favorite daughter and the problems she is facing in Dayton, Ohio." Mother put her traveling basket on the kitchen table and filled it with three homemade cherry pies and other treats for the Kelly family. Maggie thought to herself, my mother had carried that old basket with two lids hinged in the middle for as long as she could remember. It was like another appendage attached to her mother's arm, she smiled as she watched her mother fold a pretty napkin over the contents and close the two lids. Mother handed Maggie the basket and then she slipped on her lightweight fall coat and of course one of her many hats. Her mother never left the house without a hat; she had been raised in a time in history when a lady always wore a hat. Her great aunts were milliners and kept her in the latest fashion as a child and young woman. The aunts were no longer able to work in their shop, but still made beautiful hats for special occasions.

When Maggie and her mother pulled into the drive of the Kelly residence the few children that were still at home, came out to greet them. The oldest took the basket from Maggie and gave her a hug and kiss. Maggie's mother had one Kelly child that reminded her of her little son, Harold, who had died. Harold was only six years old when he died during a flu epidemic; this was before Maggie was born. Mother always gave the younger Kelly child a special little gift; it was their secret. Today, it was a whistle that Mr. Mann had carved for him; he slipped it into the pocket of his pants and smiled up at Mrs. Mann. She patted him on the top of the head and he walked her up to the house, then he took off to the barn. Mother knew he would climb into the hayloft and play his whistle and be contented with his small gift.

Mother Kelly was in the kitchen as she always was, she was so happy to see the two of them together. We hardly ever visited at the same time, but I wanted to check on Mother Kelly's health and I needed my mother's opinion on the subject. We felt right at home here in the Kelly kitchen; Mother Kelly put the kettle on to brew tea for my mother. She knew her best friend a well as

I knew her daughter, Glenda Faye and what she liked. I was not happy with the condition I found Mother Kelly in; you could see her cheekbones sticking out with the skin barely stretched over the bones. I nudged my mother; she knew exactly what I meant by this action. We would discuss this later, when we went home. For now, we all sat together and related all of the news; she told us Glenda was staying to care for her ex-mother-in-law. Scottie was already in Britain working day and night sometimes above ground and other times in air raid shelters. We all agreed that Scottie had turned out to be a, "Stand up kind of man," as my father would say.

I told Mother Kelly all about Ace and the disastrous plan he cooked up for his proposal to me. Then I showed her my engagement ring, which brought back memories of the day, Glenda Faye had displayed her own ring to her family. Mother Kelly looked at her third finger, where her own husband had placed a gold wedding band at Glenda's wedding. She could not believe that I was marrying the son of the wonderful people who had anonymously helped Glenda Faye, Red and myself through nursing school. I told her I could not believe it either, but God has a plan, we just have to be patient.

I asked Mother Kelly if Glenda had heard from Josh Wakefield, she said that Glenda received several letters, but still did not know where he was. She said they had a kind of code and Glenda thought he was on a battleship, in route to Pearl Harbor. Maggie thought that was good, Red had written about the beauty of Pearl Harbor when she was laid over there for a few days. I thought of the coincidence of Ace referring to my pearl earrings and me figuring out where he might be stationed. It would be great if Josh and Ace were to meet, but that was really stretching a coincidental happening!

On our ride home, my mother and I discussed the health of Mother Kelly, my mother, being her best friend and was beside herself with worry. I assured her that some how, some way, I would get Mother Kelly to a doctor at the hospital for a complete check up. I would not take, "No," for answer when the time came to go. This helped my mother to clam down, but I could see the worry in her beautiful Irish blue eyes, they were glazed over with tears. I could not even imagine losing one of my best friends, now this was a worry that I wish I could take away from my mother's mind. I would get right on this when I returned to the hospital and speak of her condition with my friend, Dr. Lucas Anthony.

Chapter 28

Glenda Fay Kelly
"Glenda Faye heals old wounds"

Mrs. McAtee was returned to the mansion by ambulance; just the way she had been taken away when she had her stroke. Glenda had been taking care of Angela for a few weeks now; they had reached a silent agreement of forgiveness. Not on Glenda's part, but on Angela's, for treating Glenda less than human. Mr. McAtee was a different person; he also was released from his bondage by the old, Angela, who was a tyrant. Now he was always pleasant and did absolutely everything he could to make Glenda happy, which did not take much. In the evenings he would sit and read the classics to his wife, it was their private time. Glenda had no idea that Angela could barely but two sentences together, but she would soon find out why.

Glenda worked with Angela everyday, helping her to regain enough speech to be understood. They started with just a blink of her eyes to let it be known if the answer to a question was, "Yes or No." Glenda would bathe Angela with a gentle touch, rub her with lotion and put her favorite scented dusting powder on. She could tell that Angela was grateful for the care this wonderful young woman gave to her without any monetary motive. Glenda seemed to be the only one who knew exactly what Angela needed or wanted to say, Mr. McAtee was glad that his wife had finally seen the light. It was just so sad, that it took her almost losing her life to learn the real meaning of life and unconditional love.

It seemed like magic to Mr. McAtee and the family servants how quickly Angela progressed, she was now able to sit in her wheelchair while Glenda would brush her long blonde hair. Angela had always worn her hair pulled straight back and twisted into a figure eight bun at the back of her head. She was never seen with one hair out of place, even her husband commented on this. He came in one morning while Angela's hair was down, it took his breath away, and once again, she was beautiful to him. Angela looked at her husband and gave him her biggest smile, even though it was a crooked smile; it meant the world to him.

Glenda had helped Angela eat her breakfast and was holding a napkin under Angela's chin while she sipped her tea; this was their morning ritual. Angela was telling Glenda something that she could not understand; she called for one of the oldest servants that knew Angela well. Angela repeated her request in front of the servant; the servant turned to Glenda and said, "The elevator, she wants to go up in the elevator." This was the first Glenda had heard of an elevator in the mansion, but it did not surprise her, the house had four floors including the attic. Glenda pushed the wheelchair while the maid led the way to the back of the house behind the kitchen. There in the corner was a crude elevator, used only by the household help to transport items needed on different levels of the home.

Angela made it known that she did not want the maid to go with them, so she just smiled and went on with her daily chores. Glenda backed the wheelchair into the elevator, she pointed to each button, until Angela nodded her head. They were going to the attic, when Glenda pushed the wheelchair out of the elevator she gasped! This room ran from one end of the house to the other with many center support beams holding the roof up. Angela gave Glenda a crooked smile and pointed in the far direction, and straight ahead. Glenda could not get over the orderly fashion of the attic; Angela had a place for everything and everything in its place. Maggie's daddy would have loved this attic, he would have appreciated the days it must have taken to make all the shelves and bins to hold the treasurers that belonged to the McAtee's.

Angela put up her hand and Glenda stopped in front of a very old and battered trunk. She could not imagine why Angela would have anything like this in her home, even in the attic. Angela felt along side her robe and pulled out an old rusty key, Glenda took it and put it in the lock. She stopped and looked back at Angela, she muttered something to Glenda and Glenda continued. She had a very hard time getting the key to turn, finally the lock clicked open. Glenda lifted the lid of the trunk, a strong musty smell came wafting out, Angela muttered again and Glenda picked up an old photo album. She laid it on Angela's lap, Glenda helped her to turn the pages, and the first page was a picture of Angela's parents. It must have been their wedding day, but they were dressed in the poorest of clothes, this puzzled Glenda. As Glenda kept turning the pages there were more family members added, it was as if she were looking at her own family album.

Angela started to cry; Glenda stopped and asked her if she wanted to go on, she nodded, yes. There were also eight children in Angela's family, but compared to the McAtee's, the Kelly's were upper class. The photos were taken in front of an old broken down home, out in the middle of nowhere. Her mother looked old, weather beaten and worn out. Her father wore overalls with holes and patches, as did the many children in the photo. Glenda was now beyond words; she asked Angela if she could explain her childhood in some way that she could understand. Glenda thought maybe Angela had been given to a rich family because her own family could not afford to raise her. Angela motioned for her to keep turning the pages, in the turn of three pages; it became a rags to riches story. Their family farm was setting on a rich field of oil; the farm was passed to her father by his father. Somewhere back in their history, a grandfather participated in a race for land that you could stake out for free or the price of one dollar.

Glenda was fascinated, Angela just smiled, she wanted Glenda to know that she was considered white trash or even less at one point in her own life. What Angela did not have was the breeding to be accepted in the social circle of her time. She moved to Dayton, where she reinvented her history, no one knew her there. She set out to snag a gentleman of high breeding to make her acceptable in high society. She had the money and Mr. McAtee had the breeding, but his family had fallen on hard times. Angela took care of that and then put her husband and two sons under her tyranny for fear of being told on or found out.

Mrs. McAtee took a turn for the worse, Scottie was somewhere in Great Britain, but Thomas and Lillian Claire came in from New York. Dr. Edelman was in attendance; Glenda was sitting with Mr. McAtee beside Angela's bed when Thomas and Lillian Claire came bounding in the room. Lillian immediately asked to see Angela by herself, Mr. McAtee only agreed to her request if Glenda was there to make sure nothing happened health wise. Everyone left, Lillian Claire went to Angela's bedside and patted her head and gave her the slightest kiss on the cheek.

Lillian Claire then went to Angela's beautiful antique dresser and opened the top drawer; she pulled out a beautiful velvet box. Lillian Claire looked at Glenda and said, "The old lady won't be needing these any more." Glenda looked at Angela, she could see the fright and anger in her eyes, and Angela was moaning and trying to grab Glenda Faye's hand. Glenda calmed Angela with a squeeze of her hand and a wink, as if to say, "Watch this Angela." Glenda got up, slapped Lillian Claire across the face and grabbed the large velvet box out of her hands. Glenda then opened the bedroom door and pushed Lillian Claire out into the hall.

Mr. McAtee and Thomas ran into the bedroom, Glenda was seated beside Angela, and for the first time in weeks, Angela had her normal smile. Lying beside Angela was her beautiful velvet box that contained her most precious jewelry. No questions were asked about what had just taken place, but Lillian Claire made herself scarce. The two men sat down with Glenda and Angela, she looked like an angel, with her blonde hair lying on her shoulders. They held her hands and watched a tear run down Angela's cheek, a tear of joy and happiness, but it would be her last tear. Angela's ragged breathing stopped; Glenda listened to heart and shook her head. The two McAtee men held Angela's hands and wept together for the lost of their mother and wife. Glenda excused herself and left Thomas and his father alone with Angela, to grieve her passing in private.

Chapter 29

Sister Margaret Faye
"Red flees in fear for her life"

The village people could not believe their eyes when Philippe and his search party returned with Sister Susan Marie's body. Sister Margaret Faye and Sister Christine Rose prepared the body for immediate burial, just as they had done for Sister Ann Francis. The men of the village made a rough wooden coffin and the women lined it with soft leaves and covered these with a white muslin blanket. Everyone gathered at the gravesite, both nuns noticed that many of the villagers not in attendance. This was out of the ordinary for these respectable people. Sister Christine Rose asked Philippe where all of the other people had disappeared? He told her many had left to return to their homes in the high hills to be with their families. They were terrified by what had happened to Sister Susan Marie.

After the burial, the two nuns returned to their quarters, they did not know what to do now that Sister Susan Marie was not in charge? They did not have to wait long with their idleness, two local women came in to the hospital, and they were ready to deliver their babies. The nuns were glad to have something to keep them busy and their minds off of the tragedy they had encountered. When the women came into the hospital, they each brought a large woven basket with them. The nuns set the baskets aside, but realized there was a small bundle in the side pocket of each of the baskets. They could not be bothered with small details right at this moment. Their two women patients were lying on the hospital beds, holding onto the metal head rail and bearing down. Sister Christine Rose was attending to one patient and Red was helping the other, both women had been through the birthing process before. This made helping them with the birth much easier.

When both babies were delivered, cleaned and wrapped tightly, they were handed back to their mothers for nursing. The two nuns were tired, it had been a long drawn out process and Sister Christine's first delivery. They fixed a light supper and served the two women supper to build back their strength. The nuns sat in the kitchen talking, Red was frightened, but she could not let Sister Christine see her fear. Red told her sister nun, it might have been a one-time happening and Japanese were probably frightened off by the scouts in the search party. There could not have been very many Japanese and to face twenty or so villagers carrying rifles would make them think twice about staying on the island. This seemed to ease Sister Christine's worry, but Red was not appeased in the least by her own story.

The new mothers were up and about the next morning, they ate breakfast with the nuns, but told them they were taking their babies and going back to their homes in the hills. Now the nuns knew why they had brought the woven baskets with the small parcels placed in the side pockets. Philippe came to escort the women into the jungle for a mile or two; a member of their own family would then meet the women for the rest of the trip. Philippe did not like leaving the nuns unprotected, so he gathered a few young men with rifles to guard the village until he returned. They had to have a plan, Philippe had the same thoughts that Red did, and he did not think this was a one time happening on his island.

Philippe returned and things seemed to get back to normal, but he was still hearing rumors about the Japanese from other islanders coming and going doing their trading. The nuns were kept busy, it seemed everyday there was another birth to attend to, but the women only stayed overnight and then they were on their way. Philippe relayed to Sister Margaret Faye, that when he last visited the air base he informed them about Sister Susan Marie's murder. The servicemen were astounded by this news; they had absolutely no information to confirm any sighting of the Japanese near their island. They told Philippe that they would immediately check this out and see if they should evacuate the nuns and anyone else who wanted to leave the island.

Red was cleaning the hospital and putting everything to right again after the birth of so many babies. Sister Christine was in the kitchen fixing supper for the two of them, she did not feel like eating, she was so tired. Red told her she had to keep up her strength and get a good night's rest; she would feel better in the morning. Philippe stopped by and relayed the message to the nuns from the air base, they were glad for the news. Now at least they had someone who was concerned for their safety.

The nuns finished washing up the supper dishes and sat to rest for a while before going to bed for the night. They heard a knock at the door that startled them! They had started keeping the windows covered with black cloth and the door locked to the outside. Red got up quietly, she peeked out of the crack in the door, and there stood a very young girl heavy with child. Red quickly opened the door and let her enter, the nuns could tell she was in the last stages of labor and quickly took her to the hospital for delivery. She told them her name was Lindita, which was all she could say; her pains were coming hard and fast. Red went to get the supplies they needed to tie the cord, clean the baby and the mother after her giving birth. The young girl looked to be around fifteen years of age; her delivery was fast, but surprisingly easy. After Sister Christine cleaned the young girl, she packed her groin with white muslin fabric and tied it around her waist, this would staunch any profuse bleeding she might have later. Sister Christine made the young girl as comfortable as possible. Sister Christine then took the infant to the next room for a bath and to be wrapped and taken back to its mother. Red was in the back kitchen, near the rear door leading to the back yard where they grew a small garden. Red laid the instruments that they had used in a pan of water on the stove, for sterilizing. She had only been away from Sister Christine for about a half hour, when she heard a loud popping noise and a moan. Red rushed in to the next room, there laid Sister Christine on the floor, she was holding her side, and the blood was gushing from a bullet wound. Red could see the large tear in the curtain covering the window. Red held her in her lap, she assured her she would be fine, but Sister Christine was already gone. Red closed Sister Christine's eyes and laid her back down on the floor.

Red went into the room where the young mother had given birth, no one was there; the girl had scribbled a short note on the pad of paper beside her bed. She stated, "My baby is a half-breed and will not be accepted by my people. One of the American soldiers at the base is the father, but I do not know his name. I am leaving my baby in your hands." All at once Red thought, baby, where is the baby? She rushed into the room where Sister Christine lay dead on the floor. There on the table was the newborn, it was all cleaned and wrapped up for presentation to its the mother.

Red did not have time to think about what had happened, she emptied her large woven laundry basket, and packed what she could comfortably carry over her shoulder. She put in a few small cans of milk, sugar, clean cloths, tins of biscuits, canned meat, a glass baby bottle and an opener for the milk. She picked up the infant and placed it against her breast and brought up her apron and tied it around her neck making a sling to carry the baby. She tried to keep silent in her preparation; she grabbed two canteens of water from the hooks on the wall. She strapped these over her shoulder and stepped out into the darkness, with her heavy load. Immediately, she was grabbed from behind, she started to let out a scream, but a hand quickly covered her mouth. It was Philippe; thank God she thought to herself, he motioned for her to follow him into the jungle. In a whisper he told her she had to try to make it to the air base, he had word that they were sending in two air planes one to evacuate the island and the second to bomb the airstrip. He told her he could not take her all the way, but would lead her through the night. In the morning her would give her good directions for her to follow going through the jungle to the air base. They began their escape; Philippe carried half of her load while he was with her. She was glad for the heavy boots she thought to grab off of the hook before going out into the dark. All she could think of was what this wonderful man had said a few months ago. " Never ever leave the jungle path, you will be swallowed up by the foliage."

Chapter 30

Maggie
"Maggie is worried about Red"

Maggie stopped in to see Mr. Murphy at the green grocers; Mrs. Murphy was there to, knitting little clothes for a baby. Maggie looked at Mr. Murphy; he motioned for her to come over to the check out counter. Maggie asked why Mrs. Murphy was knitting baby clothes, he looked so sad and answered Maggie. He said, "Mother thinks she is pregnant with Sandra Kay, her mind has slipped somewhere back in time." Maggie thought what a wonderful escape for her with all that is going on in the world right now. Mr. Murphy told Maggie that they had not received any word from their daughter going on two months now; he was beside himself with worry too. Maggie walked around the counter and put her arms around Mr. Murphy, they had a good cry together. All the while, Mrs. Murphy sat in her rocking chair with her knitting needles clacking away to a different rhythm of normalcy. Maggie went over and kissed Mrs. Murphy, she smiled up at Maggie and said, "Have your mother come by, I want to show her all of the little clothes I have made for my new baby." Maggie assured her that she would relay her message to her own mother and left the store.

When Maggie arrived home, her mother was in the kitchen; Maggie went to her mother and broke down in tears. Mrs. Mann had no idea what had happened to upset her daughter in this manner? She sat Maggie down at the kitchen table and handed her a handkerchief. She then got out their special little china teacups and saucers with the violet flowers on them. She poured each one of them a steaming cup of tea; she put a thin slice of lemon in Maggie's cup. She knew Maggie liked her tea with lemon it was a treat. The winter months were upon them it was the first of November and fresh lemons were expensive. Mr. Murphy had given Mrs. Mann two lemons the last time she visited his store, he told her they were the last of the season.

When Maggie related what had happened, she was glad for the two lemons so generously given to her by Mr. Murphy, they helped to soothe the hurt Maggie was suffering. Mrs. Mann did not know what to do to fix Maggie's problem this time, it was out of her control. Normally, she always had an answer, but she could not help what the United States Postal service did. She prayed that Red would get a letter though to her parents, this would help everyone to feel more at ease. When Maggie's daddy came home from work, they sat together listening to the overseas broadcast; the news about the Pacific operations was not good. Maggie got up and kissed her parents and went to her room, she penned a letter to Ace and hoped he would receive it. Mail delivery was sporadic, one day you might get two letters and then a week or two would go by with nothing in your mailbox.

Maggie was glad to be working long hours at the hospital, it helped pass the time. She was still volunteering at the USO, she would question all of the Air Force enlisted men for any information. Some men would have a few vague news reports, but most of the time she felt the right hand did not know what the left hand was doing. This period in time was all mixed up with the Germans and the Japanese. Her father had heard that

Washington was trying to negotiate with Japan and trying to set up a meeting with a special negotiator. All this political news was so far above Maggie, she had trouble understanding exactly which countries were fighting each other?

Maggie was busy in the maternity ward when Dr. Lucas Anthony came in to check on one of his patients, when he finished, she pulled him aside. She did not like asking favors, but this was an emergency as far as she was concerned. Maggie related the story about Mother Kelly and that she had been observing her health decline over the past year. When Dr. Anthony heard that she was the mother of eight children he looked concerned too. He went on to relate to Maggie that a woman has a higher percent of getting female cancer birthing so many children.

Maggie now had to break the bad news, Mr. Kelly worked on an hourly salary and they did not have the money to pay for medical care. Dr. Anthony had a soft spot for Maggie; in fact if she were not already spoken for her, he would love to ask her out to dinner. He thought to himself, "That is my life, a day late and a dollar short." Dr. Anthony told Maggie to make an appointment with his receptionist and bring Mrs. Kelly in for an examination as soon as possible. He told Maggie not to worry about the financial part for Mrs. Kelly; he would take care of that on his end. Maggie could not help herself; she reached up and hugged Dr. Anthony and thanked him profusely.

Mrs. Mann and Maggie were downtown in Indianapolis helping with a fund drive, one of her mother's many projects. They were setting behind a table passing out buttons with red, white and blue ribbons. The other shoppers would drop a coin or a bill in the big glass jar and they would be given a button with three ribbons attached. This brought back Maggie's memory of the day they sold their little flags to raise money for Glenda Faye's uniform for nursing school. That seemed to be a million years ago, so much had changed for the three girls since that carefree summer.

Mother agreed to go with Maggie and talk to Mother Kelly; after all she was mother's best friend in the whole world. This was an expression Maggie had picked up from her mother, and it applied to her own friendships. The day they got into, "The Old Independence," her mother could never keep still about the condition of the old automobile, it made her nervous. Maggie would just laugh; she told her that daddy would never let her risk her life while driving. Mother agreed, but still was not totally convinced this was true!

Mrs. Kelly was out in the yard with the small Kelly boy that was Mrs. Mann's favorite. The day was brisk, but sunny without any wind. Mother had her double-lidded basket hanging over her arm; the little boy came running to Mrs. Mann. She smiled at him and reached into her basket, Maggie never knew what she would pull out next. Today, it was one of the buttons with the red, white and blue ribbons attached. There was also a very large lollipop, and some for the other children in the house.

They all went into the house, Mother Kelly put on the kettle and sat down at the long table, she knew we were there for a reason. She was the first to speak to her best friend, "Ok, Sadie, what is on your mind, just spit it out?" Mother had to laugh, but what she had to ask Mary was not funny in any way. After Mother told her about Dr. Anthony wanting to check her over and that there would be no bill, she seemed relieved. Not the reaction they thought they would get from Mother Kelly. They both sighed with relief, Maggie told her she would set up the appointment and come pick her up at the appointed day and time.

Chapter 31

"Glenda Faye bids farewell to the McAtee's"

Mr. McAtee knocked on the bedroom door where Glenda Faye was packing her suitcase; she turned to him with a smile. "Come in, I am just about finished packing, she asked if the maid had called for her taxi?" He approached Glenda Faye quickly, put his arms around the young woman and could not help the tears that were falling on Glenda's suit collar. Glenda Faye hugged him tight and said, "This is a farewell, but never a good-bye!" Mr. McAtee, pulled away from Glenda, he was now smiling, she had lifted a heavy burden from his heart. He did not want this amazing young woman to leave his life for good.

Mr. McAtee asked Glenda to come to the parlor when she finished packing. She said that she would, it would be hard to say farewell to the McAtee family. She had grown to love each of them while caring for Angela. When Glenda walked into the parlor, there were two old white haired serious looking men sitting at the parlor table with the rest of the family. Mr. McAtee asked Glenda to sit down, Glenda looked around the table, when her eyes came to Lillian Claire seated next to Thomas, and she wanted to slap her again. One of the white haired gentlemen pulled Glenda's chair out for her to be seated. The other stranger stood up, he said, "We are all gathered here today for the reading of Angela McAtee's Last Will and Testament." Glenda interrupted the attorney, but he asked her to be seated, Angela had named her in the will.

Glenda took her seat, she looked at Lillian Claire, and Glenda could tell the color had drained from Lillian's face. The attorney started the reading of the will, this did not take long, and most of her estate was left to her family. Now the color was returning to Lillian Claire's face, she was smiling. The first attorney sat down and the second attorney stood up, he told the family that Angela had added an addendum to her will two weeks before she passed away.

Mr. McAtee expressed a look of surprise, as did the rest of the family. How did she do this without their help, even Glenda had the same thought? There was one person in the room that stood silent and smiling while standing in the corner of the room. This was Matilda, Angela's personal maid; as usual no one was paying any attention to her standing there. She had helped Angela with the addendum and took it to the attorney to be drawn up for signing. The legal office sent one of their office personnel to deliver the new document to Angela. She signed the document in a scrawling hand, but her signature was notarized and witnessed by Matilda. No one was the wiser and Matilda felt guilty in a way, because she was happy to be present when the addendum was read.

The attorney asked Matilda to bring the package from the other room, he then continued reading. He turned to Glenda; she looked surprised by this action. Angela had left Glenda Faye a very large sum of money. She also stated that if her first-born son, Donald McAtee, was not remarried before his death, his trust fund would go immediately to Glenda Faye Kelly. Mr. McAtee looked at Glenda Faye and smiled, he was so proud of Angela, she may have spent most of her life heavy handed and angry. He knew now, all of those years she was a very frightened woman, but in the end, she was his angel.

Lillian Claire started to get up from the table, but the attorney motioned her to sit down, which she did, taking hold of Thomas' hand. Lillian thought this was just what she had planned; she had Thomas and the McAtee fortune. Little did they know that her family had lost their fortune in the stock market? If anyone could read Lillian's mind at that moment, they would have known she had an agenda similar to young Angela's. The only difference being the reversal, she was broke, but had the high society breeding.

The attorney continued reading the addendum, he turned to Thomas, Angela's second son. He said, "Your mother stated emphatically that if you marry Lillian Claire Williams, you will be disinherited from any of her personal fortune." Everyone in the room knew that Mr. McAtee really had no personal fortune of his own; Angela had controlled all of their wealth. Lillian Claire's face turned a deep shade of red; she could hardly catch her breath, but said nothing. Matilda walked to the table and laid Angela's beautiful velvet box in front of Glenda. Matilda turned to leave; she hesitated just long enough to give Lillian Claire a smirk. The attorney told Glenda Faye that Angela wanted her to have all of the jewelry contained in this box. Now, Glenda Faye could not catch her breath, she had seen the collection she had just been given. The attorneys stood up and stated that the reading of the will was ended; they shook hands with the McAtee men and nodded to the ladies present and left. Glenda Faye waited until the attorneys were gone, she asked everyone to sit down again. She picked up the velvet box, walked around the table and laid it in front of Mr. McAtee. Glenda said, "Dear man, you keep Angela's jewelry, one day Scottie and Thomas will marry decent loving women. You give Angela's precious items to them and hopefully to your granddaughters." Lillian Claire could not stand it a moment longer; she stood up so abruptly that she knocked her chair over. She looked around the table, but focused on Thomas, she said, "Your mother was a smart cookie, she read me like a book at the end of her life. You were no more than a bank account to me, you made my skin crawl every time you touched me! I am glad to be rid of the lot of you, but I sure could have used the money." With that said, Lillian Claire grabbed her coat and hat from Matilda, she walked out of the front door and stepped into Glenda's taxi.

Glenda Faye told the McAtee's that she would put the trust fund to good use; she would not squander any part of it. Mr. McAtee was curious, he asked Glenda, "What is the first thing you will do with your trust?" She said, "I will have a beautiful home built for my family in Speedway City, I have just the spot picked out in my mind. It will be down the road from St. Christopher's Church, my mother would be able to walk to church if she felt like it." Thomas walked over to Glenda; he told her if it had not been for her, he would have lived a life of misery with Lillian Claire. Matilda handed Glenda Faye her hat and coat and the butler put her suitcases in the taxi. No one could say, "Good-bye." Mr. McAtee, Thomas and Matilda stood on the porch steps, Glenda Faye got into the taxi, as she pulled away they waved to her. She looked back through the rear window of the taxi, and watched them until they were out of her sight.

Chapter 32

Sister Margaret Faye
"Red is on her own"

Philippe and Sister Margaret Faye, with the infant strapped to her bosom, traveled by the light of the full moon. The trip to the airstrip was longer going through the jungle. She remembered that the three miles seemed more like twenty when she had arrived a few months ago. They stopped just long enough for Red to throw off her lightweight shoes. She changed into the heavy boots that she had grabbed on her way out of the kitchen. Philippe fed the small infant and put on a fresh diaper, this little child never uttered a sound. When Red was finished arranging their traveling goods, Philippe placed the infant in the sling around Sister Margaret's neck.

Every now and then they could hear popping sounds far away. Philippe said, "They are probably on the other side of the island." Red was a little more worried, if this was true, how did Sister Christine Rose get mortally wounded by a stray bullet? She could not let her mind go there, she had to stay in the present. The ground was soggy and Red was glad for her boots, but in places the ground would go out from underneath them. Philippe told her this area had many bogs that could suck you under. Red thought of the word, "Quicksand!"

They kept walking; the ground was a bit better now, more stable. Philippe suggested they take a rest; Red took care of the infants needs. She realized for the first time it was a boy; he stared up at her with the blackest eyes and a tiny dimple in his little chin. She placed a kiss on his little forehead; he closed his eyes and slept. The sun was breaking on the horizon, Red knew what this meant, even before Philippe handed her a hand drawn map to the airstrip. He told her it was not much further, but there was another area that could be treacherous and for her to be very careful. Philippe and Sister Margaret Faye hugged each other, he hated leaving this small young woman alone, but he had no choice.

Red put most of the map to memory; she took one last peek at the little boy lying warm against her breast. She could no longer hold back her tears, but had no time to wipe them away. She grabbed a sturdy stick from the ground and continued on her journey. The foliage was so dense at times; Red could swear it was the middle of the night. She stopped just long enough to take one last look at the map Philippe had given to her. Red thought she heard the sound of an airplane engine. She started running, the tree branches were slapping her face and leaving small cuts on her arms. Red prayed to God, "Please do not let us die out here all alone, we have come so far." Red felt a cool breeze brush over her face, and she picked up her pace. Then without any warning, she fell into a bog. She was waist deep in the muck; she struggled to keep the baby above the watery mud. She stepped into a hole and went under the water. She immediately came bobbing back up, she saw a branch and grabbed onto it. She gave the branch a tug to see if it would hold and it did. She pulled herself out of the bog, she checked the infant, he was dirty, but still breathing.

Red could now hear the roar of the airplane engines; the jungle was thinning in front of her. The airplane had landed twenty minutes earlier; everyone at the base was on board. One of the servicemen was pushing the rolling stairs away from the side door of the plane, when he saw movement at the edge of the jungle. Red threw off everything that could weigh her down, she ran with her last burst of adrenaline. She cleared the jungle and started running towards the plane, she stopped short, when she saw a rifle pointed straight at her. Red offered up another prayer and started running and screaming, "Help us, please wait, and help us for God's sake!" The young man in the doorway of the plane could now see that the person he was aiming at was a pregnant woman. He dropped his weapon and yelled for someone to come and help him. Red was now climbing the rolling steps to the doorway of the plane, but she could go no further. She felt two strong arms grab hers and pull her on board the plane.

The young man gave the rolling steps a hard kick so that the back of the plane would have a clear path for take off. He started to pull the door closed, but the pilot told him to care for the woman, he would get the door. He grabbed the handle and turned to the woman, he said, "My name is Ace, and I will be flying you out of this hell hole." As Ace was pulling the door closed, he felt a hard tug on his right shoulder; he looked down and saw bright red blood. A sniper hidden in the jungle had wounded him; he did not let this stop him. Ace ran to his seat, yelled for everyone to hold tight, he knew this was a life or death situation. His co-pilot looked at him, Ace gave him a nod, and they revved the engines, and held the plane in place as long as possible. There would be no second chances; Ace knew the second plane was right behind them waiting to bomb the airstrip. Ace pushed the throttle hard; he felt the blood gush from his shoulder. The plane shot down the airstrip like a pebble out of a small boys slingshot. The passengers could hear the ping of bullets hitting the side of the airplane. The young man that had helped Red on board the plane had her cradled tight in his arms. He gave no thought to his own injury; he wiped the mud from her face. Red had fainted after the young man had placed her in his lap.

Everyone on board the airplane could feel the wheels of the plane brushing the tops of the trees. They cleared the island and pulled up the landing gear, Ace smiled at his co-pilot and gave him a thumb up sign. He started to return this sign, but instead he had to grab the controls of the plane. Ace had fallen sideways; the co-pilot could now see the severe injury he had sustained. He yelled for help, two medics on board came running, they lifted Ace and carried him to the back of the plane. They accessed his wound, it was a clean shot, but the bullet had done a lot of damage. They packed his shoulder wound and wrapped his arm against his body. He was unconscious, but they gave him a good dose of morphine any way. His pain would be fierce when he woke up; this wound was a ticket home for Ace.

Red woke up, she was strapped to a folding cot, like the ones she had seen on the plane that had brought her to the island. She was frightened; she could no longer feel her little boy on her chest. Red started to wiggle, but she did not have the energy to unbuckle herself. She knew someone had cleaned her up to some extent; she looked down at the military jacket lying over her. She read the nametag, Private John Ryan, which sounded familiar to her for some reason. Red looked down from the cot and saw a well-muscled young man sitting cross-legged in only an undershirt. She could see a think bandage bound around his waist. He was holding the little infant; there was a small container of diluted canned milk beside him. Slowly he would dip a clean square of white cloth in the milk and let the infant suck on it. Red started to cry, the sight of this grown man being so gentle with her little infant was more than she could take without breaking down.

When Private Ryan heard a cry escape the woman's lips, he looked up, she returned his smile. He thought to himself, "If she looks this beautiful all caked with mud, what will she look like all cleaned up?" Little did he know that Red was thinking along the same line, John's smile tugged at her heart?

John put the sleeping infant beside Red and laid her arm around him. John whispered to Red, she stopped him, she said, "You don't have to whisper, this child has not uttered a cry since he was born yesterday. If he could make it through a dangerous, muddy jungle trek sleeping, he will continue sleeping now." John scratched his head, he could not figure out how a tiny woman like the one in front of him could give birth one day and then flee the jungle. Traveling all night and the next day? Red could tell that John was confused, she told him to sit down and she would explain on the trip to Pearl Harbor. When John heard the complete story, his heart dropped, she was a holy woman, a nun. He referred to her as Sister Margaret Faye; she put her hand up to his mouth, and said, "No, I am giving up my vocation as a nun when I return home. It is not for me, I had pretty much made my decision, but when this little guy came into my life it sealed the deal between God and myself.

Red and John had a few more hours to talk about their history; John related the story about his wife, Patricia Kathleen. She had gone into labor with their first child. There was a raging blizzard, and they had no transportation and had to walk in the freezing weather to the bus stop and wait. When he and the bus driver carried Patricia Kathleen into the Charity Ward, the situation was grave. John explained there was a wonderful nurse at St. Ann's that never left his side, until the horrible news was related to him. His little son was still born; his wife had delivered only the baby's head, when they were riding on the bus. He said, "I can still hear her blood curdling cry, before she passed out on the bus."

Red knew exactly who Private John Ryan was, she told him that she was one of the nurses that had helped to cut away Patricia's frozen dress and saw the horrific sight in front of her. She told him that she and her best friend Glenda Fay Kelly had been on duty as well as the nurse he spoke of, "Maggie Mann." She told him they were best friends and had grown up, went to school together and graduated nursing school together. John Ryan reached into the side pocket of his uniform pants and pulled out a small leather case, he showed Red a photo of Patricia. He then pulled out a piece of blue satin ribbon, he said, "Maggie had tied this ribbon in Patricia's hair, he knew it stood for a boy child. Neither John nor Maggie told his wife the reason for the blue ribbon, but he had carried it with him since the death of his wife. She never quite recovered from the birth and slowly faded away, and in a few months she died." Red could feel not only his sadness, but also the guilt of responsibility he carried for the death of his baby son. She could not imagine how he coped with the death of his young wife on top of his other grief. The two young adults were the best of friends when they touched down on the tarmac at Pearl Harbor. When Red reached the tarmac, she knelt down and kissed the ground. Red said a silent prayer of thanks to God; he brought them through the ordeal in the jungle as she had asked of Him. God, now had given her a new lease on life, she had this wonderful little infant and a strong friendship with Private John Ryan.

Chapter 33

Maggie
"Maggie finally gets word from Ace"

Maggie was sitting at the dining room table; mother had invited the Murphy's for dinner. She thought this would give Mr. Murphy a break as his role of caretaker for Mrs. Murphy. They were half through their Sunday dinner when the telephone rang. Maggie said, "I will get it, stay seated," she walked over and answered the telephone. It was Mrs. Van Camp, Ace's mother, she was so excited, but Maggie could sense an underlying nervousness in her voice. Mrs. Van Camp went on to tell Maggie that Ace was safe in a hospital at Pearl Harbor. Safe and hospital did not quite make sense to Maggie. Mrs. Van Camp did not have a lot of the details, and Ace did not know when he would be released to return to the United States. Maggie thanked her and blew a kiss through the telephone.

Maggie relayed the news to her family, they were all thrilled, but like Maggie they were worried about Ace's condition. What kind of an injury would send him home for good? With all the jubilation, she could see that Mr. Murphy was becoming upset; he had no news of his own daughter. Maggie tried to change the conversation to a more pleasant subject. Mr. Murphy stood up and said, "I think mother is getting tired, I had better be taking her home now." Maggie helped Mr. Murphy gather up all the items Mrs. Murphy had brought along to show to her friend, Sadie.

When they opened the front door, there stood Glenda Faye, Maggie was wild with happiness; she stepped in front of the Murphy's and grabbed her friend. Mr. Murphy could not help himself, he to put his arms around Glenda Faye, he felt as if he were hugging his own daughter. Mrs. Murphy seemed oblivious to the situation; she was now in her own world somewhere in time. The Murphy's left and Glenda Faye came in, Mrs. Mann grabbed her and took her into the kitchen. Mr. Mann came in and said, "What about me, don't I rate a hug and kiss from my favorite gal, too?" Glenda Faye stood up and hugged Mr. Mann; she loved this man as much as her own father.

The girls drank tea with Mrs. Mann and then put on their warm coats and went for a walk. Glenda Faye had not yet been to her own home, she came straight from the train station to Maggie's. Glenda filled Maggie in on everything that had happened to her, she told Maggie that she was now a very wealthy woman. They just laughed, being wealthy and the name Kelly did not go together in their town. What a surprise this would be in the little town of Speedway City, when the news got around.

Glenda Faye said the last letter she had received from Josh Wakefield, was over a month ago. It was now going on the second week of November, she was getting worried, but Josh had explained about how the mail was picked up from the vessel he was assigned to. With all that was entailed, she realized why it took so long to reach her and for her letters to reach him.

Maggie did not want to bring up the subject just now, but it could not wait any longer. They walked into the back yard and sat on the arbor bench that her daddy had made for Glenda Faye's marriage to Scottie McAtee. This brought back memories of happier times for Glenda when she thought her life was going to be perfect. Maggie nudged Glenda, she said, "I need to tell you something important, it is about your mother." Instantly Glenda Faye's mood changed, she listened to her friend. Maggie told Glenda that she had taken Mother Kelly to see Dr. Lucas Anthony, to have a full evaluation of her health problems. The news was not good; Mother Kelly was in the first stages of uterine cancer.

Glenda Faye started to weep; Maggie put her arms around Glenda, "The True Friend of Her Heart." Maggie went on to explain that Mother Kelly had some time, Dr. Anthony said, "She may have a year or two at the most." Maggie made a suggestion, she told Glenda Faye that Dr. Anthony was performing hysterectomy surgeries and having good results. Glenda Faye asked why her mother was not having this surgery, her ex-husband; Scottie performed the same operation in his practice? Maggie told Glenda Faye that her mother was waiting to talk it over with her before committing to the operation. Glenda Faye looked at Maggie and said, "Get her prepped, she will be rolled into the surgical suite at St. Ann's as soon as we can get her there!

In a way this was good news, Glenda would have some quality time with her mother. She thought to herself, I will start the building of her new home immediately. Glenda jumped up, and said, "Maggie, I have to discuss something very important with your father and his friend Austin Bates, it cannot wait." Maggie was perplexed by this, but followed her into the house. Glenda found Mr. Mann and sat with him for over an hour laying out her plan for the new house to be built for her mother. Mr. Mann knew exactly what to do to kick-start the project and get it completed as soon as possible. Glenda told him that money was no object, to hire as many men as he needed to get the house built. He told Glenda Faye that he would have it famed and closed in before the first snowfall. They would then start all of the finishing work on the inside of the house. Mr. Mann thought to himself, when I spread the news around Speedway City, I will have all of the unpaid help needed to complete the project. The Kelly's were admired and loved by each and every family in their community!

Chapter 34

Glenda Faye
"Josh's accident"

Josh Wakefield was whistling as he left the Captain's bridge, he, like so many other sailors, put their hands on the steel rails of the steep stairs. They would then lift their legs and slide down to the deck below. Just as Josh started sliding down, there was a loud blast that shook the ship. The thick smoke started rolling through a hole in the back deck. Josh shook his head, he was stunned, but still conscience after being thrown from the stair railing to the metal deck below.

Other sailors came running, Josh was trying to get up and did not understand why his legs would not work for him? One of the sailors calmed him and explained he had suffered an injury. Josh looked down at his legs; one of his legs was bent in an awkward position. He could see blood beginning to show through his white uniform trousers. All Josh could think, he was the one in charge of the engine room. His job was to keep the engines running in tiptop shape at all times.

The medical personnel carried Josh to the ships hospital ward; his pain was starting to set in. The doctor in charge told the medic to shoot him up good with morphine. The doctor cut away his uniform pants and pulled them off. The morphine was working, Josh could feel himself floating away, and he liked this feeling. The doctor instructed one of the attending medics to get some ether from the cabinet. He told him to put the mask over Josh's nose and administer the ether drop by drop, when instructed to do so.

The ship's doctor had never seen this kind of a compound leg fracture before. Josh's leg was broken between the hip and knee and again between the knee and ankle. The doctor set the bones as best he could and wrapped his leg in a temporary cast. The surgical team at Pearl Harbor would have to do a better job, if Josh was to ever walk on his leg again.

They were only a couple days away from Pearl Harbor. When Josh cleared his mind; he wanted to know immediately what had taken place. Josh's second in command of the engine room relayed that one of the gauges got stuck. It had registered cool, when actually it was red hot and blew up. He told Josh that he had been the only causality. He told Josh, they were running on the small auxiliary engine to get them into port at Pearl Harbor.

When they were towed into the harbor, the sailors on the docks wanted to know if they had been torpedoed? This took the crew by surprise; they had no news that would warrant this kind of happening. Josh was taken to the hospital; the surgeon sawed off his cast and told the staff to prepare him for surgery. The surgeon told Josh this would be a complicated operation and he could end up losing his leg. Josh wanted to send a telegram to Glenda Faye, but there was no time, his leg was the first priority.

Josh's surgery went better than expected; the surgeon told him that the ship's doctor had saved his leg. He had done everything just right at the time of his injury. Josh was so grateful to know he would not lose his leg. Josh decided to wait and contact Glenda Faye. In fact he thought he would just show up at her front door and surprise her. He laughed to himself, it would be like the first time they met on the beach, she came out of the water and there he was looking at her.

Josh had a lot of time to think while his leg healed, he was sorry for Scottie, but glad that he was man enough to release Glenda Faye from their marriage. Being Catholic they could never have been divorced. Josh knew he would never have had a life with the woman he loved.

One warm day Josh was sitting in his wheel chair on the front porch of the hospital, he noticed a young couple sitting at a table not far from him. Josh was never shy, he yelled out for the man to come and get him. John Ryan got up and went over to speak to Josh. They introduced themselves, John wheeled Josh over to their table, and Red was sitting with a deck of playing cards in her hand. They talked about going home, for some reason John forgot to properly introduce Sister Margaret Faye to Josh. The three had a great time together and planned another meeting for tomorrow.

Red did not like playing the Catholic card, but John said it was the only way they would be able to take the little boy home to America with them. Red, playing the role of Sister Margaret Faye, would assure the officials that she would find a good home for the little boy back in America. John and Red already knew where his home would be, with them. All that would be left to do was for Red to terminate her sisterhood with the church. She still had time without suffering any consequences from the church. Each nun is given one year to make up her mind to stay or leave the sisterhood. John's own wound was healing well, but he would always suffer with chronic pain in his ribs. That did not bother him, nothing bothered him, and he was so happy finding love again. Imagine the chance of pulling up a mud caked pregnant waif of girl onto a moving plane. Then finding out she was not pregnant, only protecting a small infant tied to her chest. God moves in mysterious ways, as it says in the Bible. How much better could his life get?

The three met again to play cards, John said to Josh, "I have to apologize for not introducing my friend, her name is Sister Margaret Faye, but I call her Red." Josh could feel his jaw drop open, he said, "You are Glenda Faye's friend, Red, Sister Margaret Faye!" Red looked at Josh and said, "You are Glenda Faye's, Josh Wakefield." They started to laugh, John felt left out, but they filled him on the history of the three girls. How they had all gone separate ways after graduation from nursing school, Glenda married Scottie, Red, became Sister Margaret Faye and Maggie had stayed at St. Ann's hospital. Wow, was all they could come up with.

Time was growing short; they were getting ready for their flight home to America, Red, John and their little boy. Josh, could not wait to surprise Glenda Faye, the three of them had made a plan for this meeting. They were all boarding the plane that would take them home. Everyone was buckled up, Red had to take a seat between John and another young officer. John immediately recognized the young officer; he reached across Red's lap and offered his hand to the officer. The young officer grasped John's hand with his left hand. It was then that John remembered his friend had been severely wounded before take off from the island.

Red was trying to figure out what was taking place; the young officer introduced himself to Red. He said, "You do not remember me or what I said to you and all the passengers on the plane that picked you up from the island." He repeated himself, I said, "My name is Ace and I will be flying you out of this hell hole!" Red thought to herself, this couldn't be Maggie's Ace. The chances are too great. Ace went on to tell Red that his real name was, Leo John Van Camp. He was flying home to surprise his fiancée, Maggie Mann, Red started to laugh as she looked at John. Here they were, the three of them, just like before, "True Friends of the Heart." On the flight to America they filled Ace in on their own plans for their surprise homecoming. Ace was so happy; he knew the timing would be perfect.

Chapter 35

"The Homecoming"

Maggie and Mrs. Van Camp had decided to invite all of the families to the Van Camp estate for the Thanksgiving Holiday. This would keep their spirits up; they were all missing their loved ones who were so far away. There was still no word from Sister Margaret Faye, Mr. Mann knew more than he was willing to tell about the military action in the Philippines. He figured the less said the better.

The ladies insisted on doing their own cooking, Mrs. Murphy was not helping; she was sitting on the sun porch knitting talking to her husband. Maggie was glad that Mrs. Van Camp was having the opportunity to get acquainted with her mother and Mother Kelly. Maggie tried to talk Mother Kelly into staying home, because of her recent surgery. She told Maggie, "I have never missed fixing a Thanksgiving dinner, yes, some were meager, but none the less we had a holiday dinner!" Mother Kelly was a determined woman, she would give birth one day and be up the next fixing breakfast for her family. I guess to Mother Kelly, her surgery was no different, and she was making excellent progress.

All of the ladies became immediate friends, Mrs. Van Camp, was as normal as apple pie, according to Maggie's mother. Sadie Mann sat beside Mother Kelly, both of them laughing like schoolgirls again. Mother Kelly had the rose blush back in her cheeks; Glenda Faye had fixed her hair. It was the first time that Maggie had ever seen her with her hair down. She looked beautiful today, sitting there with her best friend peeling potatoes. Maggie made a promise to herself, that one day she and Glenda Faye would still be sitting together fixing their Thanksgiving dinners. She was sad that Red could not be included in her promise of togetherness in the future.

It was still early in the morning, there was a huge turkey being stuffed with dressing, Mr. Bates had donated one of his special smoked hams for the occasion. He and Minerva could not attend, their son was ill and they did not want to infect anyone at the gathering. Maggie looked around the huge kitchen, there were so many side dishes being prepared. Even some of the older Kelly children were helping. Lotus Foo, or" Blossom," as she was nicknamed by the girls, was helping cut vegetables. She was home from the East, where she worked in the medical research field. Yes, even the Foo family was in attendance for the feast being prepared. They too had sons in the military that were missed by their parents. Blossom and Maggie were chattering away, playing catch up on all of the latest news from Speedway City.

Mr. and Mrs. Wakefield had come in by train from Dayton, Ohio, the previous day. While they were on the train, Mrs. Wakefield thought she saw Mr. McAtee and his son Thomas three rows in front of where they were seated. She told her husband she was going up to speak to them. Mrs. Wakefield tapped Mr. McAtee on the shoulder; he turned around and got up, and gave Mrs. Wakefield a hug. She asked why they were on the train to Indianapolis? Mr. McAtee asked her to sit down, she said, "Why don't you and Thomas come sit with me and my husband?" The three got up and went to sit with Mr. Wakefield, he was happy to see his old friend and neighbor. The trip would be more pleasant with conversation between the four of them. Mr. McAtee explained that Glenda Faye had invited them to the Van Camps for the Thanksgiving Holiday. She could not stand the thought of them being alone on their first holiday after losing Angela. Mr. McAtee's explanation for their trip, just confirmed to Mr. and Mrs. Wakefield that their son, Josh, was marrying a gracious and amazing young woman. The four friends were also invited to spend four days at the Van Camp estate to just rest and relax. When Mrs. Van Camp gave Glenda Faye permission to invite the McAtee's, she had a hidden agenda. She and her husband loved to play Bridge; Glenda Faye informed her that the Wakefield's and the McAtee were also avid Bridge players.

Red and John were tending to their little infant son when their train pulled into the Indianapolis station. Ace asked if they would mind stopping by his home first, he needed to pick up something special for Maggie. This was a lie, Ace had contacted his mother, and she knew they were coming in today, but kept his secret. It was not easy for her, but she knew what it would mean to the other families when their children walked in. Ace did not tell his mother about the little infant that Red and John were bringing back from the Philippines. He felt this was their own gift to give to Red's family.

They hailed a taxi and started the last leg of their journey, it had been a long and dangerous one, but finally the end was in sight. Red and John were nervous, the ride to Ace's home was longer than they imagined, but soon they turned into the long driveway. Ace paid the taxi driver and they stepped out and walked up to the front door. The family maid opened the door; Ace put his finger to his lips, meaning for her to be quiet. She led them to the formal dining room; she opened the door and stepped aside. The families looked up from their meal, there in front of them were all of their children and one young man they did not know. They all let out screams of joy; chairs were knocked over as everyone rushed to greet them. Maggie soon recognized the other young man standing beside Red. It was

John Ryan, a young man she had met a few years ago. His wife, Patricia Kathleen was one of her patients, who lost her newborn baby boy. She wondered, where he came from and what was he doing here with Red? She also noticed Red was not wearing her black nuns habit; she had on a regular dress with shoes to match.

Mrs. Murphy seemed to be the only one who noticed that Red was carrying a wrapped bundle in her arms. She went to her daughter and took the bundle in her own arms and said to her friend Sadie, "See, I told you I was going to have a baby!" Now everyone gathered around Mrs. Murphy as she pulled the blanket away from the infants face. The little boy stared up at them, with his big black eyes and gave a hint of a smile. Mr. Murphy looked at his daughter and then took her in his arms; he never wanted to let her go again.

Glenda Faye stood in front of Josh; he took her in his arms and kissed her long and hard. He said, "If I were able I would get down on one knee and give you this ring and ask you to be my wife." Mr. and Mrs. Wakefield came to greet their son and heard what he had just said to Glenda Faye. They stopped to listen to her reply, Glenda said, "There is no need for that, I would be honored to become your wife." Josh slipped the beautiful diamond on Glenda Faye's finger, and then the Wakefield's came to congratulate their only son and his new fiancée.

Ace saw Maggie across the room; she hurried to where he was standing. She noticed that the sleeve of his uniform hung limp at his side. She didn't care if Ace lost both of his arms, she would love and care for him the rest of his life. When Ace put his left arm around Maggie's waist and pulled her close, she could feel his right arm against her chest. He bent down and placed a gentle kiss on her lips, she took his face in her hands and kissed him all over. She ended her kisses on his mouth where he first kissed her. Maggie realized all of the people in the room were watching them. She turned bright red. Maggie's mother and daddy came to welcome Ace home, they were both in tears, and this was something new for Maggie's daddy. She had never seen him cry before, but they were tears of joy and happiness.

Mrs. Van Camp finally said, "Let us give these young folks some breathing room, they must be starved." She then said, "Mr. Van Camp and I need to hug our boy just once before we let him and Maggie set down to eat."

Chapter 36

"Explanations are in order"

Mrs. Van Camp said to Mrs. Mann, "This is what this estate was built for, it has never been used and I feel ashamed about that." Mrs. Mann, Maggie's mother, replied to her new friend, "All in God's time, we thought our children were all grown and out on their own, now look around, your house is full to bursting." The two women went to look for Mother Kelly; she was seated at one of the big round tables that had been brought in for the occasion. Mother Kelly looked up at her friends and asked Mrs. Van Camp how she was able to keep this secret? She told them it was hard, there were a few times she almost let it slip, like when Sadie asked her why we needed so much food? Mrs. Van Camp said, "It was hard to come up with one excuse or the other, I finally just said, this was the way my caterers handled things." They all laughed, they could not remember when the last time they had been this happy, not a worry in the world, now that everyone was home safe and almost sound.

Sadie Mann was not a person to let anyone feel sad or sorry for themselves. She went to sit with Mr. McAtee and his son

Thomas; she patted his hand and looked at Thomas. Sadie said, "I know you are missing Scottie, we all are, and we are very proud of him and the way he handled his life. Just look at how happy Glenda Faye and Josh are, have you ever seen two more happy people?" Thomas told Sadie Mann, that he owed the rest of his life to Glenda Faye, now he knew the qualities he would look for in the woman he would one day marry. Mr. McAtee agreed with his son on this subject, they continued their conversation about the surprise guests.

Mr. Murphy was sitting talking with Maggie and Ace, John and his daughter, Red, as everyone called her. He said, "Daughter, I am so confused, please explain who this young man is and what you are doing with him? The most important explanation I need to know about is the beautiful young infant your mother is rocking on the sun porch? Also, where is your black nuns habit?" Red said, "Daddy, my time in the jungle of the Philippines, was dangerous, but the most important thing I learned, was that the sisterhood was not for me. I was too young to make that kind of decision so quickly."

Mrs. Murphy came to her daughter, Sandra Kay, as she always called her and said, "I believe our baby needs some attention." When Red looked up into her mother's eyes, for the first time she could tell she was there; she was back in the present moment. Her father had filled her in on how her mother had practically lost her mind. Red took the baby in her arms and both she and John could tell her mother was right. There was a foul smell coming from the little one, they just smiled at each other. Red got up and found her large bag with all the baby's needs, she took him into a downstairs bathroom, connected to a guest bedroom. There she laid him on the bed to change his diaper and sprinkle him with baby powder. He just smiled up at her, she loved this child more than life its self. She had proved this, back in the jungles of the Philippine Islands.

Maggie could not stand it one more moment, she knocked lightly on the bedroom door, then right behind her came Glenda

Faye. Red opened the door; she was smiling from ear to ear. She said, "Go gather everyone in one place, John and I do not want to have to repeat our story over and over again. The two girls went running back into the dining room, they relayed what Sandra Kay, "Red," had told them. Now everyone was thinking, how long does it take to change a diaper?

Maggie, Ace, Glenda Fay, and Josh sat with John Ryan. They were talking about the good times they had recuperating at the hospital in Pearl Harbor, before their return home. Ace chimed in, he said, "I bet you were really surprised when you found out who I was?" John looked at Maggie, and thought about the first time they had met each other on that cold winter night. He could not help thinking of his beautiful young wife, Patricia Kathleen; who had passed away after the birth of their stillborn son. John could not stay with that memory for long, out of respect to his new fiancée, Sandra Kay Murphy.

Sandra Kay, "Red," Murphy, entered the large room; she motioned for John Ryan to come join her. She related her time in the jungle, her near death escape from the Japanese. She told them about the young girl that had just given birth and could not take her baby, because as she stated, "He was a half breed!" Red told them she had no time to think, she grabbed the baby and a few supplies and ran into the jungle trying to make it to the airstrip. She explained about Philippe and that he had to leave her to go on alone with just a crude map to follow.

Without any notice, Red started to cry, John took her place and continued telling the story. He told them that he had almost shot Red as she came running out of the jungle, but then saw that she was a young pregnant woman. After rescuing Red, he realized she was not pregnant, only carrying a newborn infant strapped to her chest. No one in the room made a sound, John explained that he fell in love with this little bit of a mud caked woman the minute he lifted her into his arms. Red was now composed enough to tell the rest of the story, she explained that she would immediately be giving up her vows to the sisterhood.

She had not passed her one-year date to opt out and return to her normal life as a regular citizen.

The two young people went on to explain and answer any questions asked of them by the crowd in attendance. Mrs. Murphy stood up and asked, "What is my grandson's name?" John and Red just looked at each other, they had not named the infant yet. John turned to Red, he said, "I guess I had better marry this beautiful woman, so our son will have a proper last name too.

John asked Red in a whisper, "Would you consider calling the baby, Patrick, after my late wife? John noticed that Red had tied the pretty blue satin ribbon in her hair that he had given her. It was the one Maggie had tied in his late wife's hair after their baby boy had died. This made his heart swell with pride; he knew Maggie would have noticed this too. Red answered John's question, only if you will consider calling him, "Patrick Murphy Ryan." The couple turned to the crowd seated in front of them, John held the little boy up for everyone to see. He announced to the crowd, "This is, "Patrick Murphy Ryan." He is our son, the grandson of Irene and Joseph Murphy, but most important, Patrick Murphy Ryan, has two very special aunts. Maggie and Glenda Faye are his, "True Friends of the Heart."

Chapter 37

"The Future is planned"

No sooner had the Thanksgiving holiday come and gone, there was Christmas to think about, everyone was happy, they felt that no greater presents could have already been given. It was the first week in December, all of the old and new friends had gathered at the Mann household for dinner. The women were in the kitchen planning weddings for their daughters. Mrs. Van Camp, spoke up, how about having a triple wedding, these girls do not do well being separated? Just then the girls came in through the back door, their cheeks were rosy, it was cold for the first week in December of 1941.

Mrs. Murphy was holding little Patrick, he was the best baby, and the only time he would make a sound was when he was hungry or had a dirty diaper. Red came over and picked up the little boy, she kissed him all over his face, and he jerked. She realized that her face was really cold and it scared him, Red turned to her two best friends and said, "I believe these women are up to something?" Maggie and Glenda Faye turned to their mother's and asked them if this was true?

They were all sitting around the kitchen table, the ladies told them of their plan and thought Christmas would be the perfect time for a triple wedding. They would all be starting the New Year, happy, content and joyful for the first time in a very long time. The girls were ecstatic; they were surprised they had not thought of this first, their mother's were getting the best of them. Maggie asked her mother if she could wear her wedding dress, Mrs. Mann felt so proud that she would want to wear her dress. She said she would have to take it in a bit; Maggie was smaller than she was at the time of her own wedding. Many years from now, Sadie and Maggie's wedding dress would be remade into Maggie's daughter, Saragene's First Communion dress. Saragene's granddaughter, Bailey Ann would wear the little dress too, for her First Communion.

Red told her mother that she wanted to wear the same dress that the three women worked so hard on for her when she took her vows. Mrs. Murphy was so glad that she had it safe and sound in the attic. Mother Kelly noticed that Glenda Faye was silent, she was sad that she could not offer her own daughter a family heirloom dress for her wedding. Mrs. Van Camp pulled Mother Kelly aside and asked if she could contact Mrs. Wakefield to see if she had her wedding dress packed away. If she did not, she would offer her own wedding dress for Glenda to wear, she told Mrs. Kelly the dress was beautiful. Mrs. Kelly was all smiles; Mrs. Van Camp went to phone Mrs. Wakefield, but when she returned, Mrs. Wakefield did not have her wedding dress. In fact she related to Mrs. Van Camp that she had just gotten married in a suit at the justice of the peace.

Mrs. Van Camp asked Glenda Faye if she would do her the honor of wearing her wedding dress, she explained that she had spoken to Josh's mother for permission to ask. Glenda was so excited, she turned to the other two girls and they were once again like the three young girls standing in front of their dorm room, so long ago, jumping up and down full of giggles. They all had special dresses to wear that had history and love behind them for the women who wore them the first time. Red said, "I am just sorry that John does not have any family, being raised in an orphanage, must be hard for him. This was news to everyone, but Maggie's mother said, "Well, he has more family than he knows what to do with now!" This lighted the air and everyone was once again laughing and making plans. There was so much to do and so little time. Mrs. Van Camp asked if she could take care of the reception and knew of a large hall to rent, more than likely the whole town of Speedway City would be in attendance. They agreed the only Church option was to be St. John's, where they attended High School and Sandra Kay had taken her vows. Sandra Kay let them know that this was not a problem with her, she and God were on good terms or she would not be alive and given her precious new little son.

The women were drinking tea; Maggie and her mother were using their little hand painted teacups the great aunts had made. The other women were using the everyday china cups and saucers. Maggie was thinking how happy the great aunts were at the Thanksgiving Day celebration. The aunts had already made a wonderful baptism dress for little Patrick Murphy. Now, knowing them, the three would start immediately making new hats for the wedding celebration, they loved a party of any kind. Maggie could still picture every New Years Eve, the three great aunts, sitting with their little paper hats and blowing on the whistles that rolled out and snapped back. Maggie's heart actually ached when she brought to mind all of the wonderful women God had put in her life as role models.

No sooner had this thought entered Maggie's mind, than it was interrupted, her father was screaming from the living room! He joined in by all of the other men that sat with him listening to the radio. Come, come quick, the women ran to the living room, they saw the men had tears in their eyes. What could have happened to make grown men cry in this day and age, it had to be tragic.

Listen, the men said softly, this time. President Roosevelt is going to speak about the news we just heard. The Empire of Japan bombed Pearl Harbor in the early morning hours. It was a sneak attack that came out of nowhere; there was no way to prepare for this. Red, John and Ace looked at each other and were thinking the same thing; they had just made it out of the jungle in time and destroyed the airstrip. If the five of them had stayed at Pearl Harbor recuperating any longer they too, might have lost their lives in the bombing. Everyone in the room was waiting for the President to speak; the tragic news was being repeated over and over. The telephone was ringing, Mrs. Mann went to answer it, and the great aunts were sobbing on the other end. They did not know what to do, Mrs. Mann quieted them and told them to listen to the radio, and the President was about to speak. She told them she would call them later and have Mr. Mann come and pick them up if that was what they needed.

President Roosevelt was introduced for the broadcast and he started his speech to the U.S. Congress. "President Roosevelt says, that December 7th, 1941, is a date that will live in infamy." Everyone listened intently to every word and put it to memory for the rest of their lives. After a vote of 82-0, in the U.S. Senate, and 388-1 in the House, in favor of declaring war on Japan, Roosevelt signs the declaration of war!

Red, Maggie and Glenda Faye sat together holding hands; they could never remember being so frightened in their lives. The whole world had just been turned upside down; there were people in the streets, just walking around seeking solace. Telephones were ringing all at the same time, the operators, just sat at their stations unable to do their jobs. The silence everywhere was eerie, like nothing Maggie could remember before now. Maggie, in her old age, would remember this silence again in her life, on 9/11/2001.

Chapter 38

"Life goes on, America is Strong"

Everyone who had gathered at the Mann residence picked up what they had brought with them and said their, "Good-byes." The girls went home with their parents, John, Red and little Patrick went home to the Murphy household. John had been staying with the Murphy's since they returned from Pearl Harbor on Thanksgiving Day. Some of the neighbors were gossiping about this situation, but Mr. Murphy quickly put a stop to this in short order. When everyone in Speedway City heard the story of how these heroic young people escaped the jungle of the Philippine Islands, they were ashamed of themselves.

It took a few days for the town to settle down and make a plan on how they could help with the war effort. Mrs. Mann formed a committee of women who with the help of the Red Cross organization found plenty to keep them busy. Mrs. Wakefield sent a letter to Mrs. Van Camp asking her if she and her husband could come and spend some time in Speedway City to offer their services. They wanted to spend more time with their son, Josh and Glenda Faye's family. Mrs. Van Camp answered with an astounding, "Yes, and you will stay here at the estate with Mr. Van Camp and myself." There will be plenty to do with the war effort and planning the Christmas wedding. The three families had decided it would not change anything to postpone the wedding plans; in fact it gave the town something to look forward to.

The news that was coming in almost daily on the overseas broadcast got worse by the day. The Secretary of the Navy told Congress that 2,729 military were killed during the Japanese attack on Pearl Harbor. During the rest of the month the United States were concerned about the founding documents of the United States in wartime Washington. The Declaration of Independence and the Constitution were removed from display and transported in sealed containers to temporary storage at the U.S. Gold Depository at Ft. Knox, Kentucky. This was kept top secret from the public until much later in the war, they were returned in October of 1944.

The ladies tried to keep busy with wedding plans, but the men could not help but listen to the news whenever possible. Everyone had to do their regular jobs; Maggie's daddy had orders stacked all over his desk, for wood working production. There were many positions left vacant, due to so many young men joining the military, the Allison General Motor plant had hired women to fill these positions. Mr. Kelly worked at the plant and he wondered how this was going to work out? Mrs. Kelly had his answer, "Try to run a household and raise a family of eight children!"

John was working with Mr. Murphy in the green grocers, they too were very busy, Mr. Murphy had been given a government contract to order and ship canned goods to the various military posts. John also helped at the Allison General Motor plant, he was considered 4-f by the military, which meant, not fit for duty. This depressed John, but he did not let it get him down for long, Red and little Patrick were always there for him when he came in from work. All it took was a smile from the two of them to lift his spirits.

Maggie was working a part-time shift at St. Ann's, in order to prepare for the triple wedding that would take place on Christmas Eve. She and her two friends were so excited; everything was falling in place, just like a jigsaw puzzle. The girls really had a light load to carry, their mother's and mother-in-law's had taken the reins and everything was under control. In fact, the girls were told to just sit back and take it easy. Of course there were dress fittings and other small details that they had to be present for.

Maggie, Red and Glenda Faye were gathered at Mrs. Mann's house, Maggie was standing on a small stool, while her mother pinned her dress. There was a knock on the front door, Mrs. Mann, with her mouth full of pins, muttered for someone to go to the door. Glenda Faye ran to the door, it was a very chilly day and she did not want to keep anyone waiting outside in the cold. When she opened the door, there stood the Great Aunts, she helped the three women in and took their coats and hats. Mrs. Mann was so pleased to see her aunts; she smiled as she removed the pins from her mouth. She patted Maggie on the behind and told her she could step down for a moment.

Mrs. Mann took the great aunts to the kitchen for a nice hot cup of tea. Mrs. Mann placed the two hand painted teacups in front of them, she could see tears in their eyes. She knew exactly what they were thinking and what theses two little cups and saucers meant to them. Aunt Lena spoke first, she looked at her two sisters sitting in front of her and said, "and we have a surprise for Maggie and Glenda Faye." Red spoke up, "What about me, don't I rate a surprise too?" Aunt Lena, laughed, she told Red that she did not need one more surprise, little Patrick Murphy, was surprise enough. All the women laughed, Aunt Lena had a wonderful sense of humor even at her age.

The other two great aunts placed two boxes on the table for Maggie and Glenda Faye to open. When the girls opened their boxes, they found hand made wedding veils, similar to the one the great aunts had made for Sandra Kay. Now, Red new why she did not need a surprise, she already had her beautiful veil that went with her wedding dress. The great aunts had outdone themselves this time; they must have worked day and night to complete these two veils. When asked, they confessed that a few of their lady friends had helped with the stitching of the many pearls and sequins adorning the veils. Aunt Lena told them that the tiny strips of lace came from the same roll they used to make Sadie's wedding dress. This was the dress that Maggie would wear, Mrs. Mann broke into tears, and this was so unlike her that the girls all got up and gave her a big hug.

Glenda Faye got up from the table in Mrs. Mann's kitchen; she asked to be excused, because she had an important appointment to keep. Her two friends looked puzzled, what was she keeping from them? Out of respect to Glenda Faye, no one asked her where she was going or what she was doing. Glenda Faye grabbed her hat and coat, wrapped a warm scarf around her neck and left the house.

Glenda was driving a brand new black sedan, she loved this automobile, and it was one of the few luxuries she afforded herself from her trust fund. She pulled up in the driveway of her old family home and shut off the motor. Glenda took a moment to look at the shabby house she had called home for as long as she could remember, and then got out of the automobile. Glenda found her mother standing in the kitchen, where she spent most of her time. Mother Kelly was feeling better than Glenda could have hoped for, Mrs. Kelly was still recovering from her recent female surgery. Glenda walked over and gave her mother a big hug and kiss; she untied the apron from her mother's waist and hung it over a kitchen chair. Her mother gave her a look of surprise, Glenda said, "Put on your coat and bundle up, I have something I want to show you!"

Mrs. Kelly rode beside her daughter wondering where they were going? When she saw St. Christopher's church in front of them, she knew they were going to talk to Father Linderman for some reason. Glenda just kept driving, passing the church and rounding a bend in the road. She turned the automobile in to a wide paved driveway; in front of them was a large white house with pillars that ran from the porch to the roof. Glenda shut off the motor, went around and helped her mother out of the passenger side of the automobile. Mrs. Kelly was embarrassed, she had not changed from her everyday dress that was faded from so many washings, and she had no idea who would greet them at the door.

When the two women stood in front of the large double doors, Glenda turned to her mother and handed her two bright shinning keys. She grabbed her mother and started to cry, she said, "Mother, this is your new home, it is long overdo, but better late than never." Mrs. Kelly could not speak, Glenda took the keys from her mother and put the key in the lock and turned it. The large door swung open, they stepped inside, and Mrs. Kelly could see that the house was not completely finished. Glenda explained that Mr. Mann and the whole town of Speedway City had been working on her house, but with all that had happened they were running behind schedule. Mrs. Kelly, put her arms around her wonderful daughter, she could only whisper, "Thank you, daughter of my heart."

Chapter 39

"Christmas Eve to remember"

Christmas Eve morning of 1941, the dawn broke clear with beautiful colors of green, pink and light blue. There were a few wispy clouds here and there, but none that looked like a snowfall was imminent. The three girls were gathered at Maggie's, where every important plan had taken place in their lives. They had spent the night together, all snuggled under one of Mrs. Mann's big comfy blankets, and no one could make a warm blanket like Maggie's mother.

The girls could smell coffee brewing, wedding day or not, Mrs. Mann was in the kitchen cooking breakfast for her husband and the three girls. The only difference was the time of day, it was early, and they had a lot to do today. This was why Mrs. Mann had insisted the girls go to bed at a reasonable time last night. She laughed to herself, like they won't stay up half the night giggling like they used to do as teenagers. The telephone rang, it was John, and he was calling to tell Red that little Patrick Murphy had slept through the night. Mrs. Murphy was the best grandmother a small child could ask for. Mrs. Murphy's senility had all, but disappeared when her daughter came home safe to her family, little Patrick Murphy was a wonderful bonus. Mr. Murphy still could not figure out how his wife knew in her heart there would be a baby coming into their lives? All of her knitting was put to good use; everything was in different shades of blue and yellow, just right for a baby boy.

Mrs. Mann had her husband move the dining room furniture to the side of the room so she could take her own private photographs of the three brides. The girls walked out of Maggie's bedroom, when Mrs. Mann saw them together for the first time dressed in their wedding gowns, she gasped, the sight of them took her breath away. Maggie was first to stand for her photograph, she was wearing her mother's wedding dress, the great aunts had sent to Ireland for the thin cotton handkerchief fabric. The hem was hand embroidered forming a scalloped edge; the top of the dress was plain with a round neckline and long sleeves. The aunts had worked for weeks making the vest that went over the top of the dress and tied at the side with satin ribbon bows. The vest was made of rows and rows of handmade lace; each row was a different pattern of lace. Her veil had the same lace; the great aunts had saved the rolls of lace for just such an occasion. Maggie's mother snapped a few photos of her, through the tears that were forming in her eyes.

Glenda Faye was next in line; she was not wearing her mother's wedding dress or her mother-in law, Mrs. Wakefield's, wedding dress. She was wearing Mrs. Van Camps's wedding dress, the beautiful lady that had made her life possible those many years ago. The dress was elegant, ordered from a famous designer in France. The material was a light cream satin, the bodice had a square cut neckline, and there was a wide cummerbund that circled Glenda's small waist. The skirt of the dress hung in many thin strips of satin that ended in points decorated with small pearls. There was a jacket that also had the same square cut neckline edged with handmade roses; little pearls were sewn to look like dew drops on random petals. The simplicity of this garment was perfect for Glenda Faye, just as it had been for Mrs. Van Camp on her wedding day. Her photo was taken, Mrs. Mann didn't bother showing her tears, and she kept her hanky handy.

Sandra Kay, "Red," took her place just as the other girls had, but she felt odd. She was experiencing dejavu, she had been married in this dress before, but that was as a, "Bride of Christ." Now she would be marrying John Ryan, she smiled and offered up a small prayer for God to forgive her. The three mothers and the great aunts made Red's dress, she looked like a fairytale princess. Mrs. Mann knew time was running short; she took Red's photographs. She took two or three photographs of the girls all together. Even with three dresses that were completely different, the girls fit together perfect, in the frame of Mrs. Mann's camera. Maggie looked at her mother and said, "Thank you mother for being a special person who loves us separately, but just as one unit."

The grooms gathered at the Van Camp estate, they were all nervous, but excited. Today all of their wishes were coming true; by tonight they would be married to the three most wonderful women in the world. Mrs. Van Camp and Mrs. Wakefield were helping the men with their tuxedos, adjusting a tie or putting in cufflinks. They paid special attention to John, who had no family present for this special occasion in his life. The women let him know in no uncertain terms, that he now belonged to them in every way possible! Mr. Van Camp, Ace's father and Mr. Wakefield, Josh's father, had arranged the transportation for the wedding parties. They would all be chauffeured to St. John's Church in long black sedans.

Time had run out, it was the moment everyone had waited for; the brides were picked up along with Mr. and Mrs. Mann. She was sorry her two sons' could not be here to see their sister be married, but Maggie's older brother had been transferred out of state and could not leave his job. Maggie's other brother was overseas in the army. The Great Aunts were being picked up along with some of their friends that had known Maggie and helped to work on her wedding veil.

Mr. Mann helped his daughter down the front steps to the sedan and then repeated the process with Red and Glenda Faye. He could not help thinking back to when these three girls were in nurses training and he had helped them with all of their many problems. He had tears in his eyes again, but he did not stop to wipe them away, Mrs. Mann, reached over and dabbed his eyes with the edge of her handkerchief. Looking at his daughter, wearing her mother's wedding dress was like looking back in time. If he had to pick who did the dress justice, he couldn't, they were both so beautiful to him. When they were all seated in the sedan, the girls started to laugh, Red's dress that was made of so many layers of tulle was sticking straight up in front of her face. It was so gracious of the Van Camp's and the Wakefield's to provide these luxury automobiles with three rows of seating to transport them to the church. Red, being the jokester, said, "I guess if we had to take, " The Old Independence," I would be riding strapped on the roof!"

Maggie and Glenda Faye could not help laughing, they were afraid their make-up would be ruined by the jokes that Red was cracking. Glenda Faye thought to herself, I would imagine this joking behavior, was do to Red being nervous and trying to make everyone else feel more at ease. Mr. and Mrs. Mann were being quiet, but smiling at the three young women sitting in front of them, they did not want to let go of them again.

Chapter 40

"Church Bells Ring Out With Joy"

When the cavalcade of black sedans pulled up in front of St. John's Church, the bells were ringing, it was a joyous occasion for all in attendance. The brides were the last to be escorted into the church so as not to be seen by their waiting grooms. Every invitation that had been sent out had been accepted, there was standing room only. The first two rows of the church pews on both sides were reserved for the families of the brides and grooms. Glenda Faye had made it known that Mr. McAtee and his son Thomas were to be seated with the family, they had chosen to sit in the second row. Unbeknownst to Glenda Faye, Mr. McAtee had received a telegram stating that his son, Dr. Donald McAtee, had been killed in Great Britain. It was all he could do to hold himself together, he did not want to spoil Glenda Faye's special day with such tragic news. He would relate this to her in a more private moment, when she returned from her honeymoon with Josh Wakefield, Scottie's best friend.

Everyone was waiting for the ceremony to begin, the organ sounded a soft melody, little Pearl Foo, came down the aisle first.

She was dressed in a little miniature bride dress carrying a basket of rose petals. She looked like a little doll; she was smiling a toothless grin at all of the seated guests. Pearl walked on the white runner, sprinkling the rose petals from her basket. She then seated herself along side her parents.

The three grooms were in place, waiting to see their brides enter the church. There was no need for best men or maids of honor; a triple wedding had them all with each other. Just as the priest walked out to the middle of the alter, the organ, sounded the wedding march. First, Maggie and her daddy walked slowly down the aisle; she was stunning in her mother's wedding dress. Mr. Mann no longer cared about the tears that were running down his face and on to his shirt. When Maggie and her daddy reached the steps leading to the alter, her daddy lifted her veil and kissed her on the cheek. He then placed her hand in Ace's. Mr. Mann seated himself beside, the woman who was his own bride, Sadie; she was radiant in her rose-colored suit and hat.

Mr. Murphy escorted his daughter Sandra Kay to the steps leading to the alter. Knowing this time it was right and that she was so in love with John Ryan. He too, lifted his daughter's veil and kissed her on the cheek and placed her hand in John's. He then took his seat next to his wife. Mrs. Murphy was holding little, Patrick Murphy, soon to be, 'Patrick Murphy Ryan." The baby was awake, but he did not make a sound, he just smiled, as if he knew what was taking place. This was his future; his happiness and these two people were his parents.

Glenda Faye held her father's arm close to her side on the walk to stand beside her friends. She felt that in reality, this was her first wedding. Josh was waiting for her, she could see the smile on his face, those dimples so deep, she remembered the first day she had seen him smile at her. Glenda hesitated for a second when she saw Mrs. Van Camp. She blew her a kiss; both women knew it was a heartfelt thank you for all she had done for Glenda over the past years. She continued walking with her father, he kissed her and placed her hand in Josh's. Mr. Kelly took his seat with his wife, she was dressed in light blue satin, and this made her blue eyes shine. Glenda Faye had given her father the diamond that Scottie had given to her when they were engaged. Mr. Kelly now slipped this diamond ring right next to his wife's golden wedding band. Mrs. Kelly knew what her daughter had done; she looked straight into Glenda Faye's eyes, no words were necessary between these two women.

This was the first triple wedding for the priest performing the wedding ceremony. He made his apology in advance, for any mistakes that might be made on his part. The girls had given the priest a copy of the vows they wanted to be read instead of the usual ones read from his prayer book. This took him by surprise, but by this time, nothing they could come up with would bother him. The priest first addressed the grooms with the vows, given to him by the three brides. Two of the words that they left out, were, "To Obey." The three grooms answered, "I do," to their vows. The priest then turned to the brides and repeated the vows as written by the girls, they too answered; "I do," to their own vows. The priest told the three couples to join hands, he said, "I now pronounce you all husbands and wives, gentlemen, you may now kiss your brides." The three couples kissed each other in a gentle fashion in front of the crowd in attendance.

Then the three brides, dropped their husband's hands, and walked in front of them. They joined their hands, raised their arms and said, "We Are The Three Sister's of St. Ann's, True Friends of the Heart."

Chapter 41w

"Maggie Returns to the Present"

Maggie was sitting at her little white wooden table, in her mother's kitchen, with her two granddaughters, Lil and Patti. She had just finished her story telling, the girls were sad that the two days were over, they loved their Grammie Maggie and they new her time was short. Lil went into the other room and came back with a little teacup and saucer with hand painted violets with green stems and leaves. She handed it to her Grammie, she said, "I have had this for some time, my mother and I found it one day while walking through an antique shop. After her death, I just could not let it go, it was the last thing she bought for you. I believe the time is right for you to have it now." Maggie placed the little set next to her own set of two; it was so close you could not tell the difference.

The doorbell rang; Maggie wondered who could be coming by so late in the afternoon? Lil went to answer the door, she opened the door and put her finger up to her lips, meaning for the visitors to be quiet. Patti joined Lil; they took the visitors coats and hats and guided them into the kitchen where Maggie sat looking at her little gift. When Maggie looked up, there stood her friends, Red and Glenda Faye, she could not believe her eyes.

Lil and Patti had made arrangements to have the two frail ladies flown in to Speedway City; they now lived with their children out of the state. Lil and Patti seated Red and Glenda Faye on both sides of Maggie. She placed the three china teacups in front of them, while Patti poured tea for them. Maggie could hardly speak, she had loved these two women all of her life and now they were here with her.

Lil and Patti came into the kitchen; they told the three ladies there was a special reason for bringing them all together. Lil was holding a cardboard box and Patti held a black garment bag. Lil opened the box as Patti unzipped the garment bag, and took out the little white First Communion dress. Patti told her Grammie Maggie, that her mother, Saragene, had kept the little white dress washed and pressed for over sixty years. They all knew the history of the dress; it had been Grammie Maggie's mother's wedding dress, then hers. Years later Grandma Sadie had remade the dress for, Saragene's First Communion, and Patti's daughter, Bailey had worn it for her First Communion. Patti looked at her Grammie Maggie and said, "This little white dress was my mother's most precious item." Maggie thought back to the day her granddaughter, Lil, had opened Maggie's little wooden cedar chest. The little chest held her most precious item, "A White Starched Apron."

Lil took three books from the cardboard box and laid one in front of Grammie Maggie, Red and Glenda Faye. There on the front cover, was a picture of them together, holding hands, little innocent children. Lil told her Grammie Maggie, "I found my mother's manuscript and had it published, but without your storytelling, I could never have completed the task. This is the story of your life, love and friendship."

The three women were crying so hard they could not speak, Patti went for tissues, and they composed themselves and smiled.

Lil and Patti were so happy to see them together like this; they could only imagine what they were like when they were young women?

Maggie looked at Red and Red looked at Glenda Faye, they joined their hands and raised their arms and said, "We are, The Three Sister's of St. Ann's, True Friends of the Heart!"

AKNOWLEDGEMENT

"I am so proud of myself," those are difficult words for me to write down for the whole world to read. I have never had much confidence in myself, but everyone who knows me, does. When I finished, "The White Starched Apron," they would not let me give up on my girls, as we all have come to call them. This book, "The Three Sister's of St. Ann's," is my favorite so far, I guess you just get better with each book.

Saragene Stamm Adkins
May 15, 2009

Clara Margaret "Maggie" Mann

We all carry precious items with us through life, for Maggie it was her White Starched Apron. Myself, I carry my most precious items in my heart, they are my family and friends. I may now add, "My Dear Readers of My Heart." I will take everyone with me when I go home to be with my God.

I hope you enjoyed the journey with the three girls. I loved writing this modest little book about friendship, love, and virtue. It was a simpler moment in time.

Saragene Stamm Adkins
sarageneann@comcast.net